After leaving university, and followi
worker, clerical assistant and leisure
worked in the events industry for th

Gavin lives with his wife and
Bobbing Heads is his first novel.

C000173482

BOBBING HEADS

GAVIN DE BIER

Best wishes

Gavin de Bier

SilverWood

Published in 2017 by SilverWood Books

SilverWood Books Ltd
14 Small Street, Bristol, BS1 1DE, United Kingdom
www.silverwoodbooks.co.uk

ISBN 978-1-78132-682-4 (paperback)
ISBN 978-1-78132-683-1 (ebook)

British Library Cataloguing in Publication Data
A CIP catalogue record for this book is available from the British Library

Page design and typesetting by SilverWood Books
Printed on responsibly sourced paper

*In purples, yellows, greens and reds were
rows and rows of bobbing heads…*

CHAPTER ONE

If it hadn't been for those beige slippers then things would have been so different. They were a present from my Aunt Isa who, at eighty-three and widowed, still never forgot my birthday and instead of just sending some money or a gift voucher, which shamefully I would have preferred, she always sent a present. As Isa has difficulty getting about these days, I imagine that the slippers were purchased mail order. She probably found them in that curious, almost early 1960s world that still exists in some newspapers, where you can purchase half-price thermal separates and packs of men's flannels in a choice of lovat, grey or black. Whilst I appreciated the gesture and the feeling behind it, the gents' beige vinyl full slippers with touch-and-close strap, super-soft lining and insock were simply not me. They arrived four days early and, almost a week after the big day, remained boxed and unworn.

When I received a gift from Isa I always kicked myself for not having got in touch more often, because in our calls, she was always keenly interested in me, which served only to increase my guilt. After each call I vowed that it wouldn't take another present to prompt me to phone and in future I would do so at least monthly. This of course seldom happened and at thirty-six I should have done better.

I tend to give life to inanimate objects, such as cursing the cupboard door if it doesn't close properly or swearing at a stuck zip, and in a strange way I felt sorry for the slippers. That, added to my self-reproach over Isa, meant that I couldn't just throw them out, so with a sudden sense of purpose, I decided to give them to a good cause and assuage my guilt. It was a rainy Saturday afternoon; I had been nursing a slight hangover all day and up to now hadn't left my flat, so with uncharacteristic vigour for a weekend and the slipper box in a carrier bag I left the flat and headed out to the nearest charity shop. This was for an international children's organisation that also worked in the UK, and was located about ten minutes' walk away on the High Street.

Despite the rain, I enjoyed the short walk in the fresh air and soon arrived at the bustling shop which unfortunately smelled of wet wool. It took a while to catch the attention of an assistant and whilst waiting I took a brief look round and noticed a claret silk paisley-pattern waistcoat priced at £10. With the Christmas festivities starting in little over a month the waistcoat could fit the bill for a couple of work-related functions. I picked it up, and happily it passed the sniff test, then tried it on and it was the perfect fit. Were I to go uptown I knew you could stick an extra £40 on the price tag for that quality. My mind was made up and I now felt doubly self-righteous as not only would my slippers benefit children both in the UK and abroad, I would contribute £10 to their cause as well.

The shop assistant took my payment for the waistcoat and she accepted the slippers after a cursory inspection and an equally cursory thank you. I put the waistcoat into my empty carrier bag and brushed past a couple of impatient customers as I left the shop.

Back at the flat I tried the waistcoat on again and admired myself in the mirror. Whilst I stood side-on holding in my stomach and patting down the garment, I felt something in the lining. I checked the pockets and noticed that the right-hand one had a hole in it. The object that I felt was below and underneath this pocket, and was of credit-card size. I took the garment off, felt for the object again and started working it up to the pocket. It was a simple procedure and I soon had it out. What I found was a small bank-card style wallet with two sides of clear plastic that contained a driving licence on one side and a piece of yellow paper on the other. I took them out. The driving licence was current and belonged to:

Eustace Barrington
14 Clepington Road
London
W5 4AN

Eustace was aged fifty-seven and didn't look very happy in his picture, but who does? The piece of paper had the number 2339 handwritten on it. Eustace's address was familiar to me as his street was next to the local park where I occasionally jogged. It was still only late afternoon, and as my renewed sense of purpose hadn't yet waned, I decided to return the driving licence to its owner. I got up from my default position in front of the television, pulled on a hoody and left the flat.

It was getting dark as I walked the short distance to Clepington Road where the houses were in the same redbrick terrace style as in my own street. I could see that the light was on at number fourteen which was situated opposite the park entrance. I pressed the bell but couldn't tell if it had actually rung; however the door was answered almost immediately by an attractive dark-haired female with sallow skin who I guessed was in her early twenties. She looked at me slightly suspiciously when I asked her in my best non-threatening manner if Eustace Barrington was in.

"What do you want him for?" she asked.

"I have something of his," I replied.

She didn't ask for any more detail and said, "You better go through." She turned around and walked along the short, narrow hall. As I followed, I was aware of pungent cooking smells which I found quite appealing. She stopped at the living-room door and opened it, gesturing with a nod of her head for me to go in. Eustace was sitting with his back to me in front of a television that was playing loudly. I coughed lightly to announce my presence and walked over to him. Like the young woman, he also had a quizzical look on his face, but unfortunately Eustace was obviously quite dead.

CHAPTER TWO

I was in an unremarkable room of average living-room size that had a standard floral carpet with differing floral wallpaper and ornaments and family photographs in the usual places. Eustace's chair faced a small bay window with the television in front of it; a fireplace was to his right, a small coffee table to his left and the living-room door behind him. A black backpack sat underneath the bay window and was partially covered by the drawn curtain from that window.

Until now, I had never seen a dead body in real life, if that makes sense. Both my parents are still alive and none of my friends or near acquaintances have died. When any family or friends of the family have died, my involvement has simply been to attend the funeral. I have never seen someone draw their last breath from their sickbed or at the scene of an accident and have not been to a wake and walked past an open casket or visited an elderly relative as they lay in state in a funeral parlour.

I stood and stared at Eustace, and in particular at the large kitchen knife sticking out of his chest that had caused the front of his shirt to be covered in various shades of crimson, brown, and black. His glazed eyes were open which I found even more horrific than the knife wound.

Eustace, who looked vaguely familiar, was Afro-Caribbean

with short curly hair that was almost totally grey. In his sitting position he appeared to be of average height and weight. He was wearing a white T-shirt, a pair of faded blue thick cotton shorts with a white drawstring (the type that rugby players wear on holiday), he didn't have socks on and had dirty white espadrilles on his feet. I could see that he would normally wear glasses because there was a pair on the floor next to his chair with one leg bent at an angle but with both lenses still intact.

As a crime-scene virgin, I don't recall shouting out or shaking and am not sure if time stood still or passed in slow motion whilst I took all of this in. Most likely I stood transfixed and stared like a startled rabbit for several minutes. In that time I had completely forgotten about the young woman who had let me into the house and directed me to Eustace. I suddenly remembered when there was a cough, which made me jump, followed by a click as the living-room door was closed. A young man had joined her and they both stood looking at me impassively. He was white, about five foot ten, blue eyes, tanned; probably twenty-five to thirty with thick blonde hair swept back boy-band style and very white teeth. I suppose that he would be described as good-looking. He wore designer jeans, a dark-blue branded polo shirt and was chewing gum. "What did you bring for Eustace?" he asked calmly. He had an English accent, possibly South Coast.

"This." I raked in my trouser pocket with trembling hands and produced the driving licence which I had put back into the plastic wallet. I thrust it towards him whilst still staring at Eustace. The blonde man took it from me.

"Have you anything else?" he asked as he took the driving licence out of the wallet and looked at both sides of the small laminated card. His voice remained calm and was unnaturally quiet.

"No," I answered truthfully.

"That's disappointing." I didn't know what he meant, so said nothing. "I think that you may have what Eustace was killed for," he continued.

I still didn't know what he meant, but now panic had set in and I could feel myself shake. "What do you mean?" I croaked. I looked at him and her with what I hoped were pleading, scared, good-guy eyes. The pleading eyes of an average schmuck, who had done a good turn then witnessed a murder scene but wouldn't ever, ever, ever say anything about it to anybody. They both looked at me with casual indifference.

The shock-induced serenity that I had felt when I first saw Eustace had now vanished and his body, and its condition, were nauseating and scaring me. "I don't know what you mean. I don't know him – I found his driving licence."

"Where?"

"In his waistcoat."

"Don't know him, but you have his waistcoat…?" he said quietly but tightly.

"Charity shop," I mumbled. My voice wasn't my own. What was going on? How could I get out of this?

"What?"

"Charity shop I got it…" My ability to speak was leaving me. I needed to sit down. I needed to retch. I did retch. I knelt with my shaking arms extended and palms pressed into the carpet almost like I had completed a press-up as I coughed up some bitter coffee-tinged bile. They watched impassively.

"Get up," he said, so I did as I was told and pushed myself up and leaned against the fireplace. My legs were trembling so much that I felt I might collapse. I had heard of the fight-or-flight response – would this kick in? Or would I simply collapse onto the floor like a quivering eel? The young man approached me. I could smell his aftershave and chewing gum.

"Where's the number?" His voice remained quiet, but there was something happening behind his eyes.

"What number?" was all that I could muster in response.

"His number," he gestured towards Eustace. Why was he talking in riddles? What did he mean?

"Phone number?" I asked plaintively.

"No. His number." He hissed slowly as he continued pointing at Eustace.

"Don't know don't have it." My words ran into each other. I felt very scared and very helpless. My heart was racing and I could feel sweat on my temples and the back of my neck.

"I think that you do…"

Suddenly the penny began to drop. I had barely considered the piece of paper that I had found along with the driving licence. I had taken it out of the wallet, had a look at it and now struggled to think what I had done with it. At the time it meant nothing as far as I could remember, so I had forgotten about it; my focus had always been on the driving licence. Despite my addled state, it suddenly dawned on me that my control of that number might prolong my existence. Where had I put the piece of yellow paper? It was the top half of a post-it note. Had I stuck it somewhere or scrunched it up and chucked it out?

"I don't know what you're talking about," I said. My eyes, I'm sure, were betraying me. "I found his driving licence in a waistcoat, got his address from it, here I am. I don't know any more," I added.

"Get your kit off," he ordered after a slight pause. I briefly looked at him but started to undress automatically without questioning his order. "Everything," he said. I complied. It didn't take long to undress. He told me to turn round and looked me up and down. My current state meant that despite being naked in front of the silent young female, I wasn't bashful and felt like a patient would do on being inspected in an A&E department. She wasn't looking at me anyway, but concentrating on my garments which didn't take long to search as I had only been wearing trainers, boxers, joggers, socks, T-shirt and a hooded fleece. She went through each item, turning them inside out and raking through all the pockets. I noticed sweat marks on my T-shirt and the waistband of my boxers when she picked them up. The only item she found were the keys for my flat which she put on the coffee table. He picked up the keys and they exchanged glances. "That's all you got – you got something to hide?" he said. In my enthusiasm to return the driving licence I had simply thrown on a fleece and not bothered to pick up my wallet or phone or anything else as I wasn't going to be gone for long.

"I just live up the road," I bleated, "I was just coming to hand in the licence then head back."

"Where do you live?"

"Rathgar Avenue, just up the road." I don't know why I repeated that I lived just up the road; probably because I wanted so much for him to believe me.

"Who do you stay with?" he asked.

"Nobody – on my own."

He picked up each item of my clothing, felt them in turn, then threw them onto the carpet. He put my keys in his pocket. "Get dressed. We're going to find the number." I picked up my clothes and put them on. My T shirt had landed on the wet patch. "Let's go," he added.

He switched off the living-room light and I left the room with him behind me and his accomplice in front. We walked down the corridor and they picked up jackets that were hanging next to the front door. He kept the corridor light on, we left the house and he closed and locked the front door.

"Lead the way," he said. I dragged my feet like an errant

schoolboy on the way to the headmaster's office and he nudged me forward. It was dark and drizzling, the streets were quiet and we didn't attract a second glance – why would we? They were dressed smarter than me, but both casually. She wore jeans and now had a long padded jacket on; he was wearing a leather jacket. We fitted in.

As we walked I considered my position. I had answered all his questions, stripped off and had my clothes examined, he had my flat keys and now I was mechanically walking to my flat for them to search it; all without a single threat being made or weapon brandished at me. Just seeing Eustace was enough for me to comply. If they could so casually kill a man in his own home, they could obviously do the same to me. Neither of them had even asked me my name, I was simply a commodity. I had considered trying to make a run for it, but the fear and confusion within me had reduced my legs to trembling lumps of lead. He was behind me and would react quicker and more ruthlessly than I could ever possibly hope to.

"That's it," I said and pointed towards my flat. It was the upstairs part of a terraced house conversion which was reached by going up an open brick staircase to the right-hand side of the building. There was a shared scrubby patch of garden and a tiled area that neither I nor my neighbours, the Cartwrights, tended to properly and was mainly used for keeping the Cartwright's car, our bins and general garden storage. I had lived in the flat for two years now and exchanged pleasantries when required but had a pretty neutral relationship with them. They were in their sixties, both retired and I think had stayed there for most of their married life. Mrs Cartwright didn't keep good health and I rarely saw her, but I would see Mr Cartwright quite frequently, either walking their dog which he used as his reason to get out for a smoke or washing his car that he rarely drove. I occasionally upset them if I played my music too loudly when I returned home happy from the pub, but that was about it in terms of neighbourly engagement.

The Cartwrights were in but with their curtains closed. We made little sound as we walked past their window and across the frontage towards the stairs. The young man was still behind me and I noticed that he had got very close. His partner had gone in front and he stretched past me to hand her my flat keys. There was a light on in my hall which showed through the thick glass at the top of the front door. As we reached the top of the stairs, she hesitated and straightened. There were voices coming from inside the flat. "Who's in there?" he hissed into my right ear and pulled me down and around by the shoulders to face him.

"Nothing, nobody – TV on," I stammered nervously. He looked at me and then nodded to her and she unlocked the door.

All the time in the walk up the road I had been mentally retracing my steps from when I found the driving licence until I left the flat to go to Eustace's. In that time I still couldn't remember where I had put the post-it note and silently prayed that it would somehow have vanished. As we crossed the threshold I suddenly remembered that before leaving the flat I had rinsed my coffee cup in the kitchen sink and then dried my hands before picking up the driving licence which was on the top of the kitchen table.

We entered the flat, walked along the hall and went into the kitchen.

CHAPTER THREE

We were in my kitchen, which is large relative to the size of the flat, and had probably been a bedroom when the building was one house. It is the tidiest and most attractive room in the flat, has a wooden floor, tiled walls, and several built-in pine cupboards. The clock on the oven said it was quarter to five.

I sat on one of the four chairs at the smallish table as I had been instructed to do. My first feeling on entering the kitchen was one of massive relief when I saw that the post-it note was not on the table. Blondie, as I had come to think of him, sat facing me and his partner leant against the oven and I realised that she hadn't said a word since she had let me into Eustace's. They had both taken their jackets off which were now hanging over the two empty chairs. The glazed door was open and I could hear my television from the living room.

"Before he died, Eustace told us that the number and his driving licence were together," Blondie announced. "That's why we think you can help us. Where is the number?" His manner was businesslike. I had avoided overtly looking at obvious places such as the fridge or notice board when we entered the kitchen because I thought that they would be following my gaze and looking for any flickering of recognition in my eyes.

"I'm sorry, but I don't know. I don't know what number you

mean." I had once read that no one tells a lie like a man who believes it and at least I could answer the first part honestly, all the while thinking of a way of finding and hiding the number.

"You might not know what the number is or means," he said. "That doesn't matter – that's not what I am asking. Have you seen the number?"

"No," I said. I hoped that he believed me because I didn't. I couldn't help but swallow and I looked at the table to avoid eye contact.

He looked at me, using silence as a tool, and after what felt like several minutes, but was perhaps only sixty seconds, he said, "Is anyone expected here tonight or have you made plans to go out?"

This change of tack momentarily threw me. I shook my head and said, "No." I had been out with my mate Phil last night and we had had a few beers and a post-pub curry. Tonight I had been looking forward to a night in on my own, a couple of drinks and some football on telly. The novelty hadn't worn off and I still loved satellite television for my nights in and the multiple choices of matches to watch. My mum, ex-girlfriend and sister had all at various times accused me of starting but never completing anything and they did have a point. Perhaps because of this and after reading about the Ealing Half Marathon which had taken place recently I had decided to enter next year's race and get in shape for the event. Staying in tonight was the start of my training regime.

He told his partner to make him a cup of tea, and I could see the cold beer in the fridge when she took out the milk. When he had his drink he said, "Get your phone and wallet." My wallet was still in my jeans which I had discarded last night and left draped over a chair in my bedroom and my phone was lying beside my bed. I expected him to follow me but he didn't; he must have been confident in my meek compliance. I picked up both items and returned to the kitchen. "Give her the phone," he told me and I did. She pressed a few buttons on the phone, then hers, and a few seconds later my phone rang. She then took the back off my phone, removed the SIM, put it in hers, pressed a few buttons before returning it to my phone. Now she had my number and had also presumably saved all my contacts.

Blondie ordered his silent friend to start looking in the kitchen. She threw a utility bill which had been lying in the cutlery drawer onto the table; he glanced at it then took everything out of my wallet. He put the money to one side then looked at each business card, stamp and assortment of membership cards and receipts before examining my driving licence:

Greg Stewart
25 Rathgar Avenue
London
W5 4AH

"Well, Greg, you are in a bit of bother, my son. Tell me a little bit about yourself."

What the hell do you say under such circumstances? He could see my date of birth and he knew my address. "I've lived here for about two years," was all that I could manage.

"Is that it?"

"I work as a college lecturer."

"Oh yeah, where?"

"West Thames College."

"What do you teach?"

"Teaching English as a Foreign Language."

"But English ain't a foreign language, Professor."

"It's to teach English to people who speak other languages."

"Enjoy it?"

"Yes, it's all right."

"So are you good at communicating then?"

"I think so."

"Well I don't think so, Professor. If you did you would tell me where the fucking number is before I start to get angry." I had nothing to say to either the cheap academic bating or to the number question.

"Got any family round here?"

"No."

"Where do they stay then?"

"West Midlands."

"Where about?"

"Solihull."

"Your name sounds Scotch."

"My dad's half Scottish," I replied.

"Do you have a bird?"

"No."

I did have a *bird* for over eighteen months, which was a record, up until about six months ago, but we had drifted apart and the relationship ended without any major fallout or acrimony. Apart from that, the only long-term relationship I'd had with a female was with Vicky, who I met at Leicester University seventeen years ago, and we had kept in touch ever since. She was part of an extended group that developed over four years and we often drank, smoked and partied together. To my everlasting regret I had never slept with her and we had the ultimate platonic relationship where we would discuss who we were shagging at the time and offer each other advice and support. How right on and adult.

We met three to four times a year and also forwarded funny emails and texts as friends do. Vicky was always attractive but as the years have passed she has blossomed. I felt flattered that she had bothered to keep in touch. As I was reminiscing about Vicky, Blondie got up and went out of the room to make a call. When he came back he said, "Where's the waistcoat?"

"In the bedroom."

"Let's take a look."

I regretfully put Vicky to the back of my mind and got up and started towards my bedroom. We went into the room which was obviously the bedroom of a single man with several items of clothing strewn about rather than hung up; curtains closed which remained closed all day; discarded magazines and newspapers on the floor; dust on the units; and thankfully today no used tissues near or under the bed. The wrapping paper from Isa's present still lay on the floor. Were the curtains to be open you would look out onto lock-ups and then a road.

I opened the wardrobe; the waistcoat was hanging up and I took it out and handed it to him. He looked at it inside and out then started to rip it apart. Without a word he then threw the remains of the waistcoat onto the floor and paced about the room. He picked up a magazine, glanced at the cover and tossed it onto my bed, then picked up the wrapping paper, looked at it and put it down on the chest of drawers. His partner was with us and she had been looking through all my drawers and the pockets of my clothes. "Go back to the kitchen," he ordered both of us as he became increasingly agitated.

I thought about doing a run for it in the instant that he told us to return to the kitchen; however he walked out of the bedroom first and stood in the hall whilst we went past him. He closed the kitchen door and after a moment I could hear his muffled voice as he presumably talked on the phone. We sat in silence and after a few minutes he reappeared holding my passport with my laptop under his arm. The laptop had been in the living room which we hadn't visited up to now and my passport was kept in the sock drawer of the chest of drawers. He put my driving licence inside my passport and then put them both in his jacket pocket. He sat down at the kitchen table, booted up my machine and asked for my logins. Despite my fear, I inwardly seethed at this further loss of privacy as my laptop contained so much of me. I had volunteered as little as possible to this callous bastard when he asked about me, but now he could read all my college stuff, my unfinished novel, see everything else I had stored in my folders, look at my favourite websites and read my emails.

I sat watching him as he played about with the laptop and drank one of my beers. She went and used the toilet and he shouted at her to look in the living room. He methodically went through each folder and opened it. This may sound onerous but most of the fifty or so folders contained work-related files or general fluff such as my novel. He was going through the motions of opening the folders, but not looking at every file, perhaps hoping that the number, or a signpost to it, would jump out at him. His phone rang and he left the room to answer it, closing the kitchen door on the way out. He was away for a few minutes before returning. She followed him back in from the living room carrying my laptop bag.

Blondie switched the laptop off. "We're going now," he announced suddenly and unexpectedly. For a very brief instant I felt monumental relief that they believed me. They believed that I didn't know about or have the number and that they would now leave me in peace. This feeling passed in an instant of course because they weren't that stupid and life isn't like that. I was still well in this shit.

He put my laptop in its bag over his arm then looked at his watch and said, "I know that you're lying, Professor. You've got twenty-four hours to find the number. We'll be back." I swear that he winked as he looked at the phone which was still on the table and said, "Don't tell anyone. We don't want Aunt Isa ending up like Eustace." Still looking at the phone he added, "That's tapped and we'll keep an eye on you." With that they both left.

I exhaled and sat shaking, sweating and sobbing, trying to comprehend what had happened and what would happen next.

I didn't know what to do and who to call, if anyone, so I went to the fridge and got a beer. It took several attempts to open the bottle as my shaking hands slipped on the condensation. I sat down at the kitchen table and gulped the golden liquid down my parched throat. I leaned forward and held my head in my hands trying to think, but not coming up with anything. I checked the time on the phone and noticed a missed call from Vicky. It was six-thirty so their visit had gone on for nearly two hours.

I finished the beer in several gulps and went for another. As I opened the fridge door my phone gave out a loud text alert that gave me a fright, which wasn't difficult under the circumstances. I sat down, picked up the phone and opened the text. The sender was withheld and there were no words in the message, just a picture. The picture was very clear and it showed someone wearing a Guy-Fawkes-type mask like the anti-capitalists wear at demonstrations. I have always found these masks unsettling. What I found particularly frightening about this picture was that the person in the mask was holding what appeared to be a large kitchen knife against the throat of a clearly terrified Aunt Isa.

CHAPTER FOUR

The terrified look on Isa's face haunted and alarmed me. It also engulfed me in guilt. I've caused this, I thought, Jesus Christ – I've caused this...

Isa is my dad's much older sister; he is sixty-six and she is his only sibling. He was *the mistake* they would both joke. That remark always has, and still does, make me feel uncomfortable. I can only very vaguely remember my paternal grandmother and have no memory at all of my paternal grandpa. Isa became my surrogate granny as the years went by and she was also fondly protective of my dad even when he became an adult. Neither my parents nor Isa have moved house in my lifetime and her house is fifteen minutes' walk from ours. She babysat me and my sister Frances from when we were babies. From kids to teenagers to young adults we were round at Isa's all the time. She has a crude earthy wit, ready smile, is a great cook, extremely house-proud and operates to set routines when shopping, cleaning and cooking. She had had part time jobs and helped out at the Women's Institute in Solihull, but most of the time she was a housewife. I know that this sounds like the clichéd, idealised selective memory from another, simpler age but it is all true.

Isa and Uncle Bill had lost their only child, Richard, to spina bifida long before I was born and he would occasionally be mentioned by her. Bill never spoke of him. We would acknowledge it when Isa talked of Richard but would never dream of raising the subject with her.

They had married young and celebrated over sixty years together before Bill was taken. As he succumbed to the cancer that ate away at him, she was his rock. I remember the party for their diamond wedding celebrations when all the family had gathered at a hotel function suite. By then Bill was very ill and knew that he had little time left. He had worked on the railways all his life and was a quiet, determined, respectful character. He wasn't a natural public performer but the unscripted speech he gave that night in praise of his wife and the joy at their life together was one of the most emotional experiences that I have ever had. Like most people that night I wept unashamedly as we celebrated their love, companionship and friendship, knowing that it was soon coming to an end.

When Bill died we worried if Isa would fall apart and quickly follow him. My parents would phone and pop along with increased regularity, but she remained fiercely independent and outwardly appeared not to have lost her sparkle. She was getting on with life, more interested in others than herself. Now, nearly three years since Bill passed, this bastard with the mask was holding a knife to my lovely, special, caring Isa. Seeing that look on Isa's face was too much for me.

No, no, no… She can't die! What can I do? I wailed inwardly. I didn't even keep the slippers she sent me, couldn't be bothered to call her after all she has done for me over the years. Poor, poor Isa – what an ungrateful bastard I am.

I shook with emotion and guilt.

I paced manically, desperately trying to think straight. I had to be logical and I had to move fast, but I was up against people who had already killed for this number.

Who am I, what can I do? I wondered. I'm an unambitious college lecturer, a nice guy who gets on with most people, and I haven't had a physical fight in my adult life. I am totally out of my depth, but I must do something – Isa is being held. I must do something and I have less than twenty-four hours until they return.

I thought of the person behind the mask as male but of course couldn't be sure. How had he found her? How had he got to her house so quickly? Was he on his own in Isa's house? I forced myself to look at the picture on the phone again to see if it was a selfie or someone else had taken it, but I couldn't tell.

I tried to think objectively. It takes about two hours to drive from West London to Solihull which is more time than their visit had taken. The person in the mask along with Blondie and his partner were obviously part of a gang or some kind of network. How did they know who she was? How did they find her address and get there so quickly? I suddenly felt a sickening wrenching in the pit of my stomach. I got up, left the kitchen and went into the bedroom. My waistcoat was lying on the floor in rags and the brown wrapping paper was on the chest of drawers where he had put it. I picked it up and there printed on the back of the wrapping paper in very small capitals was:

Sender:
MRS I BRAITHWAITE
17 SYCAMORE DRIVE
SHIRLEY
SOLIHULL
W MIDLANDS
B90 4XT

The card that Isa had sent with the slippers was sitting on my chest of drawers as well. After looking at the wrapping paper,

Blondie had sent me and his accomplice back to the kitchen and made a call...

Should I phone the police? Should I tell my parents? Is there anyone I know nearby who could get Isa out? What would they do with Isa? Would they take her somewhere? Would she be bound and gagged? How would she cope? Was he using bad language? The more I thought of this nightmare the worse it got.

The number was the key to all of this – what was it for? How could it be so important? Where was it? Would I find it and what would I do if I found it? Could I do this on my own? No. Who could help?

I wrote down a list of names: Mum/Dad, Frances/Brian (her husband), my mates from work – Phil and Dave, the uni group, Vicky. Anyone else? I couldn't involve my parents or my sister; I wasn't now close enough to anyone in the uni group apart from Vicky so I quickly narrowed it down to Phil, Dave or her. Phil's a good guy and I liked his company for a drink on a Friday. Ditto Dave. Could I rely on them? Dave didn't even turn up last night and didn't let us know he couldn't make it until we were onto our third pint. It had to be Vicky. She was logical, calm, smart and resourceful.

I had to call Vicky, but I wasn't going to use my phone just in case it was tapped. I would have to leave the flat and find somewhere to phone from. I checked my contacts and wrote down Vicky's number along with Phil's and Dave's. I could remember Mum and Dad's and Fran's landlines, but hoped that I wouldn't need to call them until this nightmare was over. Thinking of that caused another panic and despite having a major evacuation in the morning following my late-night curry, I suddenly had the urge for another. I sat on the toilet in the long thin bathroom, sweating heavily and legs shaking. Already an hour had gone by. Job done, I washed my hands and looked at myself in the mirror.

I looked a mess, a scared mess, the type of mess that you give a wide berth to on the pavement. I had to try to compose myself. Characters on television and in films splash water on themselves and that works a treat as they instantly wake up/sober up or rid themselves of the effect of the drug administered to them by an evil criminal mastermind.

I gave myself several large splashes of cold water, which helped, and looked in the mirror. I noticed in the reflection a piece of yellow paper stuck on the shelves behind me. It appeared to be the size of half a post-it note.

CHAPTER FIVE

It was very cold. Isa wasn't sure how long she had been lying in the back of the dirty red van. She had been sitting in the living room with her Saturday treat of a small brandy getting ready to watch *Strictly Come Dancing* when all of a sudden a man in a mask came through from the kitchen. For an instant Isa thought that she had perhaps dozed off and was having a bad dream but sadly this was all too real.

"Hello, Aunt Isa," he had said. She couldn't say anything. "Your Greg's been a naughty boy. He's got something of mine. I want it and you are going to help me get it," he told her. The man was dressed all in black and had a black balaclava on with a small rucksack on his back. Isa was terrified by the sudden intrusion and the tone of the man. Her heart beat rapidly and her legs shook. She stared at this apparition in wide-eyed terror. "Just you do as I fucking say and you will be okay," he said. Isa was shocked by such language; her Bill was a gentleman and would never have dreamt of speaking like that in female company. "Do you understand me?" She nodded, still in wide-eyed terror. "Lost your tongue? Good, keep it quiet. We're going to pose for a picture for our little Greggy."

He took a mask out of the rucksack and put it on over his balaclava. It was of a white-faced man with a cruel smile, pointy chin and slits for eyes. It was terrifying and Isa gasped; she couldn't look at it. "Now sit still," he ordered as he took a large knife out of the bag and held it in his right hand. He then knelt next to Isa, who was still sitting in her chair, and took out his phone with his left hand and stretched out his arm. He held the knife against her throat with his other arm. "Right, look straight at the camera," he ordered her then clicked the button and there was a flash. He stood up and looked at the photo, but wasn't happy. "Keep your fucking eyes open, you old cow, or I'll fucking kill you."

The language, the tone of voice and the mask were more than she could bear. He then went through the procedure again, looked at the selfie and this time was happy and took the mask off. "That's better. Now let's send this to Greggy boy. See how fucking clever he is then." He did something with his phone and put it back in his pocket. "Time to go. Stand up," he told her. Isa did as she was told and stood on trembling legs and looked at the wedding photo of her and Bill on the mantelpiece. What would he think of all this? He wouldn't have let this happen. Bill was a gentleman, not like this thug.

"Put your arms behind your back," he told her and she complied. They were bound tightly and very roughly with what felt like plastic strips which made her wince. "We're going out the back door and you're going into my van." Isa hadn't even heard a van park next to her house. Her neighbours Jim and Betty were roughly the same age as her and probably wouldn't have heard either. The neighbours on the other side, the Bradleys, were new with young children and probably would have been preoccupied with bath and bedtime duties.

He pushed her towards and then through the kitchen, out the back door and on to the van. The back door of the vehicle was unlocked and slightly ajar. He pulled one of the doors open and told Isa to get in. She looked at him worriedly; although he had removed the mask after taking the picture he kept the balaclava on and his eyes were still slits.

"Climb in before I drag you in, you stupid cow," he hissed. Isa put her left foot on the vehicle's step but couldn't climb due to her hands being bound and her legs not being what they used to be. The man pushed her upwards from behind and Isa fell into the back of the van from the head to the waist and banged her right knee off the edge of the van's floor. The man then opened the other door, bounded in and grabbed her by the shoulders and neck and dragged her across the metal floor to the back of the van. Isa was in shock and had never felt such sudden pain as he threw her down like a sack of potatoes. He put tape across her mouth and said, "Don't move a fucking muscle or you're dead."

Isa lay trembling and in great pain from her knee, neck and shoulders; she was almost in the foetal position but her arms were behind her back and there was no way of getting comfortable. It was so cold and she just had her nylon trousers, blouse and cardigan on. The floor of the van was damp and dirty and she inhaled the strong metallic smell from it.

The man closed the doors of the van, started it up, and drove for what felt like ten or fifteen minutes. She could hear a muffled telephone call from him in the driver's seat, then the back doors opened and he climbed in and closed them. "Right, you old cow, we're here for the night. Don't move and don't make a sound. If you're lucky, and if little Greggy comes up with the goods, then you might get out tomorrow."

Isa couldn't believe that this was really happening. The doctor had said that he was upping the strength of her amitriptyline after her last visit when she had told him that she was missing Bill so much and felt unhappy and unable to sleep properly. Had she muddled up her prescription and taken two tablets that were now reacting with her brandy? Surely she would wake up soon.

Isa had no idea how long she had been in the van and had never been so uncomfortable in all her life. She wondered where Misty her Yorkshire terrier was as she usually gave a few friendly barks when Isa had visitors. She worried about how the man would have left her house – would he have made a mess? Had he locked up? She worried about Greg. He was such a nice boy, what kind of trouble could he have got into? What did this monster want from him? Greg wasn't a bad lad; he wouldn't get involved in anything bad deliberately. She always liked talking to Greg on the phone and wished that he would come and visit her more often. She worried about Jack and Wilma, Greg's parents. Would some monster be at their house as well? She worried about Wilma because she hadn't been keeping too well recently.

Ever since Bill died Isa hadn't liked the dark. Every night she would read herself to sleep, wake in the middle of the night and switch the light off before rising around six-thirty the following morning. She had her habits, with a cup of tea when she got up, breakfast just after seven and she did the toilet usually around eight. She had always been regular with that. Perhaps it was the shock but it felt like she needed to go now. She closed her eyes and tried to think of other things, hoping that the need would go away.

Bill was taking Richard for a walk on the beach at Weston; she was setting up the picnic. They were both taking off their socks and shoes and going for a paddle. She watched them for a while and was so happy. Isa loved their holiday trips together, Bill and Richard were having a great time and Isa thought that she would have forty winks before they returned…

"You dirty fucking stinking old cow. You fucking animal. It's fucking stinking." She was roused as he kicked her from his sitting position and hit her right thigh. He made a phone call: "She fucking shat herself, for fuck sake…"

"Too bad," the voice at the other end said, "you stay put in the back of that fucking van 'til I tell you to move."

The man was positioned in front of the windows in the back of the van. He moved and stepped over Isa and stretched round the side of the front passenger seat and rolled down the window half an inch. That would help to get rid of the smell a bit but of course made the van even colder. He then went back to his original position.

Isa lay behind him, shaking with cold, fear, pain and humiliation. This monster must have a mother, she thought. What would she think of his behaviour? As tears trickled across her face and warmth ran down her legs, she closed her eyes and wished more than anything that she had ever wished for in her life that she could join Bill and Richard again and be with them forever.

CHAPTER SIX

2339.

I held the small piece of paper with trembling hands and stared at the number. A man had died for this number and Aunt Isa was being held because of it.

The post-it note had been next to the mouthwash. Of course! In my job where I was in close proximity to my students I was very conscious of my breath and used mouthwash and throat sprays a lot. I disliked chewing gum and used mouthwash automatically before going out. I must have had the post-it note in my hand and left it here after I gargled.

Now that I had the number had anything changed? Well, yes and no. Yes, I now had the number, but no because I didn't feel any safer. They had killed Eustace, they were holding Isa at knifepoint and I of course knew both of these things. They would kill me without blinking an eye – having the number only increased my bargaining power.

2339, 2339, 2339. I had decided that the number was too valuable to keep on me and kept repeating it to commit it to memory. To keep the number safe I would hide the original piece of paper, and so I put the post-it note into my small leisure membership card wallet, which was very similar to the one Eustace kept his driving licence in.

I switched the kitchen light back on and left my phone on the table then changed into a black hoody, dark jeans and trainers. I took Vicky, Phil and Dave's numbers and put them in my wallet, which surprisingly hadn't been taken, and put that and the leisure card wallet into my pocket.

Blondie had said that they would be watching me so I decided that it was too risky to leave by the front door and therefore slowly pulled up the bedroom window, which was stiff but surprisingly didn't make too much noise. I had never climbed up or down the drainpipe before, but always had it in the back of my mind that if I arrived home pissed without my keys I might be able to climb up and get into my bedroom – that's if I hadn't left the window lock on of course. After a furtive look out of the window, I gingerly turned round and edged my legs out and over the window ledge. I gradually lowered the rest of my body out of the window and grabbed onto the drainpipe. It felt secure and I quickly started to make my way down. I was aware of scuffing my feet off the wall and my knees kept banging painfully off it as well; however, I made it down intact.

Safely on terra firma, I brushed down my jeans, gently massaged my sore knee then put the leisure card wallet underneath the side of Mr Cartwright's shed in the back garden. I climbed over the fence and squeezed between the garages and walked cautiously and nervously down Telford Road trying to keep to the shadows as much as possible. Despite my understandable shakiness I didn't feel as if I was being followed. Having said that, I needed to get to a phone and had ruled out using a phone box (assuming I could even find one) because I felt that I could be seen making a call. I reached the junction of Telford Road and Rathgar Avenue unhindered and then continued down towards the High Street. I had decided to go to the Dog and Duck, which is where I had been with Phil the previous night, because they have a phone booth that gives the pissed caller some privacy as they call a cab or lie to their wife.

I went into the pub, and the phone booth was situated in the lobby, before you actually got into the bar area, so I went straight into it and called Vicky. The call was answered on the second ring. "Hello," she said cautiously.

"Vicky, it's me, Greg."

"Oh hi, what's up? I didn't recognise the number. Where are you calling from?"

In my anxiety I ignored her question and asked one of my own: "Are you free tonight? I really need to speak."

"Christ, Greg, she doesn't want to go out with you again?"

"What?"

"Kerry."

"What? No, no, nothing to do with that..."

She was referring to my ex, Kerry, because I had said in one of our recent conversations (after a bottle and a half of wine) that Kerry would still probably go back out with me if I asked her.

"I really, really need some advice – can you help?"

"Okay. Do you want to head up to meet me in town?"

I don't know why, but the thought of leaving my neighbourhood frightened me. "No, no, can you come to me? I, I really need to see you..."

She interrupted and said, "Greg, please calm down. I'll come out to you. Where do you suggest?"

"What about Toni's near the station?"

"Toni's? But it's a dive."

"I know, I know. Let's meet there and then we can maybe go somewhere else."

"Okay." She sounded doubtful.

"What time can you make it?" I asked.

"An hour from now."

"Vicky, please be as quick as you can. See you then."

"I'll try. Maybe fifty minutes."

"Thanks, Vicky."

I felt better that soon I could share my plight with another person, someone who I could trust and might even take the lead in dealing with this. I didn't even need to close my eyes to see Aunt Isa next to that mask…

I had time to kill and I went into the bar which was about a quarter full. I couldn't face a pint and ordered a brandy and coke. The barman recognised me from last night. "Still a bit rough?" he asked as he noticed my trembling hands picking up the glass and can. I gave a weak smile and nod and made my way to a table where I could face the door but be partially hidden by a couple deep in conversation at the next table. I played with my drink and tried to blend in. Every few seconds I looked up to the television to see what the time was on the news channel. Beyond the pool table, there were two guys playing darts, one of whom appeared to be good and the other crap and they were having a great laugh. Lucky bastards.

My thoughts turned to Vicky. Like me and lots of BA graduates, she drifted into a job with no great sense of purpose and ended up in NHS administration in the East Midlands. She got married to one of our group twelve years ago and after five years they moved to London where she got a job with a health trust in North London. There were no children and the marriage ended a couple of years after Vicky had moved south. After which she thrived, leaving the trust, and was now working in the City for a financial services company.

A huge wave of guilt swept over me as I considered what I was dragging Vicky so unexpectedly into, but then I thought of Isa and my desperate need to do something to try to save her from these bastards. After about thirty minutes lost in my thoughts and playing with my glass, which had been empty for twenty-five minutes, I decided it was now time to go to Toni's. Toni's was seven to eight minutes' walk away. As I walked, I tried to get the order of events right in my mind so that Vicky would clearly see what deep shit I was in.

Toni's café is next to the station, which was handy for Vicky, and basically functioned as a place to grab food on the go during the day and feed the munchies at night. I had chosen Toni's because even when it wasn't busy it was still quite noisy between the staff banter and the radio and I didn't imagine that we would be overheard. Toni's doesn't do romantic and I expect that the majority of profits are generated in the last two hours of business each night. It is basic in the extreme with chipped Formica tables, tired, grubby, greasy wooden chairs, laminated menus, a radio playing eighties hits quite loudly in the background and there is more empty floor space than that occupied by tables and chairs to accommodate the queues of hungry late-night revellers.

Three guys of Mediterranean appearance worked behind the counter who, to their eternal credit, could not be more welcoming, which made me feel guilty about my sneering regard of the premises. To avoid standing out, I ordered a plate of chips and a coke and took a seat in the corner. "Come on Eileen" was playing in the background. This was the first time that I'd been in here sober, I realised. I was restless and so to kill time and avoid wasting it when Vicky arrived, I went for a pee.

The toilets are in a subterranean labyrinth, reached by squeezing along a corridor populated by empty frying-oil cylinders and large cardboard catering chip boxes and then negotiating a set of damp, slippery stairs before crossing through a dark room lit only by the emergency exit signs. It was always damp in here with a constant dripping noise. The gents had a permanently broken window and the autumnal chill poured in. The only saving grace was that in the autumn and winter the smell of stale urine wasn't as strong as in the summer. I stood peeing and contemplating, then suddenly recoiled as I realised that my forehead was leaning against the cold wet tiles above the urinal.

When I re-entered the upstairs café, I immediately saw Vicky. She had a slightly panicked look about her as she scanned the café patrons looking for me. Our eyes met and she instantly relaxed. "Hi. Thanks for coming – do you want anything?" I gushed. She took a can of orange juice and we sat down at my table. I offered her a chip.

"Yeah, I was just calling to catch up – I didn't expect this. Right, Greg, what the hell's wrong?" she said quietly, looking at me intently. I had worked out how I was going to tell her calmly and methodically the chain of events that I had experienced, but it didn't work out like that. Everything rushed out in a torrent of distressed statements, phrases and pent-up emotion. She told me to pipe down and slow down. She took out a small notepad and pen from her bag. "I'll go through the main points and you help me out okay?" she said. I nodded. I realised that I was sweating again.

"Do the slippers have anything to do with this?"

"No, yes, no well they are the reason that I was in the charity shop and got the waistcoat."

"Right, and the waistcoat had a number in it?"

"Yes – a driving licence and a number on a piece of paper."

"You took them to the owner?"

"Yes – well, no. I took the driving licence but not the number."

"Why?"

"So that the person could have his driving licence back."

"Why did you leave the number?"

"Because it meant nothing to I didn't consider it, I thought it was meaningless."

"And the man you took the driving licence to is dead?"

"Yes. Yes, with a knife in his chest…"

She was noting the key points and staying very calm. "Who did it?"

"I suppose the blonde guy. There was a girl there as well. The dead guy looked vaguely familiar."

"So then you all went to your flat?"

"Yes, we couldn't find it – the number I mean. I didn't know where I had left it. They asked questions, searched the flat and then left. They didn't believe me. Fifteen minutes later I got the text with Isa's picture with the mask and knife…" I trailed off.

Vicky remained focused. "Have you told anyone?"

"No of course not, just you."

"Not even the police?"

"Of course not. They are holding Aunt Isa; he has my passport, driving licence, laptop and phone contacts."

"Do they know about me?"

"I told you no, apart from being in my contacts lists like thirty other people."

"And you have left your phone in the flat?"

"Yes, in case they could use it to track me."

"So, have you found the number now?"

"Yes."

"Have you got it with you?"

"No, I hid it in case they followed me and searched me."

"Where is it?"

"Hidden in my garden."

"What's the number?"

"233…shit I've forgotten it. It's definitely four digits and I think it's something like 2338 or 9."

Slippers, waistcoat, dead man, number, blonde man, girl, Aunt Isa. I knew this must sound like madness to Vicky – did she believe me? Perhaps she thought that I was having some kind of breakdown.

"Greg, we need to go somewhere to work through this and decide what to do." Good. She believed me.

"Let's go to my place," she added, "but we will need to go to yours first to get the number."

I didn't want to go back to my place just yet. "I've told you the number, why do we need to go back?"

"You aren't sure of it. The number is crucial; we need to know what it is to try to work out why it is so important."

"What if we are being followed?" I asked.

"You have less than twenty-four hours, we have to risk it. I'm going for a wee then we'll head to yours then mine."

"Okay," I agreed reluctantly. She went to the toilets despite my advice on what to expect there. "The Only Way is Up" was now playing. I picked up a newspaper not because I wanted to read, but for a distraction and something to hide behind. It was last week's *Ealing News*, the same copy that I had read and after which entered the Ealing Half Marathon. I looked at that article again and ruminated on the fact that when I had originally read it and decided to enter the race my life was carefree and now I was up to my neck in shit with no idea of how to dig myself out.

There was the picture of the mass field from this year's race which looked so impressive and inspiring. As I looked at it something jumped out at me. I looked again. The picture was in black and white and somewhat grainy but there on the right-hand side was someone who looked a bit like Eustace and the number on his vest was quite clearly 2339.

CHAPTER SEVEN

When she came out of the toilets Vicky looked drawn; perhaps the reality of what she had got herself involved in was sinking in. I felt guilty, but needed her help too much to suggest that she back off from this. I told her on our way to the station that I definitely knew the number and how I had remembered it. After some initial resistance, she was suitably reassured that I did absolutely know it so we headed straight to hers. I held the newspaper and sat close to her. We were on the Piccadilly Line heading into town; we would then change for the Jubilee Line and Canada Water in Docklands where her flat was.

I closed my eyes and could see Bill and Isa's wedding photo. I then saw Isa and the mask. Vicky sensed my distress and gave my neck a gentle rub. From the original uni crowd, only Vicky and I were without long-term partners, I mulled as she continued to caress my neck. Perhaps the current circumstances had concentrated my mind, but I now realised that I should have grown a set of balls a long time ago and asked Vicky out. We should be an item. We were compatible, we liked each other, we laughed at each other's jokes and were still friends after seventeen years for Christ's sake. Why had I wasted all this time? That small tender gesture that she had just made showed it. Christ you can't see the wood for the trees and I was suddenly clear that if we got out of this shit I wanted to spend my time with her. Vicky's hair when I first met her would have to be called ginger or at best red, but as the years went by it became a luxurious auburn colour. Her skin was blemish-free with an almost alabaster look. She was gorgeous and she was my best friend.

Vicky is from Edinburgh. I had once been there for the New Year celebrations with her and seven of the uni crowd. She stayed at her parents' in the suburbs with two of our female companions and the rest of us stayed in an expensive and extremely basic youth hostel off the High Street. I had enjoyed the visit, but would have preferred to go at a less busy time and had always meant to return but never did. Another plan not seen through. Perhaps with my father being half-Scottish I felt some form of affinity to Edinburgh and the next time I visited I vowed it would be with Vicky as my partner.

As we walked through the crowds at Green Street to make our connection, all I could see were the happy, excited, expectant faces of those travelling at the beginning of their Saturday night out. I thought of the darts players in the pub earlier and now these happy crowds and again thought what lucky bastards they were. With no idea of how our evening was going to pan out, how I wished that I were them.

We got off at Canada Water and Vicky's flat was literally just round the corner from the station. She unlocked the front door of the apartment building which let us into a very well-appointed foyer decorated with modern art and pot plants. We took the lift to the third floor and entered her flat. There were no lights left on which I found surprising, although I expect that the security measures in place at her apartment block were more comprehensive than at my flat. It was certainly a bit more impressive than mine. An estate agent would describe it as: 'a stunning flat overlooking the River Thames, consisting of two bedrooms, a spacious living room and fully fitted kitchen.' The flat had laminate flooring, probably triple-glazed windows and no doubt an under-floor central heating system because it was pleasantly warm but I couldn't see any radiators. The place was spotless and had an aroma of expensive leather mixed with ginger or some other spice. I was now slightly glad that she hadn't visited my place and seen how I lived. I took a moment to stand on the balcony and take in the view. I am not normally overly impressed by material goods but must admit that this was impressive. What did Vicky do again? How had she moved into this stratosphere from an NHS trust?

Vicky and I were always a bit left of centre, although both our sets of parents are at different points on the Conservative spectrum. My parents are working-class Tories, my dad progressing from clerk to middle management, my mum managing the haberdashery section in a large department store. Vicky's are part of the Edinburgh establishment with her dad at a very senior position in insurance and her mother available as prop for all business and social requirements. I think that I have stayed more or less within my original political leanings but perhaps Vicky has moved elsewhere. "Right, stop dreaming and sit down," she said as she indicated for me to sit at one of the two black leather settees in the living room. I did as I was told and was glad that Vicky was, as I had hoped, taking the lead. She went into the kitchen and came back with two opened bottles of beer and put them on the long glass table in front of me. She then went into a bedroom and came out with a tablet.

"How long have you stayed here now?" I asked.

"This will be my second year."

"City life must suit you," I mused. I don't know what I really meant by that. "How did you move from an NHS trust to this?"

"It was thanks to Philippe. He was a Swiss banker and I was

still at the trust when I met him. Bit like *Love Story*; me and a friend had gone Christmas shopping then skating at Canary Wharf and met him or at least bumped into him on the ice after a few mulled wines. We had a hot chocolate, exchanged numbers and after a while became an item. He told me that I was wasted in what I did and that I could make a career and serious money working for him. He got me in."

"A big move culturally and philosophically," I ventured.

"Yes, but my current job was stressful, poorly paid and not stimulating. Plus after divorcing John I needed a change of focus."

"Is Philippe still there?"

"No he moved on, but I'll always be grateful that he got me out of where I was. Anyway, enough about me. Your aunt is being held at knifepoint, a man is dead and we need to move. It's nearly nine o'clock and we haven't even started. We need to find out about Eustace and the number," she said. "I'll work from my phone and you use the tablet. I'll search for details on Eustace and you search on the number. We need to try to work out what the number is for, how Eustace had it, who Eustace was and what he was up to at the very least. We need to know who and what we're dealing with," she said forcibly.

"What is the number? What does it represent? Is it a pin?" I asked.

"It's unlikely to be a pin number," she announced. "A gang that will kill would have the resources to crack a pin. We have to think like Eustace – he has taken four digits from his runners' number...are there other digits in this code?" she asked. "You said that the number was on half a post-it note. Could there be more numbers on the other half? I am sure that we are looking for another four digits at least."

I wasn't sure of her logic in coming to this conclusion, but didn't press her on it. Instead I asked, "Where do I start? How can I look for more numbers when I have no idea how many or for what reason?"

"We've got to start somewhere for Christ's sake," she responded. Vicky almost never swore and that was as near as she came. She must be serious. "Use all the information you have on Eustace and consider how he might think whilst you're searching."

"Sorry," I said, "and thanks so much for helping." It sounded a bit weak but was the best I could do. Mind you her advice wasn't exactly leading me anywhere. As I had said to Vicky, I didn't know where to start, so, out of interest and to get me going, I typed in 2339, realising that I was wasting my time because we knew that this number had come from Eustace's running number but interested to see what else it represented. I was surprised to find over fifty million references to this number including as an Electrical Power Engineering qualification, an American Legal Code relating to the harbouring, concealing or providing material support to terrorists, a reference number of a Lego brick, flight reference numbers for both Alaska Airlines and Southwest Airlines, a sewing pattern, an air squadron number and so on. It made me think of the infinitesimal combinations of digits and letters that we could be looking for with no real leads. I did as Vicky had suggested and kept thinking of Eustace whilst searching in case something sprung out from the back of my mind which could lead to a possible signpost to the number.

Vicky was finding next to nothing on Eustace apart from confirmation that a Eustace Barrington resided at Clepington Road. He was not on any social media forum so she couldn't dip into any of those outlets. His times in a few road races were listed. Widening the search to "E Barrington" massively increased the results but nothing of any relevance appeared. She tried various permutations of his name, initials and domains to find an email address but got nowhere.

"Can I have another beer please?" I asked.

"Last one then. We need to be clear-headed. I can't have you getting quite happy when we have to work out what's going on."

"One more will help me think," I said. I was getting frustrated. "This is impossible. How can we search for a number when we don't know what it's for or how long it is?"

"Write down the key points. We think we know that Eustace produced the number or was given it. What do we know about him?" she asked.

"He's Afro-Caribbean, fifty-seven, lives – sorry, lived – in West London," I said and then added some more questions: "What was his job? What were his hobbies? Can we find out any of his friends? He was a runner. Was he in a running club?" Vicky went on to the Ealing Half Marathon site and found the results page with Eustace and his number 2339 listed. Unfortunately he was listed as unattached, meaning that he was not a member of any running club, so no leads there.

"We have to think logically. What would crooks be involved in that uses numeric codes?" she asked rhetorically. "In order of importance I would say security boxes, money transfers and possibly bar codes. Most money transfer codes are twelve digits – we do them all the time. Could he have been involved in the illegal transfer of money? I'll look into this."

"Credit cards have sixteen digits. A phone number has at least six plus the area and or country code," I offered.

"Bar codes usually have between twelve and sixteen I think," she added. "Right, you find out everything you can on safety deposit boxes as it could be a code for one of them and I'll look into money transfers."

We resumed our online search and I started under "security box codes" as single words and as a phrase, finding thousands of results under whatever title I searched for with the results being broadly similar. There was nothing to suggest what the ideal amount of digits for a security box code should be. Many banks, financial institutions and specialist security companies seem to operate a combination of a pin number and a set or sets of keys. Sometimes the company keeps one key and the box is only opened in their presence and in other cases it is not. As well as this there is a whole variety of ways that codes are formed, such as biometrics, or using part of a bank's code to form a new code. Of course some codes could have letters as well as numbers, some have an alphanumeric check number and so on, and I noted that some boxes are operated by robotics. Interestingly it appears that the major banks are moving out of this line of business and are being replaced by other commercial operators and I quickly found examples in Ireland, Panama, the Czech Republic and Bulgaria where you can set up your own number without the need for a bank reference number as part of the code and conduct all business outwith the prying eye of a bank employee.

After we had been searching for over an hour Vicky said that she was going to call a colleague. "I just need to check something, don't let me distract you," she urged. She got up and went into the kitchen and switched the coffee machine on. I could hear her speaking over the noise of the machine but couldn't make out what she was saying. She came back from the kitchen with two coffees and put them down on the large low table then picked up her notes and added several bullet points.

"Who did you speak to?" I asked.

"Barry from my work."

"Who is he?"

"A fund manager."

"Wasn't he a bit surprised to hear from you at this time on a Saturday?" Despite the shit I was in, I was a bit jealous. "What did you ask him? You didn't tell him about our situation did you?"

"Of course not. Money never sleeps, Greg. I told him that I've got a potential client I'm dining with that's interested in transferring money about. Barry explained some of the basics which I'll get to in a minute." Vicky announced that it would be unlikely that the number that we were looking for would be for a money transfer because all schemes have codes that are composed of a twelve-digit alphanumeric code which is partly formed by adding a country code and check digit to the beginning and end. To give an example of what she meant, she went online and showed me pages of detail on the International Securities Identification Number (ISIN) which is used worldwide to identify specific securities such as bonds, stocks, futures, warrant, rights and trusts. Therefore if Eustace had formed the number himself, it wouldn't have been for an international money transfer because he would have had no control over forming it. I don't understand high finance, but I nodded to indicate that I understood what she was explaining because as I had discovered, some security boxes also use alphanumeric codes.

I updated her on what I had found on safety deposit boxes. It was now almost eleven; I had exhausted my list of search options and my resolve was disappearing. How I wished that I was having the night that I had planned: a couple of beers followed by a couple of wines and watching either extended highlights of a Premier League game or a live Spanish game on the telly, whatever took my fancy, then off to bed and up sometime after nine and out for a two- to three-mile jog as part of my half-marathon training programme. I had to force myself back to the present and reality. "Can we go over where we are?" I asked.

I had become increasingly exasperated and was now at the point where I thought we should just go to the police, tell them everything, and let them take charge and hope for the best. I said this to Vicky and stared at my notes, which were a page and a half of scribbles, then chucked them down. I picked up and looked at the A4 pad that Vicky had been writing on and at first thought that she had spent the last couple of hours doodling before realising that she had produced a mind map with several linked odd-shaped circles stretching out from a central point. The central point was Eustace and all of the odd-shaped circles had varying numbers of bullet points in them. I am aware of mind maps and the thought and planning processes involved, but am too literal and not lateral enough to be able to think and work like that. I handed them back to Vicky.

"Right, let's go over what we've got," she said, transferring her gaze from her notes to me. "One – Eustace. Aged fifty-seven, male, apparently single. Fit – we know he's a runner and has done more than one race. We know where he stays.

"Two – Aunt Isa. Held at knifepoint. It's highly unlikely that they would stay in her house. It's highly likely that the house is being watched. Unlikely that they will have taken her far.

"Three – the gang. Who are the blonde guy and his partner – what do they want? They have killed for the number. They are both quite young – both in their mid-twenties you think. The man in the mask – who is he and how did he get there? Unlikely that the two you've come across and the man in the mask are at the top, so who is the big boss? How many are in the gang? How did they end up at Eustace's?

"Four – the code. Eustace has probably formed the code because part of it is his running number. What does the code represent? It's unlikely that it would be for a money transfer if Eustace has indeed formed the number. The number of digits used for bar codes which can identify a product vary. Could the code be for a bank vault or security box? If so what length is it going to be?"

I listened intently to all that she said which was a well-presented case of everything that we knew and the key points and questions that we had considered, but I still didn't feel that we were any nearer to finding out who we were dealing with, what the number was for and how we would get Isa back. "So we still know next to nothing on points one to three. Do you think Aunt Isa is okay?" I asked.

"They want something from you, and your Aunt Isa is their guarantee that you will do as they say. It's in their interests to make sure that she is okay. If she wasn't you would be straight off to the police."

"I know, I know that, but I don't know if she is okay. They could come round to my flat tomorrow, I give them the number and Isa has had her throat cut..." I trailed off.

"What we need to do is to try as hard as we can to work out what the number is for and what the number consists of, then work out bargaining tactics for tomorrow." I could see how Vicky was doing so well in her work environment because she could assess situations, summarise them and work out the next steps logically, quickly and calmly.

"Okay," I said, "moving on to point four, we reckon the number from the waistcoat is most likely part of a code for a safety deposit box but we have no clear idea how many digits or letters it may have." She nodded. So on recounting what we had found and what we still needed to find, it didn't look like we had made much progress in our first few hours of searching. However, maybe Vicky's influence was working and I was beginning to think laterally because just after, or even while I was speaking, something struck me. I picked up the tablet, visited the Ealing Half Marathon site again and sat back feeling a little bit better. The cause behind the sudden improvement in my mood was that I was sure that if the number that we were looking for had eight digits I had just found the next four numbers in the code. Not only that, but if we were looking for a twelve-digit number then I think that I knew those next four digits as well. The reason for my confidence was that I now realised that I had definitely seen Eustace before and where I had seen him.

CHAPTER EIGHT

"If the number that we are looking for is more than four digits then I think that part of it is 9326," I stated.

"How do you know that?"

"Take a look," I said, gesturing for Vicky to look at the tablet. The results page of the Ealing Half Marathon was open.

"Stop playing games. Just tell me."

"Sorry." I realised that self-pride at my apparent discovery was making me milk this. I scrolled down to Eustace's name and finishing position. "He ran the half-marathon in one hour, thirty-three minutes and twenty-six seconds – that's ninety-three minutes twenty-six seconds. 9326. He's taken the number on the post-it note from the race so why shouldn't the second bit, if there is a second bit, come from it as well? You told me to try and think like him." She frowned but nodded in agreement at the same time. "We are always advised not to make passwords from kids' names, house numbers or favourite football teams – it needs to be something a bit obtuse yet still easy to remember."

"Christ, Greg, you may be right!"

"So we have 2339 9326 and we may need another four or eight digits if Eustace has made up and saved the number in four-digit blocks."

"Yes," she agreed, "but remember that the number may be

the other way around. We are assuming that it is twelve or sixteen digits. We are also assuming the order of the numbers. It could be any number of numbers and have letters in it as well."

"You're right but I think that the digits will have been stored in the correct order within their block of four. That makes them easier for Eustace to set and then remember them," I said and she agreed. "I think that I may know the next lot of numbers as well," I said.

"What? Really? Christ, Greg, you're on a roll."

I went to the Race Information section on the half-marathon website and under baggage it said:

> Baggage can be stored in the baggage tent near to the Start/Finish line or, thanks to our friends at Ealing Leisure Trust, the Nelson Leisure Centre has 200 lockers available to runners on a first come, first served basis. The lockers require a £1 coin which is refunded after use. Nelson Leisure Centre is less than ten minutes' walk from the Start/Finish.

I read this out to Vicky. She looked quizzically.

"So what?" she said.

"I have a membership for that leisure centre," I told her. I'd been a member for two or three years and been an occasional user until recently, when over the past six months I had tried to visit it at least once a week. My favourite time was a Saturday morning, cobweb-clearing visit, comprising of a small gym session mainly on the cardiovascular machines, then a swim followed by a sauna and steam. It had become a routine that I enjoyed and I always came out feeling better than when I went in. I hadn't gone in this morning because I was feeling too rough after my beer and curry with Phil. I told Vicky this. "That's where I've seen Eustace, in the gym." She frowned again.

It was a well-appointed fitness room with plenty of cardiovascular and fixed weight machines along with a free weights section. It was usually quite busy when I went at my normal time and there were always a lot of the same faces. I even knew one in particular by name, Doug, because he and his mates must have visited virtually every day and they knew the staff and the staff knew them. Doug engaged in banter with everyone he knew and eyed anyone that he didn't know slightly suspiciously. He recognised me as a fairly regular Saturday-morning visitor and I would get a slight nod of recognition which I reciprocated. He was one of those annoying bastards that think they own the place and would have shouted conversations over the loudish music and the heads of other users with a mate three machines away. Sometimes they'd be at opposite sides of the room but he would talk to a mate with them both looking at each other in the wall mirrors.

One of the group that Doug engaged in banter with was Eustace. Definitely. Some people who knew Doug just wanted to do their routine and not engage in banter on how QPR were getting on, or what they got up to last night. Eustace was like that – he would have a bit of a laugh initially, but then work away intently and Doug would find someone else to talk to. Doug was older than me – I would guess forty-five to fifty – and despite the fact that he used the gym regularly and, it appeared from his conversations, many of the fitness classes, he didn't look particularly fit. He was approximately five foot nine, slightly tubby and for no apparent reason almost always wore a beanie-type hat. I sometimes wondered what he did that allowed him the flexibility to visit the leisure centre so often and had narrowed it down to being either a taxi driver or unemployed as the leisure centre operated a free membership for those on benefits. I told Vicky all of this.

"Okay, Greg – but so what? What are you getting at?"

"My leisure centre membership number is four digits with

three letters at the front. I can't remember what they are but they are on my membership card which is currently hidden under the shed in my garden. I bet you Eustace is a member and that he will have a membership number of four digits."

"Good thinking. You may be onto something."

"I know that it's all speculation apart from that we know the four numbers I found in the waistcoat are real and must mean something. Until we find out more about Eustace all of this will just be guesswork, but we can hopefully get some detail on him from the leisure centre," I said. Then I pulled my rabbit out of the hat: "I know someone who works at the leisure centre who might be able to get Eustace's number and perhaps some more details on him. Maybe he's got a corporate membership and we can get the name of his employers." I was getting in a flow and perhaps getting too confident.

"Really," Vicky said, "who do you know?"

"Piotr – he's one of my students at the college. He works as a weekend cleaner at the leisure centre. I often see him there." Piotr is twenty-eight and from Poland. He was married with one very young child and was a student on the ESOL for Adults course, studying three days a week.

"What do you suggest we do?" she asked.

"Eustace is as regular a fitness-room user as Doug, so they will be wondering where he is. If I go in and hang about the fitness room then I may find out something about him from some of these acquaintances. Piotr doesn't work on reception, but is allowed access there so if he can somehow get onto the computerised till he could get Eustace's membership number and any other information stored on it. If we work out a plan to distract the receptionist and leisure attendant, maybe Piotr can then quickly spring into action. You could pretend to faint or have a fit. I will have already gone into the gym, Piotr gets on the computer, gets the details and gives me a signal at an agreed time and point and I get the details from him."

"For Christ's sake, Greg" – she was swearing a lot tonight – "that's all very well but how do we do this and what makes you sure that Piotr will want to help us?"

"It's all very loose I know but I'll contact him and somehow try and convince him how important it is. My aunt is being held at knifepoint. I'll promise him straight A's if that's what it takes."

"Yeah, but you are asking him to commit gross misconduct – a definite sacking offence. You've just said that he has a wife and a child; he's learning English to build a better life for them and you are asking him to do this...?"

"I'm fucking desperate, what do you suggest?" I shouted. I immediately regretted this outburst. "Sorry. You're helping me and I'm losing my head at you," I blustered.

"No, Greg, you're right, don't be sorry, you're thinking of your aunt. You're going to try everything and you're right to try everything. How are you going to contact him?"

"I've got details on all my students," I said as I went to the tablet and logged into my part of the college site. "It is mandatory for all students to have registered an email address," I told her, "and there is a field for a phone number but that isn't mandatory." I got to my section and the list of students with their various courses against their names. I scrolled down for Piotr. There he was:

Piotr Bzanucxs
47 Clifton Road
London
TW8

There was no phone number listed which was a blow, but there was an email address. "I'll drop him a line just now. Can I give him your number for him to call?"

"Of course, Greg. What if he doesn't get the message?"

"Well he's relatively young and most young people feel that they have to check and reply to all messages twenty-four seven. Hopefully Piotr is like that, but he has a young child and he will be getting up early in the morning so he might be in bed. Anyway, we have to at least try and see what happens. I suppose Plan B would be that I go to the centre and speak to him when he's on duty, but if we can contact him beforehand and plan this through then so much the better."

I wrote a message.

Hi Piotr

It's Mr Stewart (Greg), your tutor from college. Hope you are well and sorry to trouble you at this time. I need to speak to you very urgently regarding something to do with the Leisure Centre.

   Please call me as soon as you can on 078765446723
Many thanks, Greg

I clicked on the red exclamation mark icon to indicate that the message was of high importance. It was now eleven forty-five. What do we do now? I thought of Isa and hoped that she was okay.

"Do you want anything to eat?" Vicky asked. It shook me from my thoughts.

"What? No, no thanks."

"When was the last time you ate?" It was a good question and I realised that it was in fact breakfast. I had had the traditional hangover cure of a fry-up that morning which had taken precedence over going to the leisure centre. I had bought a plate of chips at Toni's but that was just to blend in. I didn't eat any.

"Greg. It's going to be a long night. We need to keep going

and we need fuel. I'll make us some toasties." God I love this girl, I thought. I rubbed my eyes and massaged my temple which was tense from the combination of stress and staring at a small screen for hours. I could hear the coffee machine on again. Vicky came through from the kitchen with her phone and handed it to me. I answered it.

"Mr Stewart. It's Piotr."

CHAPTER NINE

"Thank you for calling, Piotr, thank you very much." I tried to be brief and use small sentences with basic words. I was holding the phone very tightly and starting to pace the room.

"Is okay."

"Are you at Nelson Leisure Centre tomorrow?"

"Tomorrow? Yes."

"You are working at Nelson Leisure Centre tomorrow?"

"Yes."

"Good. Can I meet you before you start work?"

"Not sure."

Piotr had picked up this phrase a few weeks ago and used it quite a lot.

"I meet with you tomorrow?" I raised the inflection at the end of the sentence so that it was more obviously a question.

"Tomorrow?"

"Yes."

"Okay."

"We meet before you start work?"

"Work?"

Breaking many of the rules of Teaching English as a Foreign Language, but in desperation, I scribbled down *Can we meet before you start work?* and mouthed "Google translate" to Vicky.

"I need to meet you."

"Okay."

She handed the tablet over with her instant translation. I had no idea how to pronounce the words so spoke them slowly and deliberately. *"Możemy się spotkać przed pracą?"* It didn't seem to work.

"Not sure."

"Piotr I will email you just now. Do you understand?"

"Okay."

"Thank you, Piotr, please look for my email."

"Okay."

"Goodbye, Piotr, and please look out for the email. Thank you."

"Goodbye."

I quickly scribbled out:

Piotr we need to meet up tomorrow morning. Can we meet at 7.30 in the Bridge Café on Harrow Road? Please give me your mobile phone number. Many thanks, Greg.

"Translate that," I said to Vicky as I handed it over. It was hard to believe that I had been teaching foreign students how to speak English for many years, and in my desperation I was behaving like a novice, but we didn't have time. She typed it in and we had our instant translation. I took the tablet from her and copied and pasted the text into an email and sent it to Piotr.

Vicky got up, and on her way to the kitchen told me to eat the toasties that she had brought through. She said that she was going to phone her colleague Barry again as he was keen to see how she was getting on with her client and that this would help her to keep the charade going. I nodded that I understood, but secretly thought that she had actually blown a date to help me and this was her way of trying to maintain contact with that chap. Despite my feelings for Vicky growing stronger by the minute I did feel genuinely sorry that I had put her in such a position, not only of personal risk to herself but torpedoing her social life as well. Whilst I thought this I ate my toasties that had now become lukewarm. After a few minutes she came back into the lounge. "Well?" I asked.

"I just told him that nothing had come through yet and he's fine with that. I'm sure he believes me." She didn't sound too convincing but I wasn't going to pursue it.

"I'm going to write down the key points for Piotr. As you can see his English is basic and he's a pretty average student to be honest," I said.

I wrote down:

Eustace Barrington – 14 Clepington Road.

We need his membership number.

I will go into Leisure Centre and go to fitness room.

When Vicky comes in and pretends to be ill, you get number from computer in reception.

Find me – I will be in the Fitness Room. Give me the number.

It was now just after midnight. Piotr's email came through with his phone number. I replied with thanks, scribbled down the number and gave it to Vicky. "Good," she said as she saved his number into her phone.

"Is there anything more we can do just now?" I asked Vicky.

"I think that we should try and get some rest. Obviously if

anything springs to mind when you are sleeping or trying to sleep then get up and look into it and get me up as well if required. I'm going to bed and will be up by five at the latest. We need to get you a phone and some kit for the fitness room first thing in the morning." She left the living room and came back a few moments later with a continental quilt and put it at the end of the settee that I was sitting on. "This has been a crazy day, but we're making progress and let's hope tomorrow is better and successful. Try and get some sleep," she said. "Night, Greg."

"Night," I said. She left the room and dimmed the lights; there was just a small light on the coffee table left on. I was a bit disappointed that I didn't get a peck on the cheek at least and was sleeping on the settee when there was a second bedroom. Despite that, the thought that I was sleeping so close to Vicky's bedroom did excite me. I know that it shouldn't have under the circumstances, and that all my mental energy should be used on the number and Eustace and how I could get Isa back, but I couldn't help it. In the war, hasty relationships happened all the time when people got together under the most dangerous of circumstances for an unlikely coupling; hence war babies. I must admit that was what I had hoped for. Well not the baby bit.

I lay down and pulled the quilt over me and closed my eyes. I hadn't bothered to kill the remaining light. I thought of Isa and felt guilty for thinking of my sexual gratification in front of working out how we find the number and how we free her. Then I had a shuddering thought that gave me butterflies and heart flutters. I sat up with a start. What if my parents had gone round to visit Isa? What if they were being held? Fuck. I hadn't even thought of that until now. What should I do? I looked at the tablet – twelve thirty. Should I phone them? Would this make things better or worse? Should I phone my sister? Should I ask Vicky what I should do? Would she just think that I was trying it on?

I need her advice, I thought reluctantly, I have to ask Vicky. I got up and gingerly walked through the lounge and along the hall. I hesitated outside her door. I listened in case she was speaking to Barry again. She didn't appear to be speaking to anyone and I couldn't hear a television or any other sound. I took a deep breath, and then gently tapped on the door. No response. I counted to ten, and then knocked again hoping that I wasn't left with a dilemma of what to do if she still didn't answer. "Is that you, Greg?" a muffled voice said.

"Yes. Yes. Sorry but I need to ask you something, Vicky, please…" I sounded a bit pathetic.

"Come in."

Here goes. I gently opened the door and walked in. The light was on and Vicky was just getting herself into a sitting up position in bed. She was wearing a baggy T shirt and felt no need to coyly pull the cover up to her chin as they seem to do a lot in TV sitcoms. "What is it?"

"My parents stay very close to Aunt Isa and visit her all the time – what if they have gone to visit her and have been taken by this bastard in the mask? Should I phone them or my sister now? It's so late, but I don't know. What if they haven't been round to Isa's and I phone now – then they might go, which will makes thing worse, but what if they have gone and have been taken? I've got to do something."

"Sit down and let's talk this through." She was calm and firm. Good she was still taking the lead. She started repeating the options in list form.

"Let's look at the possibilities. One, they have gone to visit her and have been taken – then no use phoning them. Even more reason to find out what this number is and what it represents. Two – they haven't visited Isa. If so they will be asleep in bed, so don't call them and scare the shit out of them. We have until teatime tomorrow to sort this. Three, don't call your sister. What will that achieve? Same as in point two."

As we were going through these she climbed out of bed and I did my best to avert my eyes from looking her up and down, but I did catch a good glimpse of thigh. She sat next to me and rubbed my neck like she had done on the train. "What do you think, Greg?"

"I don't know," I sighed. "What if we get nowhere with this number? What'll happen when they come back tomorrow afternoon?"

"I think that the best thing to do at this time is nothing, for the reasons we have discussed," she said. "I am so sorry for you, Greg, you should never have had to deal with this, but if we can get the number and find out what it's for, then that gives us the bargaining power for when they return. You can tell them you know the number, what it's for and they're not fucking getting it 'til you know Isa is free." I was shocked. That was the first time I think I had ever heard Vicky use the F word. But it helped convince me. She had got closer to me; her scent was strong and intoxicating as she continued massaging my neck.

"Thoughts?" she said.

"I trust you, Vicky. I'm not used to having to weigh things up and make big decisions. You are. I'll go with whatever you say." She turned me round and I finally got my kiss, which was more than just a peck on the cheek. Worth the wait. We continued kissing and our tongues met. I could feel her hands underneath my shirt. Tentatively at first, then with more confidence, I moved my right hand under her T shirt and gently caressed her right breast. Her nipple was hard.

Here we go…

CHAPTER TEN

The sandwiches had gone down a treat and now Bill and Richard were away gathering driftwood to make a small bonfire so that they could roast their marshmallows. She could almost burst with happiness. The sea air was so good for Richard and it was also good for Bill to be away from work and spending time with him – and her. He so liked being with Richard and was such a loving father it was a pity he had all this overtime to do on the railways, but as he said it was bringing money in for the family.

The two of them were very far away now and she could just make out their happy voices as they shouted encouragement to each other. She could feel a warm tear of happiness slowly run down her face and dabbed a hankie at it. She looked up and saw Bill waving happily to her and she stood up and waved back. He shouted something that got lost on the wind. She mimed – outstretching her arm then cupping her hand to her ear to show that she couldn't hear him.

"What?" she bellowed with a huge laugh.

He shouted again.

"Shut the fuck up, you fat stinking cow."

She felt a kick on her hip and the cold metal floor of the van. Her prayers hadn't been answered.

CHAPTER ELEVEN

I woke with a start and it took me several seconds to get my bearings. I was lying on my own in Vicky's bed, but could still smell her scent and sense the warmth from her body. I thought back to our session, after which I had lain with Vicky snuggled against me and drifted off into a contented sleep.

I don't know if Yin and Yang is the correct expression to use here but on the one hand I thought back to that incredible experience with Vicky; one which I had craved for years and was better than I had ever imagined in my many solo sessions. On the other hand we were soon going to embark on a plan that we had no idea if we had the skills, nerve or luck to carry out. Last night before going to bed it felt as if we had made some form of progress with our online searches. It seemed plausible to try and find a code that we thought might be twelve digits but in reality could be of any length and then try and find the security box to which this code applied. If it was a security box, and if we did all of that in the next twelve hours or so, I might see Isa again.

I wondered how Isa's night had been and hoped that these bastards were looking after her.

I had no idea of the time and couldn't see a clock nearby. Vicky's bedroom had an en suite but I couldn't hear the shower going or any noise from in there so assumed that she must be in the kitchen. That was a bit disappointing because I hoped that she would come into the bedroom with nothing but a towel wrapped round her head and let me take in her naked gorgeousness. As I was thinking this, Vicky did appear, fully clothed in jeans and a blouse and carrying a cup of coffee. "Right, sleeping beauty, get that down you, have a quick shower and then we have to go."

"What time is it?" I asked.

"Five thirty." She was being pleasant but a bit neutral. I had expected a bit more from her after last night, but then when two friends finally have sex after knowing each other for so long, I suppose it can be awkward. I just hoped that we could get to see our plan through and get Isa back.

After that me and Vicky... No, no time for wistful romantic thoughts just now.

I gulped down my coffee and went into the en suite shower. It was very modern and took me a while to get it working. When I did, it pinned me against the gleaming tiles with a ferocious jet of water. I must have had three and a half to four hours of sleep, which was okay under the circumstances I thought, and the shower did enough to blow the remaining cobwebs away. I came out of the shower and used some of Vicky's deodorant, but had to put on yesterday's clothes of course.

We had decided last night that we would visit the twenty-four-hour supermarket in Canary Wharf, one stop down the line from Canada Water, to get me a mobile phone which would be more convenient than Vicky's tablet and some gym kit that I could use at the leisure centre. "Are you ready?" she asked.

"Yes," I replied. Maybe the big match nerves were kicking in but she hadn't even offered me breakfast.

"Right, let's go."

I went into the lounge and picked up my wallet and the prompt notes for Piotr, plus the notes that I had made in the online search for security boxes and related matters, which I folded neatly and put in my hoody pocket, zipping it shut. Vicky handed me a carrier bag with a towel and some shower gel for the leisure centre. "Oh thanks," I said, noting that she had thought of everything, her planning being way better than mine.

It was dark when we left the apartment and took the lift down. In the lift there was an almost embarrassed silence between us. Making love to Vicky probably meant more to me than her, and to me signified that we were closer than ever and was hopefully the start of something. However I wasn't totally naive and considered that she may have regarded our session along the lines of the wartime analogy that I'd thought about earlier. A one-off, good at the time, but over. I put that depressing thought to the back of my mind and decided that today we had to think and work as a team. She was definitely the captain and we couldn't have any awkwardness getting in the way of how we were operating.

If I thought about what I was going to say for any longer I wouldn't have said anything, so I took a breath and as we were leaving the apartment block and heading to the station said, "Vicky. The only good thing about yesterday was being with you and sleeping with you last night, which was amazing. I don't know how you feel about me or about last night but let's just get on with things today like we had done up to then and try and get this sorted and Isa home. Then we can talk about the future." I thought that I had done okay up to the end and was then inwardly cringing. What the hell did I mean by saying, "Then we can talk about the future?" What a prick. Hey ho.

"Yeah, Greg. No bother, of course. Let's get this plan underway and work it through." Phew.

We waited about ten minutes on the cold platform for the train and then boarded it for our one stop. The warmth of the compartment as we got on the train made me do an involuntary shudder. Soon it was time to get off and we headed down the escalator and into the huge shopping area below the Canary Wharf tower. The supermarket was at the far end and had several dozen shoppers in it. What did these people do, I wondered, that they were in here at this time on a Sunday morning?

We selected the cheapest pay-as-you-go phone option and a pair of dark-blue leisure shorts, white sports socks, a white T shirt, and a small black backpack. Vicky paid despite my protestations, peeling off some notes taken from a bundle inside her purse which I found quite surprising as I expected everything was done by plastic in her world. She threw the receipt into the nearest bin. I don't suppose we will be bringing them back, I thought as I put my carrier bag into the backpack.

We sat at a table in the café area in the main concourse and got two coffees from one of the few cafés that had already opened up for the day. I let Vicky set up the phone and she of course did it in what felt like seconds. Vicky called her number from my phone and it rang reassuringly. She saved the number and then saved Piotr's into my phone.

"Right, text Piotr and remind him to meet us at the Bridge Café at seven thirty." I did as I was told.

"What now?" I asked.

"Let's go over the plan again, starting from us meeting Piotr in the café," she said. We did so and I felt as if we may have a chance of getting the number, which even if we didn't find out any more about Eustace at least would give me some more bargaining power with Blondie. After we had covered every point, Vicky announced that it was time to go. I checked my phone for the time, glad that I had a phone back again and a way of telling the time. It was just after six thirty. We made our way to Canary Wharf station and I desperately wanted to hold Vicky's hand as we walked and then

71

stood waiting for the train; however, I sensed that she had her businesslike head on and that I would be rebuffed so fought the urge for contact. The train arrived and we got on in silence. We were both lost in our thoughts on the short ride to Green Street and the journey passed quickly. As we made our way to change platform on arrival at the station I felt marginally more optimistic than I had done when I was there last night, but now the nerves were beginning to kick in. As we stood on the platform I felt my phone go. It was a text from Piotr. C U @ café. His English might not be great yet but texting must be universal, I thought.

Thanks, Piotr, I replied.

"That was Piotr. He's coming to the café," I told Vicky.

Vicky smiled. "It's coming together, Greg," she said and I nodded rather too enthusiastically, but I was like a smitten teenager and overreacting to any positive vibes given off by her. I felt in my pocket for the notes that I had written as prompts for Piotr last night. I had done this several times since leaving Vicky's apartment. They were still there.

Our train arrived, we got on a nearly empty carriage and I tried to snuggle into Vicky, but she was far less responsive than on the equivalent journey last night. I straightened myself up, fiddled nervously with the straps of my new backpack and stared at the adverts to take my mind off what was to come. We were now living the plan.

We got off the train and made our way to the Bridge Café which was a good fifteen-minute walk from the station. However I chose it because I knew it opened early every day, having once stopped off there from a particularly good and late night out. It was on a main road populated with the usual convenience stores, bookmakers and takeaways and was near to a small industrial estate. The window of the café had the customary condensation on it and the smell of bacon frying could be picked up from some distance away. A thought struck me that between Toni's and the Bridge you could get 24/7 grease in this neck of the woods. Vicky must have read my mind. "You sure can pick them, Greg," she said somewhat snottily. "First Toni's, now this dump."

"It's open, it's near the leisure centre and Piotr's coming – what's the fucking problem?" I snapped. Who said this? Was this the same man as "we can discuss the future"? Yes it was. I had just had the most unusual, stressful and unbelievable day of my life culminating in shagging the object of my dreams who was now coming over all Lady Muck. I was very nervous, I didn't know what to expect or how to cope, my aunt was in danger and maybe my parents, I'd maybe worked out what the number was and what it might be for and she was speaking to me like this. "I'm sorry," I immediately followed up with, "but I'm fucking nervous."

"Okay, no bother, Greg, you're right."

We went into the café, which had three other customers who were all on their own. We sat down and after a few minutes I realised that we wouldn't get table service in here, or a skinny latte for that matter. "What do you want?" I asked Vicky.

"Black coffee." I noted the lack of a *please*. Despite everything that we were about to embark on, at that moment my biggest concern was that I had just screwed up everything with Vicky. "Anything to eat?" I took her rolling eyes as a no. On my walk up to the counter I noticed that the three other customers – two men and one woman and each sat at separate tables – were of roughly the same age, fifty-five to sixty-five. They all looked like smokers with grey pallor and leathery complexions. None of them were eating; both men studied the sports section of their tabloids intently and the woman muttered to herself as she drank her tea. I tried to imagine what this place would have been like before the smoking ban in public places; you would have had to cut your way in.

The price list was fixed to the wall opposite the counter and was about a metre tall and half a metre wide. It had those white letters and numbers that clip into holes in the black plastic board. I noted with approval that all the letters and numbers appeared to be in place. Just like in Toni's my condescending attitude towards this place was countered by an extremely welcoming café assistant. She was well built, appeared to be in her sixties, and in fact was like a younger, rougher London version of Isa. Yes – I'd think of her as London Isa. "Hello, my luv, what can I get you?" she asked with a big welcoming smile. I have always been partial to a bacon roll and surprisingly despite my nerves I was hungry so I ordered one along with a cup of tea for me as well as Vicky's coffee. "I'll shout when it's ready, my darling," she told me. She was true London salt of the earth. I liked her and wished that I could stay in her café all day.

I went back to our table and sat down. Vicky looked slightly nervous, at least for her. "You okay?" I asked. "Sorry to have got you wrapped up in this mess. I really, really appreciate your help, Vicky. I shouldn't have snapped at you." I was being genuine and suddenly felt so sorry for snapping at her on the way into the café. She didn't even need to be here. I hoped to Christ we'd get through today, get Isa safe and then hopefully be together. Ever the romantic, here I was again planning our long-term future after one night and not knowing if I'd make it through today.

"Bacon roll, tea, coffee, my darling," London Isa shouted. I got up to get our order and I felt that my eyes were watering slightly. I'm not built for such a rollercoaster of emotions. On my way back to my seat, I spotted Piotr coming in. Because I had his details on my work system I knew that Piotr was twenty-eight, but if I didn't have them, and if he wasn't a couple of inches over six foot then I would think that he was about twelve. He had a round face, very pale skin, a bowl haircut and small hazel eyes.

You had to be very close to him to see that he did in fact shave, but only on a very small area directly on his chin. He had a wide-eyed innocence about him and I found it hard to picture him as a parent. Piotr smiled warmly when he saw me. I gestured him over.

"Hi, Piotr, this is Vicky."

She stood up and shook his hand. "*Dzień dobry*," she said.

He smiled and almost bowed. "Good morning," he replied as he took off his large padded jacket and put it on the back of his chair. He was wearing his work uniform of navy tracksuit trousers, yellow polo shirt and navy fleece.

"Piotr. Thank you very much for coming."

"Is okay."

"Do you want anything to drink or eat?" I asked. I was miming drinking and eating actions very badly like some pissed Brit would do to a Spanish waiter on a Mediterranean holiday. My voice was getting louder and I saw Vicky frown at me.

"Tea please," he said softly. I went up to my new friend and ordered the tea. Back at the table, I pulled my chair beside Piotr so that we were sitting side by side and Vicky was facing us. I took out my notes and pointed to them as I took a bite of my bacon roll.

"Piotr, we have a problem. Eustace Barrington, – 14 Clepington Road, is a member of the leisure centre. We need his membership number."

"Why?" Piotr looked puzzled.

"It is part of a code. Like a pin code. I took out my wallet and pointed at it. Do you understand?"

"Yes."

"White tea, my darling." Shit, just when I was getting into a flow. I went up to the counter and got the drink. Vicky and Piotr were conversing. I handed Piotr his tea and he added three sugars to it. At least he won't run out of energy, I thought as I continued eating my roll.

"The membership number is very important," I said. "We must have it."

"You want card?" He pointed at the pocket that my wallet was in.

"No. No. We just need the number. Don't worry, it is not to steal from him."

Piotr looked confused. "I not know why you want number."

Vicky looked up from her phone and said, "Does this make sense?" She held the screen in front of him.

He read the words – Eustace jest martwy. Kod jest ważny.

"Do you understand?" She asked.

He frowned but said, "Yes."

"What have you told him?" I asked.

"Eustace is dead. The code is important."

Christ, she was good. "Good thinking," I said.

"So you understand, Piotr?" I asked – or was it pleaded?

"Yes. Is okay."

"Okay," I said, referring back and pointing at the notes. "I will go into the leisure centre and go to the fitness room." I looked at him and he nodded. "She will come in five minutes after me." I held up the fingers and thumb of one hand. "When Vicky comes in," I pointed at Vicky, "she will pretend to be sick." Vicky mimed swooning back and rolled her eyes. Piotr smiled at her mime and nodded his head. "You get Eustace's number from the computer in reception." I pointed at Eustace's name on my notes and then mimed typing to indicate that I was referring to the computer at reception. "Understand?"

"Yes. Of course."

"Good. You will have to be quick. Understand?"

"Yes. Of course."

"Find me – I will be in the fitness room – and give me the number." I gave a pathetic mime of doing some kind of arm exercise.

"Understand?"

"Yes."

"Do you need to ask any questions?"

He looked slightly quizzical.

"*Pytania?*" Vicky said.

He shook his head, "No. Is okay."

I looked at the time on my phone. It was seven twenty. I expected that he would have to be at work half an hour before opening. "Do you want another drink?" I asked, pointing at his empty cup.

"No. I go." I was right.

"Piotr, many thanks," Vicky said. She held his hand and gazed at him with her most sensuous look and I knew then that he would walk through walls for her. "Thank you so much," she repeated. He got up and I stood with him, shook his hand and gave him a little man hug.

"Thanks, Piotr, this is so helpful." I gave him a thumbs up which he reciprocated and he made his way out of the café. I sat back down. "Well here we go. Do you think he understood everything?" I asked.

"He understands the main points and what we have asked him to do," she reassured me. "What time are you going in?" It sounded like military speak.

"Five minutes after opening – five past eight. Then you wait five minutes to let me get in and changed so that they can't tell that we're together before you come in and throw your wobbler."

"Right, okay. I'm going for a wee."

"Want another coffee?" I asked. She shook her head as she walked towards the toilets. I needed to go as well but thought it best to wait for Vicky to come back. One other customer had come in who seemed to be a regular and had ordered the full works for breakfast. Again; it was becoming a recurrent theme, like the darts players in the pub and the Saturday night revellers at the station: lucky bastard, I thought – wish that was me.

Vicky came back to the table and I went to the gents, via the counter where I ordered a coffee for myself just in case I needed the caffeine energy. The toilet had a top hat and cane symbol on the door to indicate gender and when I opened it discovered that it was a single WC unit minus the seat. There were two small wooden guard rails screwed into each side of the ceramic toilet bowl which had the obligatory skid marks inside it and puddle on the floor around it. I stood and peed, grateful it was only that I needed, and shuddered when my stream came into contact with part of the skid mark which was a mustard colour.

I returned to the table and my coffee was there. Vicky must have got it. I normally don't take sugar, but put in a couple of spoons for energy. I blame Piotr. We sat in silence and checked the time on our phones every few minutes. "Send him a text," Vicky suddenly announced. It gave me a bit of a start.

"Okay," I said and dutifully wrote: Piotr, is everything okay?

Thirty seconds later: Yes.

The minutes passed slowly but finally it was time to go. I got up and settled the bill and gave a couple of quid tip to London Isa. She was taken aback and genuinely truly grateful. "Oh thank you very much, my darling. I hope that you and your young lady have a lovely day." I don't know about lovely, more like lively, I thought.

"You're welcome. Hope that you have a good day as well," I said with what I hope looked like a cheery smile.

We walked slowly towards the leisure centre. The streets were pretty quiet and as we got nearer, Vicky told me to keep going and that she would walk around the block to kill time. "Keep in touch by text. I'll let you know how my performance went and where I am," she told me.

I nodded in understanding and confirmed, "Will do."

I looked at the time: six minutes past – perfect. At this moment it dawned on me that I didn't have my leisure card, which was under Mr Cartwright's shed with the original four digits of Eustace's number. I approached the reception and recognised the receptionist. She was sitting behind the glass screen, having just served someone and there was no queue. There was also no sign of Piotr. Shit. I hesitated for a second but knew I had to go ahead and just hope that he got in the right place soon. "Morning. Gym and swim please. Sorry I've forgotten my card."

"What's your name please? Do you have any other form of ID?" she asked, sounding a bit agitated.

"Greg Stewart." I took out my wallet to get my driving licence, then suddenly thought: fuck, Blondie took that.

I'll just pay cash, I thought, then my heart skipped a beat when I opened my wallet as my bank card wasn't in it. The bastard must have taken that as well and I had about £3 in cash. This might be tricky.

"Anything with an address on?" she asked.

I couldn't find anything apart from a college business card which had my name and the college address. "This okay?" I asked slightly pleadingly as I handed the card over. She looked at it then typed something into the computer.

"Fine. Change for your locker?" she said quickly without looking up.

"Sorry?" I asked.

"Change for your locker?" she said in an exaggerated slow voice.

"Oh! No, no thanks." Phew. I had made it in. I walked past reception and through the automatic doors which led into the main foyer and had corridors leading off to activity areas on both the wet and dry sides of the building. I saw Piotr, who was beside a large notice board with a buffing machine. He had his back to me but instinctively looked up and said, "Okay?" as I walked past. He was better at this than me.

"Okay," I replied as I carried on walking and made my way to the dry-side changing rooms. I quickly got changed into my new kit, stuffed my gear into my backpack and put it in a locker which was situated on the wall of a corridor outside the changing rooms. I went to the fitness room feeling nervous at what lay ahead and slightly self-conscious as my shorts were a bit too baggy round the waist despite me pulling the drawstring in as tight as possible and tying with my best knot.

It was quiet in the fitness room with only two other users in there, both blokes, neither of whom I recognised. The music was on but thankfully it wasn't too loud and I went onto an exercise bike and started to slowly pedal which made the electronic display on the machine spring into life. There was a clock on the digital display so I could see every second passing, and as they did so I felt my chest tightening. After just over four minutes I was sweating freely due to the combination of the exercise and my mental state. I knew that I could rely on Vicky but I doubted Piotr, not just because he didn't know what this was all about, or that he was foreign, but because it was up to chance if the receptionist left her station to allow him the opportunity to get access to her machine. She seemed lazy and stroppy and I had my doubts that she would move off her fat arse to help any poor customer in distress. If she didn't, who would, and how would Piotr get onto her machine? I was shaken from my thoughts by Doug, who burst in.

"It's all go out there," he announced to the room. "Some bird has just had a wobbly in reception. Looks like she passed out."

CHAPTER TWELVE

"Is she okay?" one of the other users asked.

Doug loved this, being the centre of attention.

"Don't know, mate, looked like she was just coming round. Staff are dealing with it – think they're going to call an ambulance. Nothing I could do so I just walked in. Nobody was covering reception. She's a cracker by the way – pity she's wearing trousers, hoped to see her knickers."

The person who had spoken to Doug guffawed, "Should have given her the kiss of life, my son!" Doug found that funny. My heart skipped a beat, not at the caveman remarks but at the mention of the ambulance. I was hoping that Vicky's acting skills hadn't been too convincing. It crossed my mind that we had not worked out our course of action after getting Eustace's membership number and any other details that we could. Piotr was going to get it to me some way and that was it. We had assumed that we would just meet up, but being amateurs had not specified a location or time. I had decided to do at least half an hour in the fitness room to make it look convincing and to try and see if any of the other users knew Eustace and said anything about him. Doug being in was a bonus because he knew everyone. Also Doug said that there was no one in reception when he came in. Good.

I had been cycling for over fifteen minutes now and the sweat was pouring down. Another two people had come into the room, bringing the total users to six. They nodded to Doug and the person Doug had been speaking to and went to their chosen machines. I was disappointed because I thought that an early-morning Sunday session would be more popular; I expected a few more people to be self-righteously working off the excesses of Saturday night. As I was thinking this another person came into the room and I didn't recognise him either, although he was from the Doug school of communication.

"Looks like some bird collapsed out there," he announced.

"Yeah, saw that," Doug immediately answered." Have they got an ambulance for her yet?" he asked. He couldn't be outdone.

"Nah," he said, "they were trying to but she kept on saying she was alright and to leave her alone. I tried to help and she told me to fuck off."

"Fuck sake," Doug contributed.

"Fucking fruit cake. Bit of a looker though."

"What happened?" Doug asked.

"She got up and fucked off."

"They say the good lookers are the crazy ones," was Doug's balanced assessment.

Good, I thought. She's done her bit, but has Piotr? I had now been cycling for over twenty minutes and was getting thirsty. I hadn't thought to bring some water with me or buy a bottle from one of the vending machines on the way in. There were several water machines in the fitness room but they didn't have cups as users filled up their own bottles from them. I could of course nip out to the changing room and get money from my wallet to buy a bottle, but didn't want to risk leaving the fitness room in case Piotr happened to come in when I had just left. I had told him to meet me here and didn't want to deviate from that.

The room was filling up now and there were a few shouted conversations across the machines from Doug and his mates as if they owned the place. Swearing was commonplace and as well as the standard use of *fuck*, I heard a couple of *cunts* as well. I am no prude and swear a lot myself, in context and with friends who know me and how I think, but definitely not in a room of strangers. Perhaps that's why there were no females in.

"Where's The Man?" I could hear Doug shout to the guy who had seen Vicky's performance. "He never turned up last night."

"Don't know. Maybe *The Man* is doing some horizontal jogging!" he replied. He said this in a much exaggerated Jamaican patois. My ears pricked up. Could they be referring to Eustace?

"Yeah he's maybe fucked literally." They both laughed. "He's not been the same since he clicked with Cassie."

"Yeah. Lucky bastard. What does she see in him? Good night last night?" the man asked Doug.

"Yeah, mate, the best. Lost a few fucking quid though," Doug complained. They carried on this shouted conversation for a few more minutes. It seemed to revolve around something called a race night which was in a pub. I had never heard of a race night and didn't really understand what it meant but it obviously involved a lot of drinking and gambling. The person they called The Man was supposed to be there but didn't turn up and also didn't finish *the job* yesterday. Could this be Eustace and what was the job?

Another person came into the room and I vaguely recognised him. "Hi, Bri!" Doug shouted. I presumed he was called Brian.

"Fucking Spinning's off," he announced. Doug was not amused.

"You. Are. Having. A. Fucking. Laugh."

"No, straight up, mate. Cassie has phoned in sick."

"That's no fucking good to me," Doug announced. "If that fucking bird wasn't rolling around the floor they could have told me that when I came in."

"What the fuck are you talking about?" Brian asked.

"Some bird had a wobbler in reception," the man who had spoken to Doug earlier enlightened Brian.

"Fuck. I was looking forward to that class – blow the cobwebs away. It's fucking Eustace's fault. I'll do thirty minutes on this fucker instead," Doug said as he moved onto a stepper machine.

Eustace. The magic word.

I had now been cycling for over thirty minutes and decided I needed to get nearer to Doug. I wiped down the cycle and myself with paper towels from the dispensers then went on to a jogging machine which was one machine away from Doug's stepper to my left. There was no one in between us and Brian was on the other side of Doug. There were a further three jogging machines to my right and only the furthest one away was being used. I was hopeful that I'd pick up some useful Eustace snippets from Doug and Brian as they continued their verbal exercise whilst they gently worked the machines. I had already picked up two things –Eustace was, at least to some extent, part of their group outside the gym, and Eustace appeared to be involved with someone who might be the spinning instructor.

As I slowly jogged, I wondered where Vicky was and how her performance had gone. I assumed that it had gone well and it appeared that she had managed to convince the staff that an ambulance wasn't necessary. But what about Piotr? If he had got the number I thought that he would have given it to me by now. If he hadn't got it I thought that he would have at least told me that, but of course I hadn't given him any instruction on what to do in the event of not getting it. What if he had been caught? It would look like fingers in the till and he would be hooked straight away. A silent *fuck* muttered under my breath was the best that I could come up with.

I had set the jogger at just over walking pace to ensure that I wouldn't run out of steam whilst attempting to eavesdrop on Doug and Brian. I was onto my fifth minute when I saw Piotr come into the room in the reflection from the wall mirrors. He appeared to be checking the machines and gave some of them a quick spray and a wipe with his cloth. He worked his way over to me and I surreptitiously looked over at Doug or Brian to see if they were watching him, but no, he was the foreign cleaner – part of the scenery. Piotr wiped the machine next to me. "What is your locker number?" he asked quietly. I couldn't think and moved my wrist to look at the number on the plastic wristband that contained my locker key.

"965," I said out of the corner of my mouth.

"Okay," he acknowledged. Piotr then moved away and picked up a checklist on a clipboard from the wall next to the paper towel dispenser, made great play of noting the time, then marked off the sheet and left the room. He's definitely better at this than me, I thought. I realised we must have the number. I had butterflies in my stomach at the thought that we had cracked it – we'd got the number!

But had we cracked it? Well yes, but maybe no. We didn't know how long the number was or what it was for. Still, I had something for Blondie that must be good enough for him to let Isa go. As I was thinking this Doug enlightened Brian on his movements. "I'm off to the lockup after this." My ears pricked up. Maybe he was a taxi driver after all. Maybe Eustace was as well. Had he got the code from a customer? The clock on the wall told me that it was now nine fifteen. I'm going to follow him, I thought. I've got the number, what else can I find out before Blondie's return visit?

"Fuck this," I heard Doug say, "that's enough for me."

"Me too," said Brian. They dutifully wiped down their machines, which surprised me. They refilled their water bottles and each had large glugs from them, exchanged a bit of banter with a couple of the other users and left the room. I'll give it five minutes, I thought.

After just over five minutes had passed I slowed the machine down and then stopped it. I wiped it down, wiped myself, went out of the room and made my way to the bank of lockers and opened mine. There was my new backpack and in front of it was a piece of A4 paper folded into quarters. I calmly picked up the paper, put it in a side pocket of the bag and made my way into the changing room. I wanted to kiss Piotr.

Annoyingly, Doug and Brian had not yet made it into the showers. They stood bollock naked arguing about a dodgy penalty decision by a fucking moron of a referee. I went to the furthest part of the room and tried to make myself as inconspicuous as possible as I fiddled with my backpack and surreptitiously unfolded the piece of paper. I inwardly urged the pair of them to get in the showers. Finally they did and I looked at the paper – NLC 7126. There was nothing else on the paper. I folded it and put it in the zipper pocket of my hoody.

I followed Doug and Brian into the showers a minute or so later. They were old-style showers, no cubicles but ten individual showers next to each other where you let it all hang out and had your wash.

"Got your motor?" Brian asked Doug loudly as he shampooed himself.

"Left it at the lockup – wanted a bit of a walk to clear me head on the way here."

"Want a lift?"

"Nah – no thanks, mate. The walk will help me cool down."

I left the showers, dried myself, dressed and left the changing room. Doug was standing preening himself in the mirror. As I was out before him, I hung around the foyer area and read the posters on the notice board like a keen user would. It was the usual stuff regarding classes, club activity and so on and I noticed that one was for the Ealing Half Marathon. I was only half reading them when one jumped out at me: *Spinning with Cassie!* There was a picture of Cassie, who was in a leotard on a spinning bike, and had a huge smile. She had a lovely complexion, swept-back hair and deep brown eyes. I'd seen her before. She was the quiet young woman from Eustace's flat.

Suddenly Doug and Brian's chat made sense. Class cancelled; "Eustace's fault"; "horizontal jogging"; "What does she see in him?" Just as I was thinking this Doug came out of the changing room on his own and walked past me towards reception. He was glowing and wearing jeans, a polo shirt, trainers and a sweatshirt but no jacket. I hung back for a second, then quickly took down the A4-sized poster for Cassie's classes, hurriedly folded it and stuffed it in my backpack. I sent a text to Vicky to tell her that I had the number and I was going to follow Doug to his lockup. After that I went through reception and watched Doug go out of the main doors of the building and then started to slowly follow him.

In my excitement I realised that I had left my pound coin in the locker. More importantly in my haste to send the text I had forgotten to tell Vicky about Eustace and Cassie. My thoughts turned to them: they were an item – how and when had they hooked up? It struck me that as they unfolded, the various elements in this nightmare were in some ways revealing but in other ways just confusing the issue more. Where did Cassie fit in? She was a fitness instructor and apparent partner of Eustace but didn't seem particularly upset with Eustace sitting in his living room with a knife in his chest. That thought gave me a shudder and reinforced to me the deep shit that I was still in. Was she in a gang with Blondie and Eustace? And Doug – was he involved and if so how?

I tried to put Cassie and Eustace to the back of my mind for the moment and concentrate on following Doug. He was walking along Harrow Road, the same street that Vicky and I had walked down on our way from the café to the leisure centre. I kept diagonally opposite Doug, who was on his phone from the moment that he left the leisure centre, and he seemed blissfully unaware of anyone around him and talked loudly as he made his way to the lockup. There were enough pedestrians, cyclists, joggers and traffic to feel comfortable that he wasn't aware of me following him. We passed the Bridge Café and as I walked past the café I couldn't help but look in and London Isa saw me and waved and I waved back. More work to be done on my deep undercover surveillance technique then. Despite that, Doug didn't see me.

After a couple of minutes' walk past the café, he approached the entrance to a small industrial estate and headed towards the lockup. At the junction of the main road and the industrial estate there was a sign which was made up of around twenty individual aluminium strips, each with a company's name on it. Doug's lockup was the third on the left and was in fact a garage called Zach's Motors that appeared to specialise in MOTs. I felt my phone go. It was a text from Vicky.

Why u following if u have number??? Where r u?

He is friend of Eustace. 2 find out more on E. Near bridge café. Will text in 10. Where r u?

I was carrying out the text exchange whilst I watched Doug unlock the lockup.

Martin's in High St, she replied. This was a coffee shop that we sometimes met in.

Ok. Will txt back shortly, I replied.

The lockup was converted into a garage from a semi-detached warehouse. Like the other units in the industrial estate, it was on a single level and had good parking space in front. It had two large retractable roller shutter doors into the actual garage side of the building and also a conventional door that looked like it led into the front office. There was a metallic light-blue Austin Mini with a personalised number plate parked in front of the roller doors which was presumably Doug's. Doug was currently unlocking the door to the office side of the building, dealing with a number of different locks that had to be attended to, after which the warning beep from the intruder alarm started to go. He went inside, closed the door and the beeping stopped after a few seconds.

Now that I knew where Doug worked, what next? I felt that Eustace must have worked there too. I think that this was *the job* that Doug was referring to when speaking to Brian at the leisure centre, but how could I know for sure? Suddenly with a resolve and sense of purpose I was unaware that I possessed I decided to go in and speak to Doug to try to get a feel for the place and any hint of Eustace. I had decided that my reason for being in the garage was that I was going to book an MOT despite not having a car. I hoped that my acting skills would be as good as Vicky's.

I had allowed for perhaps seven or eight minutes to pass since Doug opened up the garage and then I went straight to the door and gave a cursory knock. There was no reply and I could hear some banging and clattering from the workshop area and I knocked again and still received no reply. I tried the door which was unlocked so I opened it and went in and took a tentative look inside. I closed the door behind me and noticed that it had a wire cage at the back of the letter box containing several letters. I was in a corridor that led into a workshop area ahead and to the immediate right was a reasonable-sized office made from a stud partition. The office had two large windows with a small square grid-style design in the glass through which I could see a large desk with an old cracked, stained leather seat behind it with two other chairs in front. There was also a water dispenser, a small circular table with two further seats and a kettle with several white cups, tea bags and a jar of coffee next to it. There appeared to be a toilet and kitchenette running off from the office as well.

As it looked like there was no one in the office, I headed towards the workshop area. It was large enough to accommodate four cars alongside numerous bits of machinery, tyres and an MOT viewing area. One of the cars, a small Fiat, was on a ramp and another hatchback, a Renault I think, was parked over a service pit. Another Fiat was parked adjacent to the tyre bay and the fourth car which was parked in front of the large closed doors was a gleaming white Audi that looked a bit incongruous amongst the other three. I couldn't see Doug and so I decided to get his attention. "Hello," I shouted. No response. "Hello. Hello." His head appeared above the pit.

"Fuck sake, thought I heard something. What do you want?"

"I was looking to book in an MOT."

"We ain't open on Sundays, mate."

"Yeah I know, it's just that I was walking home and saw you open the garage and it reminded me that my MOT's due, so I thought that if I book it in today I can score it off my to-do list." He gave it a moment's thought.

"Okay. Head into the office and I'll be with you in a minute."

"Thanks."

I went back to the office, working on my story. It was cold and had a musty smell but despite this I realised that I had started sweating again. The walls had a few standard MOT information posters and the de rigueur garage wall decoration of a topless calendar but apart from those and a locked metal key box that was it. There was a stand-up desktop daily calendar block on the desk of the type where you tear off the paper strip each day to get the date. This one still showed that it was Friday.

I sat at one of the chairs facing the desk, which as well as the calendar had a phone and a desk tidy containing a variety of pens, pencils and paper clips on it. There were no photos either on the desk or the wall, which was disappointing because I had been hoping that there may have been a standard lad's-night-out type picture showing the staff at a Christmas party or similar event with Eustace beaming along with the rest of them – but nothing. "Fucking stalking me?" It came loudly from behind. I jumped in my chair. Doug had come into the office and I hadn't heard him approach. He had obviously recognised me.

"No, I…" That was as far as I got before:

"You were in the fucking fitness room and the fucking showers."

"Yeah. Like I said, I need an MOT." I sounded weak as cats' piss.

He walked past and sat down at the desk. He was wearing a dark-blue boiler suit and had several letters in his hand which he put down on the desk. He looked at me suspiciously. "Why didn't you ask me in the leisure centre?"

"I didn't know you ran a garage. I just happened to see you open the garage so I came over. I was about to go in the café." That at least sounded plausible.

"Not a faggot are you? Lots of them in that centre."

"Nah, not me, mate. Just need my car done; I like to keep it local." I think that he liked that. My voice had lost some of its middle-class tone and was becoming a bit mockney.

"Okay. I'll book you in, then I'll lock the fucking door so that I can get on with my fucking work." I think that he believed me because he said this in a neutral tone. He sat down in the big leather chair and took out an A4-sized diary and put it down on top of the letters. It had two lined pages for every day and he started leafing through it. "What day you looking for?"

"This Tuesday?" I asked.

The diary was heavily dog-eared with most pages smudged and contained numerous entries in a variety of writing styles and different coloured ink. He got to Tuesday's page which had, it looked like to me, three confirmed bookings. I was, however, looking at his diary from upside down. Each booking had the customer's name and phone number, vehicle make and registration number. A line was drawn under each booking. As he had leafed through the diary I could see a large tick through previous bookings that had presumably been completed and paid. "Looks like you're in luck, mate. We can fit you in on Tuesday afternoon – about three. What's your name?"

"Stewart."

"What's your surname, Stewart?"

"That is my surname. My name's Greg Stewart."

"Ah. Okay and the make of car?"

"Astra."

"Reg number?"

"Sorry. Can't remember – just got it a few weeks ago."

He looked up.

"Engine size?"

"Think it's 1600."

"Think?"

"Yeah, sorry, but apart from putting in the petrol I know fuck all about cars." He nodded. This probably pleased him as he could easily bullshit me on the work required and fix the price accordingly.

His phone rang as he was putting the details into the diary.

"Yeah? No he ain't here." He got up and walked into the kitchen area and continued speaking. I could still hear him clearly but couldn't tell who he was talking to. "Wasn't in the gym neither. I phoned and got no reply. I'll give it an hour then I'm going down to his. He's holding me up. I need that car out today." My heart fluttered – this must be Eustace he was talking about. Perhaps I am so insignificant that I appear of no threat to Doug at all, I thought as he continued speaking. "If he ain't in, I'll let you know." He must have been listening to the caller because he stopped speaking apart from a few grunts and "I knows".

Doug had put the kettle in the kitchen on, perhaps to cover his voice. "I'm with a customer. I know – he just turned up. I'm booking him in for next week. Anyway, I'll call you back in an hour or so." The diary was still on the desk so I risked a look at it by swivelling it round quickly and flicking through a few pages but nothing jumped out. I lifted it up and looked at the letters that had been lying underneath it – there were five. Three were addressed to Zach Motors, one to D Zacherelli (presumably Doug; I made a mental note to check with Piotr) which were all in window envelopes and appeared to be official receipts or invoices for the business. The fifth was A5 size; it bore no address but handwritten in neat black capitals was simply the name E MANLEY. As I was looking at this I could hear from the kitchen, "Like I said, I'm finishing this job, calling him again and if he don't answer I'm heading down to his gaff. Right. Catch you."

I hurriedly put the diary back on top of the letters as Doug came back into the office with a cup of coffee. He sat down and looked at the diary and said, "Right, where are we. Oh yeah – what's your best contact number?"

As Doug spoke to me, all I could think of was:

Eustace Barrington.

"The Man."

E Manley.

Eustace Manley…?

It was time to start looking for the real Eustace.

CHAPTER THIRTEEN

"Number?"

"Sorry?"

"What's your phone number?" Doug sounded agitated.

"Oh, sorry. It's…" I brought myself back from thoughts about Eustace and concentrated on the task in hand. "Sorry. I can't remember it. New phone."

"New phone. New car. Christ. Got your phone with you?"

"Yeah."

"Right, call this number." He gave me a grubby business card with his name, Douglas Zacherelli (no need to ask Piotr now), and the number of Zach Motors on it. I took out my new phone and dialled the number. It was for the landline and after a second the phone on the desk rang plus a bell in the corridor and workshop area went off. He looked at the display and wrote down the number into the diary then told me to hang up. "Right, see you on Tuesday."

"Thanks." I got up and felt that Doug now had some doubts about me. I could feel the sweat run down the back of my neck and I think that he would have said more to me but his phone rang again.

"I haven't seen him," I could hear him say as I got up from the chair in front of the desk and walked out of the office.

I had to tell Vicky and phoned her as I left the industrial estate. "Where are you? Still in Martin's?" I asked breathlessly.

"Yes. Why are you phoning when we were going to do this by text?"

"It's quicker. I've got lots to tell you. Do a search on Eustace Manley. I think that is his real name or a name that he uses. Blondie's partner is called Cassie. Eustace and Cassie were an item. See you in ten."

"What? Okay."

As I made my way to meet Vicky in Martin's I realised that I had probably made a couple of grave errors. Doug now knew my real name and my phone number. I attempted to put this to the back of my mind as I tried to work out what Eustace did and why his job was so important. I made it to Martin's and tried not to burst in. I saw Vicky sitting with her coffee, Sunday broadsheet and tablet, and as I sat down I couldn't help myself. I repeated my previous message with a bit more detail. "Eustace is almost certainly Eustace Manley. The female I saw at Eustace's with Blondie is a fitness instructor called Cassie. Eustace and Cassie were an item."

"Slow down and calm down," Vicky instructed me. "Do you have the number from Piotr?" She sounded stern, which disappointed me. I expected a back-slapping.

"Sorry. Yes I've got that."

"What is it?"

"Can't remember – it's in my pocket, but listen. Eustace works – sorry, worked – at Zach's garage opposite the Bridge Café for this guy Doug that uses the leisure centre. Doug and other people have been looking for Eustace for over a day because he has a *job* to finish. It must be to do with cars. They call him The Man and I saw an envelope addressed to E Manley so I think that Eustace was going by another surname and, wait for this, they were talking at the leisure centre about Eustace shagging the fitness instructor." I took out the poster from the leisure centre and showed it to Vicky, holding it almost under the table. She looked at the poster, but her expression didn't change. I carried on: "Eustace and Cassie were an item. Cassie is the person that let me into Eustace's house and came with me and Blondie to my flat. She is part of the gang. Cassie hasn't turned up for her classes this morning." I pointed to the timetable on the poster. "Doug is going down to Eustace's in the next hour. We've got to do something to find out what Eustace was doing with a car and why it's so important and we've got to do it quick. If Doug finds Eustace with a knife in his chest and calls the cops then Blondie might think it was me that informed them and Isa…" I tailed off.

Vicky was impressed. "Christ, Greg, you've done well. I've searched for Eustace Manley and there are a few references to that name, but nothing of consequence to us. What do you think he's been up to?" she asked.

"I think that he is using another name to avoid the taxman." I replied. "There are three crappy old hatchbacks in the garage that look like the standard type of car they deal with and also a large new-looking white Audi with customised number plates that stands out. I reckon that is what he was working on and needed to finish today. I think that we need to somehow have a look at the Audi because if it was some ordinary job, they would just get another mechanic on the case, but they seem to be panicking that they don't have Eustace to finish it off. I think that he does cash-in-hand work for dodgy customers and Doug is the middle man. Doug will get a cut from Eustace for using his garage but the work will be set up and done by Eustace. Some of the dodgy characters may know that the work is done at Zach Motors which will explain the calls to Doug looking for Eustace."

"I follow all of that – but we've got the full number, or we at least think we do, so what do you suggest? Why don't we just go back to yours and wait for your visitors?" Suddenly it was Vicky asking and me leading.

"Yes we've got the number which hopefully is what they're looking for, but two things: one, we don't want Doug anywhere near Eustace's for the next few hours, and two, if we can find out what Eustace has been up to then we might find out what the number is for and where the security box is, but we've got to move fast."

"Like anything to eat or drink, sir?" the waitress asked. I hadn't seen her approach the table. Third café, first time we'd had table service.

"What, sorry, pardon, oh a coke please and can we have the bill?" I said somewhat stiffly. The waitress smiled thinly.

"Certainly, sir."

"How can we get Doug away from the garage to let me in and how do we keep him away from Eustace's?" I was back asking the questions and getting brave. Set off the fire alarm, burglar alarm? No, that would just attract unwanted attention. "What about you going to the office and trying to distract him?" I suggested.

"What do you mean – get my tits out and seduce him?" I didn't like her talking like that. "Wouldn't work – he has seen me, he climbed over me rolling about on the leisure centre floor. He'll recognise me and know that I'm up to something and he might twig that you and I are together."

"Yeah, you're right. What about phoning him, we've got his number," I said as I showed her Doug's business card. My coke and the bill arrived. "Thanks," I said and gave a weak smile. I don't think that the waitress liked me. Oh well, I thought, I'll go back to the Bridge Café then if I want a cheery welcome.

"What about phoning him and kidding on that you're Cassie?" Another weak suggestion.

"And what? If I say I'm her he'll want to know where Eustace is," she countered.

"Fuck. Of course." I must have said that too loudly judging by Vicky's stare and the waitress's body language. Her talk of seduction got me thinking and despite my views of a few minutes ago: "I know it's pretty lame, but what about phoning Doug in your best damsel in distress voice. Say that you're a friend of Cassie which is how you know the number of the garage and that your car has packed in just round the corner. You know it's Sunday, but could you help out a friend of a friend...and so on. Sound desperate and sexy. Hopefully he might nip out of the garage long enough for me to nip in and look at the Audi." I was getting increasingly brave in my anxiety to solve and finish this. Vicky looked at me slightly quizzically.

"Worth a try," she agreed.

"Good. Let's go," I said and got up. We went to the counter with the bill and the waitress's dislike of me grew when Vicky, rather than me, paid.

As we walked along the High Street, I suggested to Vicky that she phone Doug when we got near to the Bridge Café, then go into the café and watch to see if he left the garage. If she told him that the car was on Harrow Road opposite the council offices then he'd turn right from the industrial estate and head up the road and I could nip in. She could sit at the window in the café and text me when he made his way out and then back to the garage. "Okay," was all that she said. I couldn't believe that I was suggesting all this and planning to carry it out. As we got nearer to the café she said, "Give me your phone."

"Why?" I asked.

"I don't want him knowing my number and I can't exactly withhold my number because that will make him suspicious," she said.

"He knows my number," I said with a sigh.

"What? How?"

I told her.

"Christ, Greg." She sounded annoyed.

"I know, I'm sorry, but I'm not used to this and I had to give him a number to make my false MOT booking seem real. I'm not great at thinking on my feet."

"Let's head back down to that shop," she said calmly. We turned round and headed in the direction of the Ealing Mini Market which was a standard Asian grocer shop. We went in and Vicky bought a SIM, politely declined the offer of having it installed and did it herself in seconds. We then walked towards the café and the industrial estate. When we were close to the Bridge Café I gave her the business card and she started dialling. The phone rang and rang. I couldn't think of a Plan B at the moment. The phone kept ringing, but at least it hadn't gone to answer phone. It kept ringing, then I could hear a tinny, "Zach's Motors." Vicky leapt into action.

"Hi, is that Doug?"

"It might be," was his predictable response.

"It's Sandra – I'm pals with Cassie from the leisure centre. She suggested that I call you. My car's packed in just near the Bridge Café. I was going to meet Cassie when it just died. I phoned Cassie and she told me to phone you."

"Cassie ain't at the leisure centre," he said dryly.

"I know, I know she's with Eustace." She sounded so reassuring, and sexy. I hoped that Doug thought that as well.

"Is she?" I think that he sounded interested and from Vicky's expression, she thought that as well.

"Yeah he's not been well but she says she is going to kick him out the door and up to yours to get on with the job," she continued.

"Is she?" It sounded like his tone was lightening. Vicky was playing a blinder.

"Anyway, can you help me? I'm stopped on Harrow Road opposite the council buildings. I'll make it worthwhile. I'll even buy you a coffee if you want…" A sexy damsel in distress and Doug was biting.

"Okay. Give me ten minutes, love."

"Thanks so much, Doug – you're a star," she simpered, and for good measure, "Can't wait to see you…"

"Right – you go in the café and I'll stand over the road. Text me when he leaves," I said. I handed her my backpack to look after. Vicky nodded then went into the café. I stood for what felt like an eternity, pretending to text and make phone calls to appear normal and blend in. The text alert went – Move was all it said. I did as instructed and made my way to the entrance of the industrial estate and stood with the sign to the estate as cover when I saw the familiar figure of Doug in his car. He got to the junction and turned right and headed up Harrow Road. I reckoned that I had a little over five minutes. I started to jog. The kit I was wearing looked a bit like running gear, so I wouldn't stand out, and I was at the garage in thirty seconds. I hoped that with him just going round the corner Doug would have left the door unlocked. I tried the door but it was locked. Fuck.

I tried again as if that would make a difference then stepped back, looked around the deserted estate and ran and kicked the door with everything that I had. It gave a bit. I ran against it again, this time leading with my right shoulder, and it fell open with a large cracking sound. I stumbled into the building and ran along the corridor, straight into the garage and through to the Audi. I tried the doors of the vehicle and they were unlocked. I opened the boot which was empty inside, picked up the carpet and looked in and under the spare-tyre compartment, then jumped in the front passenger seat, opened the glove compartment, raked through it and also found nothing. I then picked up the thick carpeted mats with a rubber underlay from in front of the driver and passenger seats and found nothing. Conscious of time, I hurriedly went to the back seat and picked up the mats there, and again at first couldn't see anything, but then behind the front passenger seat, I found what I was looking for.

Time to go.

CHAPTER FOURTEEN

I closed the car doors, ran out of the workshop, past the office to the front of the garage. At the threshold I took a deep breath, poked my head out of the door had a quick look, saw no sign of Doug and trying to appear natural, pulled the broken door back to the frame to make it appear closed and then turned left and started jogging further into the estate. Despite living in the area for several years I had never visited the estate before and didn't know the layout. I soon realised that it was basically a very large cul-de-sac with only the one entrance and exit, which of course I didn't want to use in case I bumped into Doug on his way back.

I made my way towards and between units eleven and twelve which were for an engineering company and a printers. Behind the units was quite long scrubby grass and then a large fence effectively sealing off the backs of the units from the adjoining road behind them. The thick mesh fence was about two metres high and attached to concrete poles at approximately five-metre intervals. I didn't want to wait because Doug would be on his way back and when he found the broken door hard on the heels of the phantom phone call he would be putting two and two together very quickly. I yanked at the wire fence but it wouldn't move so I kept moving along and as I headed towards unit thirteen I saw some hope. A batch of pallets was stacked in the yard, which would give me the height to get over the fence. They were about a metre from the fence, which might be a bit tricky but I had to risk it.

I was sure that I could hear squealing tyres nearby. Fuck, he's back, I thought. I scaled the pallets and then leaned over and with quivering hands grabbed the top of the fence and pulled myself onto it. It shook and it was hard to get the purchase necessary to pull myself up and over but I managed it. I was coming to believe in fight-or-flight syndrome. Flight for me every time.

I lowered myself over the top of the fence and gingerly scrambled down onto the thankfully deserted street which seemed to mainly consist of fairly run-down domestic garages on one side for the flats whose backs looked onto the road from the other side. I knew that if I continued walking along this road in the direction away from the Bridge Café that it would meet up with Harrow Road further down. My heart was beating wildly and I gasped for breath. I had felt my phone going a couple of times whilst I was working out how to scale the fence. I took it out and saw two texts from Vicky: He's coming back and Where r u?

I started walking down the quiet road and was about to answer her text when this time I definitely did hear tyres squealing. I dived for cover in between two wooden garages as the noise from the car got nearer. The car had to slow down on the narrow road and as it passed I saw that the driver was Doug and he didn't look happy. His car carried on down the road and turned right at the junction with Harrow Road, so he was heading back to the industrial estate. I remained in between the two garages whilst I tried to work out what to do. A few seconds later the car roared past again. If cars have a body language then this one was *angry*.

I kept watching the road from my hiding place pressed between the garages for several more minutes. They had quite a pleasant creosote-type smell which was unfortunately offset by a strong smell of dog shit either near or below me. The car hadn't passed again and I hadn't heard tyres squealing for a while so I quickly sent a text to Vicky. Hiding. Near H road. He's looking for me.

The phone rang which surprised me because I thought that she would text back. I was instinctively about to answer it when it dawned on me that I had only two saved numbers, Vicky's and Piotr's, and no one else knew my number apart from Doug. I didn't answer the call. When the phone had stopped ringing, I sent another text. Meet me at the flat. Txt when near.

I felt that it would be easier, quicker and safer to make our way separately to my place. Doug definitely suspected me, but he may not suspect Vicky yet. I doubted that he would make the connection between me and the writhing redhead on the floor of the leisure centre. Vicky had never been to my flat but she knew where it was and I was sure that she would make it there no problem. It was how I got there that was the issue. I waited a further five minutes but there was no sign of Doug's car and he hadn't phoned me again or left a voicemail message.

I gingerly stepped out from between the garages and made my way down the road. If I could cross Harrow Road then I could make my way down an alley past the backs of houses into Wardlaw Park, cross the park and make my way up Spennymoor Road and towards my flat. The only downside of this of course would be that I would be passing Eustace's house. Would Doug be there, or more worryingly Blondie and Cassie? I decided that I would use the park exit further along from Eustace's which would take me away from the High Street and then do a loop back to Rathgar Avenue.

I decided to do my jogging act again. I hadn't imagined my training regime for the Ealing Half Marathon would have started in such a fashion. I put the hood up; I dislike running or even walking with a hood because of the limited peripheral vision it gives; however, I felt that it might offer some form of disguise. I started off and decided not to look back, just keep running like lots of other mid-morning Sunday joggers. I got lucky when I reached Harrow Road because the pedestrian crossing lights just along from the junction turned to green as I approached. I crossed the road then made my way towards the alley which led to the backs of the houses on Skipton Avenue before leading on to the park. I entered the park which was busy with numerous joggers, walkers and parents with children at or going to the play park. I ran a diagonal across the grass to take me to the park gates at the bottom of Spennymoor Road rather than the nearest option which Eustace's house looked onto. As I made my way to my chosen exit, I glanced over a few times at Eustace's but could see no sign of any action. It got me thinking about what would have happened in the aftermath of Eustace's killing, which up until now I had barely had time to think about. What had Blondie and his partner, who I now knew was Cassie, done with his body? I'm sure after leaving my place last night they would have returned to Eustace's and disposed of his body somehow.

Suddenly my legs almost gave way as I thought about this. This was who I was dealing with, cold-blooded murderers. They would kill me if necessary and God forbid Aunt Isa. What for? This fucking number. What would they do if they found out about Vicky? Also, what would Doug and his pals do with me and are Doug and his pals in any way associated with Blondie and Cassie? These and all sorts of thoughts tumbled around in my head as I ran through the park.

I started to think of how to deal with Blondie and Cassie when they returned to my flat in a few hours' time. The reality was sinking in: very soon I was going to have to deal with a murderer, a desperate murderer who needed something very badly. So badly that I imagined he was probably under a death threat himself if he didn't come up with the goods.

I arrived at the park exit and made my way up Spennymoor Road along and towards Rathgar Avenue. Nearly there. I slowed down after I realised that in my stress the pace had picked up and I was out of breath and sweating heavily. I was just above walking pace as I made my way up Rathgar Avenue and towards the flat. I walked across the paved area and over to the stairs to the flat. I noticed Mr Cartwright outside having a smoke and waved and said hello to him then climbed the steps and got to the front door, at which stage I realised that I didn't have my keys. They were in the backpack that Vicky now had. Fuck. I didn't want to talk to Mr Cartwright so I sat on the top step and texted Vicky and told her I was at the flat. 1 min, came the reply.

Sure enough, one minute later I made out the beautiful silhouette of Vicky on the other side of the road. She wasn't entirely sure where number twenty-seven was and she slowed down to find her bearings. I started down the stairs when she looked up and saw me. She looked nervous; a look that worried me, as I saw her as the cool level-headed one in our partnership dealing with the nightmare of the past day. She made her way towards me. "Hi – the keys are in the backpack," I said. She handed them to me without a word. I took them, unlocked the door and we went into the flat. It seemed so much longer than twenty or so hours since I had left. The curtains were closed, of course, and everything was just as I had left it, including the waistcoat lying in tatters on my bedroom floor and the open window that I had climbed out of. We went into the kitchen. "Drink?" I asked.

"Just water," she replied, looking drawn. I ran the tap until the water was as cold as it could get and gave her a glass. I took out a beer from the fridge, removed the cap and downed half of it in one big gulp. I took my hoody off and wiped the sweat from my forehead on it. I looked at the time on my phone which told me that it was quarter to two. The clock on the cooker told me the same.

"Did you find anything?" Vicky asked.

"Yes."

"Come on then."

"The code is for a security box hidden behind the front passenger seat in the white Audi. I picked up the rubber mat and the box is hidden underneath it. The last bit of work required is to seal a cover over the box and stick the carpet down. The security box needs a twelve-digit code which is split into three four-digit sections, just like we thought. The box is about this size by this." I held up my arms with them about a foot apart to indicate the length, and then put them about nine inches apart to indicate the width. "I guess it will be about six to twelve inches in depth. The box was obviously locked and I didn't have the time to play about with the combination."

"Christ, how do you know that and how did you find it?" She was definitely impressed.

"Given the concern between Doug and some of his contacts at Eustace disappearing, it made me think that it must be something very important that he does in the garage. It was obvious that Eustace must have had a skill that other mechanics don't readily have and that this skill was in demand. Listening to the banter at the leisure centre and seeing the white Audi at the garage along with the envelope addressed to E Manley made me put two and two together and actually come up with four. I reckoned that he must be doing some form of adaptation to cars that's not a run-of-the-mill skill like panel beating or resetting the mileage. You got me thinking about security boxes and at first I was only thinking of a security box in the context of being in a vault or similar secure building. I heard Doug refer to having to get a car out that afternoon and I guessed that it had to be the Audi he was talking about. On my way to meet you at the café I had a whole bundle of thoughts in my head, but suddenly everything clicked and I guessed that the security box might not be in a building, but in that car. That's why I was so keen to get back up there and have a look and I was right. I reckon that the security box has something in it that Eustace may have stolen or was not letting on to the big boss. He maybe got greedy and double-crossed the big boss and paid the price."

"Holy Christ, Greg." I think she was impressed but I had no time to bask in my revelations. My thoughts on the run back to the flat through the park had made me realise how much danger Isa and I were in, and Vicky as well if they knew that she was involved.

"We've got three or four hours until they arrive I guess. What do we do when they arrive? How do we play it?" I asked.

"Let's look out the number," she said. I picked up the backpack and took my notepad out which had the first and second parts of the number on it and then took out the piece of crumpled paper with Piotr's handwritten third part from my hoody. I realised that I had forgotten about Piotr – he had been key in getting the last part of the number and I hadn't thought about him since I left the leisure centre. I'll text him later, I thought. I turned the pages of my notebook and wrote 2339 9326 7126 on a fresh page.

"I didn't have time to try it out, but I think that's the number," I said. "The three sets of four-digit numbers may be in a different order but that's what Blondie is looking for, I'm sure."

"Give me the number," Vicky said.

"Why?" I asked.

"So that I can keep it safe when you are negotiating with your blonde friend." I handed the pieces of paper to her, got up and went to get another beer. Vicky glowered at me.

"Last one I promise 'til this is over," I said. I sat back down at the kitchen table and something struck me. I was sure that when I left the flat last night my phone was on the kitchen table, but it wasn't there. Maybe I had inadvertently moved it, because then, as now, I was working under huge and unexpected stress.

"Can I have a cuppa?" Vicky asked. I got up again, put the kettle on, chucked out the previous empty beer bottle and made her a cup of tea. I handed it to her and sat down. "Thanks," she said. She didn't look frightened anymore and seemed calm and in control. Good, I needed her as I couldn't do this on my own.

"How do we use this number to ensure that Isa gets freed?" I asked nervously.

"As I see it, you have to act calmly – don't be bravado but don't be cowering either. You have to tell them that you have got the number and it is twelve digits long. Tell them you know who Eustace was, what he did and that you know where the security box is because I'm sure that they don't. Tell him that you have hidden the number and won't give it over or any other details until he agrees to let Isa go and can prove that she is free. Let them respond to that and then ask how Isa is and how she is going to be released if you give over the details." I nodded, taking in what she said. It all sounded so straightforward.

"Where will you be when he comes?" I asked.

"I'll be nearby, watching the flat."

"How do I know Isa is safe before I give over the number?"

"Tell them that you have given the number to someone for safe keeping and that they will only give it over when you have evidence that she is free. Get them to Skype you with proof that Isa is safe."

"We need to plan this better," I said. "I can't fuck this up or Isa, and maybe me, will get killed."

"Okay, we have still got a few hours," she said. "I'm going for a wee then we can go over everything again."

"Okay."

Vicky went to the toilet and I sat trying to work out how I was going to play this in order to get my aunt free from a psychopathic gang and persuade Blondie to believe me and take the number. I had to convince him that what I had found out and what I knew were real and of value to him. I was happy to give it up but only if I knew for certain Isa was free.

As I was ruminating and swigging beer, there was a loud banging on the door. I looked at my phone and then the cooker and they both told me the same thing: it was three fifteen. Fuck, surely not – he was early. For some reason I had it fixed in my mind that they would turn up after five; twenty-four hours after they left the flat. But why did I think this? Why should I have trusted these bastards?

My heart rate increased and my legs turned into jelly. Vicky was still in the toilet and I walked gingerly out of the kitchen and towards the front door, hissing, "They're here," down the corridor. His banging was so loud that I was sure that Vicky would have heard it and would stay hidden in the bathroom or somewhere else. As I approached the front door I could make out the familiar blonde hair through the thick glass. I slowly opened the door and was surprised to see Blondie on his own.

"Afternoon, Professor, got anything for me?" he said quietly.

"Come in," I said in neutral. My heart was fluttering but I was trying to stay calm and focused. I turned and walked towards the kitchen and went in. He followed and we sat down at the kitchen table. He looked at my bottle of beer and Vicky's cup of tea and glass of water. Shit.

"Thirsty?" he asked.

"Yes," was all that I could muster. His early arrival had taken me by surprise and I was working out in my mind the best way to deal with negotiations. He got up and took one of my beers from the fridge.

"Okay, Professor, have you been busy and found me my number?"

"I think so."

"Are you going to give me it?"

"No. Unless you let my aunt free. I know the number, what it's for and where the security box is, but I'm not telling you unless you let Isa free and can prove it to me." My voice was holding quite firm as my heartbeat continued to race.

"Ever so brave ain't you?" He seemed so relaxed. He didn't look like he was about to kill me. "So you know all of that, Professor, but you ain't going to tell me?"

"No," I grunted. My throat had suddenly become very dry.

"Well if you won't tell me maybe Vicky will." What? I froze. What did he just say? How could he know about her? Before I could try to answer my own questions he said loudly, "Right, Vicky, you can come through now." Again I wondered how the hell he could know about her.

Seconds later Vicky came into the kitchen and walked straight over to Blondie. She stood beside him and said, "We've got it all. Greg's been very useful." After she said that, she didn't avoid eye contact with me or look in any way sheepish with an *I couldn't have helped it* expression. In fact she looked straight at me as if I was something unpleasant that she just had the misfortune to step in.

CHAPTER FIFTEEN

They say that people with near-death experiences see their life go by them in some form of sequence and that car-crash victims see everything unfold in slow motion. I experienced both of these feelings and, as well as that, I think that for some moments I was above the kitchen looking down on the poor pathetic shocked me sitting open-mouthed at the table staring at Vicky and her blonde accomplice.

I think that I was even more shocked than when I first saw Eustace. For the past day I had thought that we were working together to find this number to free my poor Aunt Isa and this bitch was playing me like a banjo. I thought that this nightmare had finally brought us together and that some good would come out of all the shit. I thought that Vicky and I had outsmarted the bad guys and done enough to free Isa. I had felt pride at what we had done and huge gratitude to Vicky for coming to my aid at such short notice, listening, advising, steering and supporting me, and all along she had... I couldn't think anymore.

I sat at the kitchen table and stared at both of them feeling vacant. My mind drifted back over the past twenty-four hours. Absolute chance had brought us together and she had maximised that opportunity. She hadn't been at home when I called her and she hadn't dropped everything to meet me at Toni's because she was in the area already, maybe even at Eustace's. She knew Eustace was dead before me. That's how we ended up looking for a twelve-digit number; I had thought that we had used reasoning and logic to come to that conclusion, but she had known that it was a twelve-digit number all along and used subtle suggestions to steer my malleable mind in that direction.

She paid cash everywhere because she didn't want to be traced. She hadn't moved from middle management in an NHS trust to high-flying City slicker, she had conned her way there. She sympathetically listened and helped me along, she massaged me, soothed me, even fucked me – Jesus fucking Christ…

My thoughts were interrupted by Blondie. "Have you got it?" he said to her.

"Yes, Greg's been very helpful. If it wasn't for him we would never have got the number. And not only that, we know where the security box is as well." She handed over the number that I had written out about fifteen minutes before.

"Thank you," he said. "Now what are we going to do with you?" he said to me.

"Where's my aunt?" I blurted out.

"Don't know, don't care. Probably dead," he answered. All along I had worked to find this number to get Isa free. I always thought that if I had the number they would be happy and let her go. Not only had I found the number but I had found out what it was for and where the security box was. I had honestly felt that I'd have at the very least a fifty-fifty chance of getting her back. Her life, her family meant nothing to them. After his cruel casual remark, the grief, anger, pain, rejection rolled into one and erupted. I sprung from my seat and lunged across the table at Blondie, but he anticipated the move, sidestepped and then spun me round, twisted my right arm behind my back and held a knife against my throat. My forehead was pressed against the fridge. He had done this all so easily.

I had reached a point of no return; these bastards had no feelings, they just got the job done. Me or Isa and of course Eustace were just expendable pawns to be used then disposed of when our usefulness had passed. I had no doubt that he intended to kill me, probably here in my own kitchen. Sudden random thoughts came into my head: who would find me? How long until Mum and Dad found out? Had they heard about Isa yet? What would Frances think? Would they get away with it? What about the college? Would Piotr understand what I had become embroiled in?

In my naive way I simply couldn't work out how something was so valuable that it made people behave like this, snuffing out life with a casual indifference, using people then disposing of them. Had Blondie been like this from birth? How had Vicky ended up like this? I thought I knew her. Was some inherent badness always inside her and, if so, what had flipped a switch to cause this? What a fucking actress.

I thought of Vicky going to the toilet and now realised that she had gone there so that she could contact him and, for some reason, this particular act felt the most treacherous. We had sat and worked out our plan and all the while she was waiting to choose the moment when she could tell him to get to the flat and bring my world tumbling down.

I could feel my heart rate pump in my chest and my pulse throb in my neck as well as feel his breath and smell his aftershave, the same one as yesterday. The pain in my arm was intense and I could feel a line of something trickling down my neck but didn't know if it was sweat or blood from where he held the knife. Fight or flight? Neither. I was a spent force and had used up my reserves of bravery, strength, determination and willpower.

I had never really considered my own death before, just imagining in that idealised way that people do that it would be somewhere in the distant future after a fulfilled life, possibly surrounded by my family. People sad at my death, but thankful for my life. However, like so many tragic and violent cases reported in the news on such a regular basis, I, and possibly Isa already, would join a long list of violent random killings, and if our deaths and the circumstances were reported at all, they would engender a few *that's terribles* in the wider world and perhaps be the subject of some small talk for a day or so then be forgotten when the next big thing came along.

"Come on, Kev – time to move," Vicky said. She had just sealed my fate as I now knew his name. I couldn't see if any looks were exchanged between the two of them because I was still held with my face pressed against the fridge.

"What's in the box?" I croaked. I wasn't trying to buy time because what good would that do? No one knew of my fate apart from these two, the cavalry weren't on their way. No, I was resigned, but I did want to know what was in the security box. What it was that had caused such carnage and was about to bring an end to my average but content life.

"What did you say?"

"What's in the box?"

"This ain't a film, Professor – you'll never know." He yanked me round, still holding my right arm and knife to my throat. "Move slowly to the bedroom."

This is it, I thought. Kill me in the bedroom and hide me under the bed or in the wardrobe. I suddenly thought of Eustace and wondered what they did with him, then thought of Cassie. Where was she? He steered me towards the door. I didn't look at Vicky because I knew that I would see nothing in her eyes. I was resigned to my fate and had gone beyond scared as I moved towards the kitchen door and out to the hall. He seemed very calm like it was just another day at the office.

Suddenly there was an eruption of the loudest noise that I'd ever heard which completely stunned me. I didn't know what had happened, but I couldn't hear and I had fallen to the floor. I looked up and there were black-clad people everywhere, shouting and moving quickly throughout the flat with the sound of smashing glass, footsteps and what sounded like furniture being thrown about. As I lay dazed on the floor I was grabbed by someone and manhandled to my feet. "This way, son," the person said and he pulled me towards the kitchen. The glass in the kitchen door was smashed and I could see blue lights flashing from outside. Blondie was on the floor under the weight of a black-clad person, his arms behind him and handcuffed. Vicky was standing, being held, and was also handcuffed. She didn't look so in control now.

"Sit down," the man who had picked me up said. Someone straightened up the kitchen table and I was led to it and then sat at one of the chairs. The floor was covered in broken glass and was also wet, which I guessed was from his beer and her tea and water. My backpack was lying against the fridge and my notes were face down and had been trodden into the broken glass and wetness. That was of no concern as I tried to take in what was going on.

The person in charge said in a very loud voice, "Read them their rights."

One of the officers started on Blondie, then turned and did the same for Vicky. "Take them away," the man in charge instructed. They were manhandled and moved along without offering any resistance. It was their turn to be resigned to their fate and there were loud crunching noises as they stepped on the broken glass as they were led out of the kitchen. Just then my neighbour Mr Cartwright walked in and passed them. I expected that with the commotion half the neighbourhood would have gathered outside the flat and Mr Cartwright as my nearest neighbour had decided to see what was happening. Unbelievably he was let in and seemed to exchange a nod with the officer in charge.

Everything had happened so quickly and was so unusual and frightening that I thought that I was perhaps hallucinating. I looked at or through Mr Cartwright and felt almost as if I was having another out-of-body experience. Then I collapsed with my head on the kitchen table and cried. I had never howled like that in my life. The wailing came from the pit of my stomach and my body shook violently. This scared me and made it worse.

My crying gradually subsided and my big snotty sobs lessened. Mr Cartwright was sitting at the table next to me. I realised that I had the side of my head on his chest and that he was gently holding and soothing me. It felt natural and at that moment Mr Cartwright was my best friend in the whole world.

CHAPTER SIXTEEN

"Where's the fucking number? I repeat, where's the fucking number?"

"Don't know."

"Yes you fucking do."

"Don't know, man."

"Yes you fucking do and you are going to fucking tell me." The young man wasn't shouting but was very angry. He was also very blonde and as he spoke forcibly his face was getting redder, making his hair seem even blonder. The television was on in the living room with a news channel playing quite loudly. The young man had turned up the volume before he had started questioning the older man.

"Don't know what you mean, man," the older man said.

"Yes you fucking do. Do you want me to hurt you?" The middle-aged man was sitting down in the front room of his house. It was just after one o'clock on Saturday afternoon and he was surrounded by two females as well as the young man. His glasses lay on the floor, having been knocked off when the young man slapped him and pushed him into his chair. All three of his assailants wore latex gloves.

"Watch him," Kev, the young man, told his accomplices and went to the kitchen, returning with a large kitchen knife. "My patience is running out – you know where the number is and you're going to tell me." He held the knife against the man's neck. "I've done time before and I'll risk it again. If you don't tell me, I'll fucking hurt you."

One of the females became good cop. She was in her mid-thirties and had striking auburn hair. "Eustace, you know that we will get the number. It's how we get it that's important to you now…"

Eustace, the middle-aged man, could see that the threat was real. As soon as the three had got into his home he knew that the game was almost certainly over. He considered his options then replied in almost a whisper, "The driving licence and number – in the lining of the waistcoat."

"What?" The young man had taken over again and thrust his face close to Eustace's.

"I hid it with my driving licence in the lining of a waistcoat."

"Get the waistcoat."

"I can't – it's not here."

"You fucking liar."

Kev grabbed Eustace by the jaw. Eustace keeled back and Kev let go. "What the fuck do you mean it's not here?"

"I hid it in a waistcoat and handed it in to a charity shop."

"Are you having a laugh? Why the fuck did you do that?"

"To get it out of here and maybe someone would find the driving licence and the number and return them to me after you have gone."

"What colour is the waistcoat?"

"Claret, paisley pattern."

"What charity shop?"

"The kids' one in the High Street, next to the bakers."

"When did you hand it in?"

"Yesterday."

"Time?"

"In the morning."

"Go and find it," Kev ordered Vicky, his auburn-haired accomplice. Vicky knew the area quite well because she sometimes met an old university friend for a coffee in the neighbourhood. She nodded and left the living room, put her coat on and left the house. She and Kev had arrived at Eustace's separately. They knew that Cas, the other female, would already be inside. Vicky had appeared at his front door with a clipboard as if carrying out a survey and as she was talking to Eustace on the step Kev appeared and they forced their way into the house quickly and silently.

Now on her way out of the house, Vicky picked up her clipboard to keep the façade going, removed her latex gloves and put her hat on as it was raining. In the walk to the shop she kept going over everything in her mind with the overwhelming feelings of *What the fuck is going on?* and *How did I get into this shit? When this is over – never again.* She hoped that Kev would stay calm, but more than that, she hoped that she would find the waistcoat. It was a short walk to the High Street where the charity shop was and Vicky was there in ten minutes despite having to weave between Saturday-afternoon shoppers on the busy pavement. She had disposed of the clipboard into a litter bin en route.

The busy shop was bustling and she forced her way past the shoppers blocking the narrow aisles. There was lots of stock, too much for it to be properly displayed, and customers leant in front of one another when trying to reach for an item to inspect. Men's and women's clothing were at least kept separate and Vicky made her way towards the back of the shop where she could see men's jackets and suits.

She reckoned that waistcoats would be next to shirts and as she made her way in that direction, she froze. A man was trying on a paisley-patterned claret waistcoat that matched the one that Eustace had described. The man had his back to her; he took off the waistcoat, put his hoody back on, picked up a carrier bag from the floor and made his way to the counter. It was easy to hide behind stock and people and Vicky hung back behind a display and watched as he paid for the waistcoat and handed in what appeared to be a shoe box. He was in his mid-thirties, five foot eleven, thick dark shoulder-length hair, quite slim. Her heart raced. Jesus Christ…it was Greg, her friend from university! What the fuck is he doing here? she wondered.

He then left the shop and Vicky quickly gathered herself, then walked to the waistcoat rail to see if there were any other garments similar to the one that Greg had taken. There weren't, so she made her way to the shop door and looked through its window before leaving. Greg was waiting to cross the High Street at the pedestrian crossing. Vicky slowly walked out of the shop, put on and lowered her hat and followed Greg, who had now crossed the road. Vicky remained on the other side and kept a discreet distance behind Greg, who was oblivious to being followed. When he reached the junction at the end of the High Street he turned right and made his way up Rathgar Avenue. Vicky had never been in Greg's flat but knew where he stayed and it was clear that he was making his way home.

Her walking pace increased as she made her way back to Eustace's. She had a mixture of emotions: surprise at seeing Greg, more surprise that he had the waistcoat, massive disappointment and fear that she hadn't got it, but hope in that she could surely work out a way to get it or more importantly the wallet with the number in it.

She got back to Eustace's; the door was locked and she rang the bell. After some time Cas opened it slightly. "For fuck sake, Cas, let me in," she said. Cas had a naturally sallow complexion but it appeared that this had lightened by several levels. "Looks like you've seen a ghost," Vicky said as she brushed past Cas in her eagerness to update Kev. "You won't believe this," she said as she went into the living room. "I didn't get the waistcoat but I know who's got it…" she tailed off.

Eustace was still in his chair but with a kitchen knife deep in the right-hand side of his chest. Kev was trying to clear up the mess with kitchen roll and a damp cloth. He was concentrating on his clothes and bare arms. Vicky gasped but couldn't say anything; she looked away and then crouched, holding her knees, taking deep breaths and trying not to hyperventilate. She didn't expect this – using a knife to get the information required was as much as she expected and way more than she was used to. Cas stood in the doorway, she too in shock. "Holy fuck – what happened?" was the best that Vicky could come up with.

"I couldn't help it," was all that Kev managed.

"You've fucking killed him for Christ sake."

"I couldn't help it. He was dissing me and her," he gestured towards Cas. "No fucking respect – calling me a boy-band faggot. I snapped and stabbed the thieving fucker and we held him down while he fucking twitched."

"What the fuck do we do?" was Vicky's response. "You've killed him."

Kev grabbed Vicky tightly by both arms and hissed, "Too fucking bad, lady. You're in this as much as us. Now shut the fuck up 'til you've got something useful to say. I'm going to the bathroom to wash the blood off me and my clothes." Kev was wearing a dark-coloured T-shirt and jeans and there didn't appear to be too much blood spattered on him. Most of it was on Eustace, the chair and the floor.

"Who's got the fucking number?" he asked. Vicky told him about Greg and the waistcoat.

"You two work out how we're going to get the waistcoat back from her fucking friend."

Cas appeared to be unable to think or speak. Vicky talked through her hastily formed plan to phone Greg and arrange to meet up, even if it meant sleeping with him to get the number. Kev came back down; he'd had a shower and smelt fresh, having used some of Eustace's aftershave. There were no apparent bloodstains about him. Vicky gave her plan to Kev, to which he agreed. Vicky phoned, but Greg didn't answer, so she left a message.

"Where does he stay?"

"Rathgar Avenue."

"Where's that?"

"Just up the road."

"Right, we'll give it an hour, then you're going there. Now you – fucking pull yourself together," he said, looking at Cas. He went to a drinks cabinet in the living room and found a Bacardi. "Follow me," he ordered Cas and they went into the kitchen where he found a glass and poured her a large measure. There was coke in the cupboard and he added that. "Get that down your fucking neck and start functioning," he ordered.

A pot of chilli that Eustace had been preparing for lunch fizzed on the hob. Kev switched the ring off and they went back into the living room where Vicky was staring and shaking. "For fuck sake, you pull yourself together as well. You're supposed to be the fucking brains behind this operation. Okay, he's dead, so what. Shit happens. He bit off more than he could chew, tried to get clever and paid the fucking price. He gave me no respect – that's what happens. Now we need to get the fucking number, get rid of him and get the fuck out of here."

Vicky inwardly prayed that Greg would call her back. She expected him to. She knew that he had the hots for her and wouldn't knowingly ignore a call from her. She wanted the number like nothing else on earth, but at this moment she wanted out of that house almost as much.

"Right, we'll sit tight here for an hour then you're heading up there," Kev said, looking at Vicky.

"I know," she said. "You've already said that."

"Don't get fucking lippy with me, lady. You go upstairs and wipe away all trace of us."

"What rooms have you been in?" she asked quietly.

"Just the bathroom. Sweep that and the stairs and landing," he instructed and she dutifully went.

"We need to hide his body and get out of here and away. Cas, you and me are going to put him in the hall cupboard and put something on the chair to cover the blood." He called upstairs. "Vicky, bring a blanket down that will fit over his chair – oh and bring a couple of sheets for us to wrap him in," Kev said as he regained his composure.

Vicky put her gloves back on and took out a cloth and wiped all the surfaces in the bathroom as instructed. She then went into the bedroom to get a blanket and sheet as required. As she walked past the window on her way to a large cupboard that she hoped would contain bedding she froze.

"He's coming! He's coming," she yelled. She bounded down the stairs and into the living room. "It's Greg. He's coming! He's coming!"

"Fuck. You get upstairs, don't move and don't say a fucking thing. Go," Kev instructed her. She went and moved fast. "You," he said to Cas, "you're going to answer the door and say as little as fucking possible. You're going to take him into here and then leave it up to me. Make sure he goes past you and into the room." He pointed in the room for emphasis. "I don't want him loitering – open the door straight away and get him in. Understand?" She nodded. "Get there now."

She walked slowly to the door and took a deep breath. Vicky's friend Greg arrived at the door and the bell rang. Cas opened the door straight away. "Is Eustace Barrington in?" he asked pleasantly.

"What do you want him for?" she asked.

"I have something of his."

She didn't ask for any more detail and said, "You better go through."

She turned around and walked along the short narrow hall and he followed.

CHAPTER SEVENTEEN

Vicky listened from upstairs. She could hear them talking, but could not make out anything that was being said. Kev was doing most of it and she could hear short responses from Greg. After perhaps twenty minutes there was activity downstairs and she heard them go through the hall and out of the front door. After a few seconds she took a look out of the bedroom window and saw the three of them go up the road, presumably to Greg's house.

She felt a bit guilty that Greg had become involved in this and sorry for him to an extent because she had always liked him. However, thinking about it, she didn't know why she had bothered to keep in touch for all these years. He was useful to show her around when she first arrived in London, but she should have cut contact with him years ago as he now served no purpose, had little in common with her and was fucking boring if she were honest. He was a bit of a wimp and was like a childhood toy or object that you kept for sentimental reasons to serve as a reminder of simpler, less complicated times. She made up or grossly exaggerated much of the bedtime activities that she related to Greg because she knew that it turned him on, which she found so amusing. She remembered that she screwed one of his friends within a week of arriving in London, a fact that both Greg and her then-husband were blissfully unaware of.

She knew what would happen to Greg because he had witnessed a murder and knew who did it. Although she had only worked with Kev for a short time she knew that he wouldn't just let him go. Poor Greg; but at the end of the day they needed the number or they would be fucking dead.

Being alone in the house with a dead body spooked Vicky and she remained upstairs. She found bedclothes in the big cupboard and looked out a couple of sheets and a blanket. Her phone rang: the number was withheld. She answered and it was Kev. "He's fucking lying. He fucking knows about the number, I'm fucking sure," he said quietly.

"Did you find the waistcoat?" she asked.

"Yeah, ripped it to fucking shreds but couldn't find any number. He has seen the number I know it, but I don't think he knows where the fuck he's put it. He's scared shitless and if he knew where the number is we would get it."

"Fuck – what are we going to do?"

"Up the fucking ante so to speak." He hung up.

Vicky was confused. She closed the curtains and sat in darkness on the bedroom floor and tried to think about how they had got into this mess and how they were going to get out of it. They'd had a good little number going and then got greedy and she now realised that teaming up with Kev had been the biggest mistake of her life. So she had two major problems: one, how to find the number to get out of this immediate mess, and two, how to extricate herself from this line of business full stop and retire gracefully.

She looked at her watch: Kev and Cas had been away for over an hour. Her phone rang and she answered – it was Kev.

"I'll be back in five."

A few minutes later she heard the door being unlocked, opened and Kev coming in. She gingerly came down the stairs bringing the sheets and blanket with her which she dropped onto the bottom stair.

"Well?" she asked.

"I've given him twenty-four hours," he said. He had a laptop bag on his shoulder that she recognised as Greg's.

"How do you know that he'll find it?" she asked.

"Coz I will send him something to concentrate his mind." Vicky was confused by this comment and just then Kev's text alert went off. He looked at the text, gave a little grin and said, "If this don't concentrate his mind nothing will." He tapped on his keypad then showed Vicky the screen. There was a photo of a very old and very frightened lady having a knife held at her throat by someone in a mask.

"Who are they?"

"That's Professor's dear old Auntie Isa with me good mate Dazza. Dazza's a fucking psycho and will slit the old dear's throat if he doesn't come up with the goods."

"What do you think will happen?" The picture unsettled Vicky a bit.

"I've left his phone with him so that he gets the text – which he already has. You've already phoned him so he will see a missed call. Give it half an hour then phone again and say that you have to meet up – make any excuse, tell him you love him, fuck his brains out if needs be but find out where the fucking number is."

"What about if he's already off to the police?" she asked.

"No chance. You know him, I've just met him and we both know that he's a complete fucking wimp. He's shitting himself and he won't let his aunt be harmed. What he doesn't know is that as soon as we get the fucking number, him and his aunt will be joining this cunt." He pointed at Eustace. "I've got Cas watching his flat in case he gets brave." Vicky had completely forgotten about Cas.

"Right, let's get this mess cleaned up. Where's the sheets and blanket?" Kev put his gloves on, Vicky already had hers on and she went to the stairs and picked up the bedding and then spread the sheets out on the living-room floor. They picked up the now stiffening corpse with Vicky holding the feet and looking away as they dragged Eustace and then heaved him onto the sheets. Kev brought one side of the sheet over Eustace's body then the other side. He tucked one side under the other so that the body was completely wrapped up. Kev looked for something to tie the package up with and finding nothing in the cupboards ripped the flex from the reading light in the living room for one end and sent Vicky up to get a lamp from upstairs and then did the same with the flex from that to secure the top end.

"Give me a hand," he instructed Vicky as he picked up the top end. She stooped and picked up the legs and they dragged Eustace into the large wall cupboard in the hall that Kev had already been in looking for rope. They pushed a few coats aside and then pulled Eustace in, rolling his corpse up against the back wall. Kev put a coat over the top half and some boxes on the lower half and pulled the coats in the rail along to completely hide the gruesome package.

Vicky got cleaning agents from her bag and proceeded to scrub all surfaces in the living room. Kev brought a basin of hot soapy water from the kitchen and he scrubbed the carpets and the hall floor. After they had done this, Vicky asked, "Why did you kill him, Kev?"

"I've told you he was getting mouthy, not showing me or Cas any respect. He called Cas a whore. Stupid cunt must have thought that she really wanted to be with him. I told him to shut the fuck up and he just laughed. He called me an amateur and that he worked with real men. I snapped and stabbed him. As soon as I'd done it I thought *fuck me*. I left the knife in but he was still alive and was trying to take it out. I thought we've got to finish this off now and we both held him and I blocked his mouth, while he kept twitching. It must have taken ten, fifteen minutes before we knew that he was dead and wouldn't cause us any grief. He wasn't long dead before you came back."

"Have you killed before?"

"Yes," he said as he started prowling round. She didn't pursue this because she knew he would say that and she had a good idea who else he had killed. Kev searched in all the usual places – under the stairs, under the sink – and eventually found what he was looking for: a timer switch for a socket. He set it and connected the standard lamp to it and switched it on. "The light will go off at eleven," he said.

Vicky was steeling herself for calling Greg in a few minutes when her phone rang. She didn't recognise the number. "Hello," she said cautiously.

"Vicky, it's me, Greg."

"Oh hi, what's up? I don't recognise the number. Where are you calling from?"

"Are you free tonight? I really need to speak."

"Christ, Greg, she doesn't want to go out with you again?" Vicky improvised, trying to be natural.

"What?"

"Kerry."

"What? No, no, nothing to do with that…"

"I really, really need some advice – can you help?"

"Okay. Do you want to head up to meet me in town?"

"No, no, can you come to me? I, I really need to see you…"

She interrupted and said, "Greg, please slow down. I'll come out to you. Where do you suggest?"

"What about Toni's near the station?"

"Toni's? But it's a dive."

She looked quizzically at Kev. He stared blankly back.

"I know, I know. Let's meet there and then we can maybe go somewhere else."

"Okay." She sounded doubtful.

"What time can you make it?"

"An hour from now."

"Vicky, please be as quick as you can. See you then."

"I'll try. Maybe fifty minutes."

"Thanks, Vicky."

Vicky hung up and Kev then phoned Cas, who eventually answered her phone. "Come back here. Vicky's meeting him in an hour," he told her then turned to Vicky. "Right, keep in touch and as soon as you've got the number give me the word. We'll deal with him and his aunt."

"Okay," was all that she could muster, then, "Give me a fucking drink," she demanded. He poured her a Bacardi into a smudged glass, added some coke and handed it to her.

"Knock that back and that's it. Keep a clear head and keep in touch at all times. Where's Toni's Café?"

"Not far. It's next to the station; I'll call when I have some news." Vicky stayed standing in the kitchen with her drink. After a few minutes there was a light tapping at the door. It was Cas and Kev let her in. They both came into the kitchen and Cas and Vicky acknowledged each other with a nod.

"Right, you've got ten minutes then you're off," he said to Vicky.

"Me 'n' Cas are going to finish clearing up in here then head off."

"Okay," she said.

Vicky finished her drink then turned around and without another word left the kitchen, picked her coat up from the hall, put it on and left the house. She made her way to Toni's, keeping her head down and planning her approach with Greg. She knew that Greg didn't like to be out of his comfort zone and would be looking for her to lead on things which suited her fine.

There was heavy condensation on the windows of Toni's which she got to in under fifteen minutes. She walked in. The café had only a few customers with none waiting to be served and she couldn't see Greg, which caused her heart to skip a beat. She instinctively went into her pocket for her phone, but what good would that do? No point worrying Kev yet. Just then she saw out of the corner of her eye a door at the far side of the service counter open and Greg walk out. Thank fuck, she thought. "Hi. Thanks for coming – do you want anything? I noticed a missed call from you a while ago," he said. She got a can of orange juice and they sat down at a table that had a plate of chips on it.

"Yeah, I was just calling to catch up – didn't expect this. Right, Greg what the hell's wrong?" she said quietly, looking at him. He started to tell his story which gushed out loudly. For fuck sake, she thought. He's shitting himself and the whole fucking café's going to hear.

She took out a small notepad and pen from her bag. "I'll go through the main points and you help me out okay?" she said. She listed the slippers, then the waistcoat, then the number and driving licence, going to Eustace's, finding him dead, the blonde guy and his female partner. The dead guy looked vaguely familiar, the text with Isa's picture with the mask and knife. Vicky remained focused throughout her question-and-answer session, always mindful not to inadvertently let slip that she already knew the whole story, although she didn't understand what he was doing with the number.

"Where is it?" For fuck sake, she thought. What had the stupid bastard done with it?

"Hidden in my garden." She could have screamed at his

stupidity and tried to keep the anger out of her voice and keep in the same neutral tone.

"Greg, we need to go somewhere to work through this and decide what to do. Let's go to my place," she added, "but we'll need to go to yours first to get the number." She went to the toilets and there was no one else in the Ladies unsurprisingly, given the state of them.

She phoned Kev. "Where are you?" he asked.

"The toilets in Toni's – he's found the number."

"Yes – thank fuck!"

"Wait, hold on. Two things – one, the number is only four digits, and two, he doesn't have it on him."

"Jesus fucking Christ. He's fucking lying. It's twelve fucking digits – you know that, I fucking know that."

"Kev. I believe him. He's bricking it. He's not trying to be smart. All he wants is to get out of this mess and get his fucking aunt back."

Kev took a deep breath and tried to calm down. He had to. Eustace was dead. They didn't have the number and time was running out. "So where is the four-fucking-digit number?"

"He hid it in his garden – we're just going to get it."

"For fuck sake, why is it in the garden? And you're sure he's not making a mistake and the rest of the number is on the back of the paper…?" Kev knew how unlikely this was as he spoke the words.

"He says he has looked at the piece of paper. It's half a post-it note, he's looked at both sides and also tried memorising it. Kev – I fucking believe him."

"Okay, okay. What the fuck do we do, Vicky? You know and I know that we've got until eleven o'clock tomorrow night to get that number, and where to use it, or we're all fucking goners…"

"I've said that we'll go back to mine and try to work things out. Maybe something will twig. He says that he recognises Eustace."

"That's because he saw his fucking picture on the driving licence," Kev interjected.

"Can you and Cas risk another hour at his place to see if there are any other clues? We'll go back to mine and try to think logically and maybe Greg has seen things that he doesn't realise and I'll try and get them out."

Kev looked at his watch. It was now seven forty-five. "Okay. Me and Cas will go over this place one more time and be gone by eight forty-five. You let me know anything major that you find. How will you be able to speak?"

"Don't worry about that – I'll manage."

"Remember, Vic, the clock is ticking. I need regular updates coz we might have to go to Plan B."

"Okay, I'm on my way," she replied. Vicky came out of the toilets deep in thought. Greg sat at the table holding a newspaper with a strange expression on his face. He looked up, saw Vicky, got up and went over to her.

"I've just seen something amazing," he said as they left the café. "We don't need to go to mine. I definitely know the number. It is 2339. Definitely, look here." He showed her his newspaper which he had folded into a quarter so that only the photo and some text showed. He showed Vicky the picture from a road race. "Look, that's him, that's Eustace."

"I don't know Eustace," she said.

"But I do and that's him. Look at his number. It's 2339 – that's the fucking number!" A passerby glanced over.

"Quieten down, Greg. So the number that you found in the waistcoat is 2339 and the number that is on Eustace's vest in this race is 2339?"

"Yes yes – 100%. Let's just go straight to yours." They had

been standing outside the station entrance whilst they had this discussion.

"Okay," she said, "let's go." On the train Vicky kept a watchful eye on Greg; she knew that he was a wimp and his display in the café proved it. She was worried that he would suddenly crack up, burst into tears in the busy carriage and spill out this whole crazy story to dozens of mystified passengers. They sat close together and she felt and heard a sudden gasp from Greg; he had his eyes closed and was squeezing his temple. She leant over, making sure that he got a good whiff of her extremely expensive cologne and gently massaged the back of his neck with her right hand. This seemed to do the trick; he noticeably relaxed and slightly snuggled in. Not long, she thought to herself. Whilst she thought this she sent a text to Kev using her left hand: Progress. Will let you know when at flat.

They made it to Canada Water without any mishaps as Greg appeared to have manned up a bit and was ready to go into action. In her flat she got the expected bullshit questions which she couldn't be bothered dealing with, but had to do so to keep the facade up to get Greg's help in working out this fucking number. Vicky dealt with them competently and steered Greg back to the task in hand because he did have his uses, having already worked out how Eustace had formed part of the number. They spent the next couple of hours searching online with Vicky trying surreptitiously to steer Greg to look for a twelve-digit number. She had to update Kev. "I need to check something," she said and told Greg that she was going to call her colleague, Barry. She hoped that she sounded reassuring and went into the kitchen, set up and switched on the coffee machine and called Kev. "The four numbers that he found are Eustace's from a race."

"You've lost me, what the fuck do you mean?" Kev was confused.

"The four-digit number that Greg found along with the driving licence in the waistcoat is 2339. Eustace is a runner and the four digits that Greg found are the same number as Eustace had when he ran the Ealing Half Marathon in September. We've got a newspaper with the picture! So it shows that Eustace has made up the number," Vicky explained.

"We need a twelve-digit number, lady," was Kev's unhelpful response.

"I know, I know, and if you hadn't killed Eustace we might have got it by now. We're searching for codes for money transfers and safety deposit boxes."

"Vic, we know it's a twelve-digit number for a safety deposit box – we just need to know the fucking number and where the fucking box is…"

"I know that, but Greg doesn't, you fucking prick," she hissed. "If I let Greg know that then he knows I'm involved – we need to get him to think it's a twelve-digit number and keep him working on this to try and find it." She hung up and walked into the living room with the coffees.

Greg updated her on safety deposit boxes and she summarised her discussion with "Barry". Greg was losing heart and wanted to go to the police so she had to work hard to appear positive and encourage further effort from him to get his mind off the cops. It appeared to work because all of a sudden Greg announced that he had what could be the second part of the number and then the third. Holy fuck, she thought; she could feel her heart race as she listened to the logic of how he found the second part and how he thought he could find the third. She almost snapped at him as he smugly showed her the times of the Ealing Half Marathon on the tablet and how Eustace's finishing time gave a four-digit number. When he then explained that he was sure he had seen Eustace several times at the local leisure centre he was a member of and that the membership number was four digits and that he knew a guy called Piotr who worked at the leisure centre she struggled to contain herself.

Greg explained his plan to involve Piotr and then exploded at her questioning of it, which again highlighted to her the fragile nature of his mental strength. She got him back on track, all the time thinking of how to implement the plan to get the number and then of course find the location of the box. Greg said that Eustace had several friends who used the centre as well so hopefully they would provide a lead. Maybe we're getting there, she thought as she then considered the implications of not getting the number and the whereabouts of the box. She had to agree to Greg giving her phone number to Piotr but what choice did she have?

She needed to update Kev and so told Greg she was making them something to eat and sent a quick text: Think we have next four digits and maybe final four. She had just sent the text when her phone vibrated; she didn't recognise the number and answered it. A heavily accented man asked for Greg and she walked through and handed the phone to him then went back into the kitchen to finish making the toasties.

Greg's conversation was quite brief but it seemed positive and they spent some time formulating the plan. Under the pretext of calling Barry she updated Kev: "Looks like the third part of the code might be Eustace's leisure centre membership – it's four digits. Have you found a membership card amongst his stuff?" she asked.

"Don't think so – fuck. We're not at his house now; we are at the agreed place. By the way the old dear has shat herself in the back of the van."

"Looks like we might be getting there, Kev – why don't you have her put out of her misery?" was Vicky's pragmatic suggestion.

"Not yet. She might still have her uses."

When Vicky announced that it was time for them to get some sleep she could tell that despite everything, Greg was excited and looking for some action. Time to nip that one in the bud. She took a quilt out from a cupboard in the hall and put it on the sofa, gave a quick "good night" and was off. Sad fucker was looking for a goodnight kiss.

She had just sent another text to Kev when she heard a knock on the door. Fuck, she thought. She ignored it. He knocked again. Fuck. "Is that you, Greg?" she said in her best sleepy voice.

"Yes. Yes. Sorry but I need to ask you something, Vicky, please…"

Fuck. "Come in," she said sleepily. "What is it?" He told her that he had suddenly thought of his parents and wondered if they had been taken hostage. "Sit down and let's talk this through," she told him and went through the possibilities. She needed to convince him not to call them, his sister or the police. She felt that he would take her advice but didn't want him changing his mind in the middle of the night. One way to do that: she got out of bed, started massaging his neck and then she fucked him.

To be honest, she thought, he wasn't that bad and at least he didn't snore, but she couldn't bear to be beside him all night. She lay with him and dozed for a couple of hours then shortly after three a.m. got out of bed, showered in the main bathroom rather than the en suite so as not to wake him and worked hard to scrub all his traces away. She had some cereal, egg and toast with very strong coffee which washed down one of her magic pills then texted Kev, who responded almost immediately, and they worked out their plans for when they got the last bit of the number.

At five thirty she took a coffee through to Greg knowing that he would be all doe-eyed and romantic, so that would have to be controlled. Vicky needed him on board and would play everything with a straight bat for as long as needed as he had been surprisingly insightful and useful so far. It was best to get out of the flat as soon as possible and get on with the plan. From waking Greg up to him showering, dressing and leaving the flat was surprisingly bearable, however he started in the lift and it took all of Vicky's self-control and role-playing skills not to tell him to shut the fuck up.

They picked up the required phone and sportswear from Canary Wharf and made it to the café for the meeting with Piotr. Greg nearly threw a wobbler over a fairly innocent remark by Vicky on his way into the café which again served to remind her that she was working with an amateur who was constantly teetering on the edge. When Piotr walked in her heart sank; he appeared to be about thirteen and looked more innocent and less worldly wise than Greg if that was possible. However she did feel confident that he understood what was expected of him, but she was unsure if he could carry it out. After Piotr left the café to go to work at the leisure centre, Vicky, who had experienced a number of dangerous, stressful situations in her new career, felt the most nervous that she had ever felt. Greg went to the toilet and she sent a quick text to Kev to be ready.

Greg nearly arsed up just getting into the leisure centre, but after that the next part of the plan went smoothly. She went up to the reception desk and asked about spinning and boxercise classes. The receptionist produced a programme and handed it to her and just as Vicky thanked her, the phone rang and the ignorant fat slut answered it. Vicky then let out a loud groan, looked the receptionist in the eye and slowly slid down the front of the reception desk. Even that lazy cow must have picked up on that, she thought. The receptionist hastily hung up and shouted into the back office and a few seconds later, she and a leisure attendant came out and stood over Vicky. Vicky looked at them, rolled her eyes and lay twitching on the floor. "She's having a fit," she could hear someone say. "Phone an ambulance."

"Put her in the recovery position," someone else said. She felt herself being put into that position and thought it was time to move. As she attempted to sit up a large male, presumably a customer, tried to get her back into the recovery position. As she sat up she saw a figure beside the computer in reception. She hoped that it was Piotr.

"Lie back down, love, and they will phone an ambulance," the big customer said.

"Fuck off," she replied and pushed herself up again. The receptionist was making her way back to her position behind the desk and the customer and the leisure attendant were beside her.

"Come on, dear, no need for that," one of them said.

"I'm okay, just leave me. I think it was something I ate last night. Seafood. Please leave me alone, you're scaring me," she said and then turned on the waterworks. This had the desired effect and the two men backed off. Vicky seized her chance, pushed herself up and mumbled a few *sorrys* and *thank yous* before making her way to and through the front door without looking back.

She had decided to go to Martin's Café on the High Street, which she chose because it was at least ten minutes' walk away from the leisure centre, wasn't a shithole and Greg knew where it was. At the café she picked up a newspaper from a pile by the coat stand, sat down at a table and ordered a coffee, opened the newspaper and desperately waited for a text from Greg. She was sure that she had seen Piotr spring into action and was cautiously optimistic that he had successfully done the business. Hopefully they had the correct twelve-digit number and if Greg could get the location of the security box, or at least an idea where it was, maybe she might actually survive today.

After thirty minutes of flipping through the newspaper and

regular checks of her watch she ordered another coffee. She considered herself level-headed and calm at times of extreme stress but this situation was testing those strengths as she was basically in the hands of amateurs with little control over them. This lack of control was what unsettled Vicky the most as she had achieved so much over recent years by careful planning and execution.

Just as her second coffee arrived and the friendly waitress was putting it down, her phone rang – it was Greg. She was relieved at finally being contacted, but annoyed that he was phoning instead of texting and asked him why. She listened as he explained about Eustace having another name and being with Cas. How had he done it? He had put Eustace and Cas together and worked out that Eustace used another surname. She had seriously underestimated him. Greg had come up with the goods again – *We've got the fucking number!* she wanted to scream out.

She phoned Kev and he answered almost immediately, but then told her to wait and about forty-five seconds later came back on the line and said quietly, "Okay, shoot."

"He knows about Cas and Eustace – she'll have to go," she said very quietly.

"Consider it done," came the reply.

"Greg's followed a guy called Doug to his garage. He thinks the box might be in there."

"Yeah, so do we. It's how we find it and open the box that's the problem."

She looked up and saw Greg passing the window. "Okay. Got to go." She assumed her pose of newspaper reader as she sensed him looking into the café. Greg arrived breathless and immediately started describing how he followed Doug to his garage giving the reasons why he believed that Eustace was indispensable with a skill for customising cars and creating hidden compartments. He had the number and a plan to get back in to the garage, because he thought he might know where the security box was, but obviously needed to get Doug out of the building.

She did admire his tenacity, riddle solving and yes, his bravery, but then he reverted to type when as they made their way back to the garage he had to admit that he had given his real name and number to Doug. What a clown, she thought. She remained calm though, bought a new SIM from the nearest mini market, installed it and then called to trick Doug into leaving his garage. Vicky knew that tricking Doug, like tricking most men, wasn't going to be difficult because they would think with their dicks.

After Greg went to his position near to the industrial estate she returned to the disgusting café they had been in earlier, sat at a window seat and had a cup of foul coffee served by the annoying fat loud cow. While she waited for Doug to leave the garage to help the damsel in distress, she had a quick look in Greg's backpack which he had given her before embarking on his mission. She threw it down quickly as all she found in it was his sweaty gym clothing and his flat keys. The prick hadn't put the number from Piotr in there. Very much to plan, she saw Doug leave the garage and Greg go towards it. Her phone was on silent and she felt it vibrate; she looked at it and of course it was Doug phoning "Cassie's mate". Naturally she didn't answer it and then saw Doug return a few minutes later so she texted Greg to warn him that Doug was on his way back to the garage, hoping that the prick didn't get himself caught at this stage.

When she saw Doug's Mini scream out of the industrial estate, take a sharp left and screech down the narrow road that was adjacent to Harrow Road her stomach was in knots as she feared that Doug must be hard on the heels of Greg. A few seconds later, the car came flying up Harrow Road, took a right and repeated the process. Good – Greg must still be free.

A couple of minutes later he sent her a text telling her that he knew where the security box was and they were to meet at his flat. Yet again Greg had excelled; the feeling in her stomach changed from a knot to butterflies of nervous anticipation. She got up from her seat in the café, paid the fat bitch with a tenner and turned to walk out. "Hang on, my love," she said, waving the note. "It's only two pounds for the coffee."

"Keep it," Vicky said coldly. She couldn't stand such inherent cheeriness and reckoned that it must be false. What did she have to be so happy about?

Gladys, the café assistant, had never had such a large tip in here and should have been delighted but was confused by the attitude of the attractive young lady. The way she stared at Gladys scared her and she wondered what the nice young man she was in with earlier saw in her. You never know with the young ones nowadays, she thought. Gladys rang up the amount for the coffee, put the £10 note in the till, took out the change and put it in the charity box. She didn't want her money.

Vicky sent a text to Kev: On way to flat. Start moving. She made her way slowly and calmly to Greg's flat with his backpack on her back. She couldn't quite remember his flat number but knew that she would find it when she got near. Greg texted her: the stupid prick had left his keys in the backpack. He could work out all this complicated stuff yet couldn't do the basics. Anyway, she thought; very soon this nightmare will be over.

She saw him waving from the steps at the side of his house and acknowledged him. There was a nosey old bloke smoking near the shed in the back garden; it looked like he was one of the neighbours and wanted to talk to her or at least say hello, but she ignored him. She took the keys out of her bag and gave them to Greg; he unlocked the door and they went in. They headed for the kitchen which looked like the epicentre of his flat. What a dump! The flat smelled of unwashed male. And that prick thinks that I want to end up with him, she sneered inwardly as she sat down. She asked for a glass of water which he had to run from the kitchen sink tap; he didn't even have a water chiller on his fridge she noted. He of course took a beer – his stock reaction to any crisis.

It was time to talk over the plans. Only a few more minutes of going through the motions – she talked him through what he should do and crucially got him to write down and give her the full twelve-digit number. Okay, she thought, here goes.

"I'm going for a wee."

"Okay."

As soon as she got in the bathroom she locked the door, sat on the toilet seat and texted Kev. Ready.

Ten seconds later he replied: OK coming. 5 mins max. Stay hidden.

She now did need a pee, so went, washed her hands and waited. She inwardly implored Kev to hurry up. Finally she heard loud knocks at the door and a few seconds later, Greg nervously hissing to her to stay hidden. The poor sod! She could hear them talking, but not make out the words. They then made their way into the kitchen and she slowly and quietly opened the bathroom door and padded a few steps along the hall. The kitchen door was open and she could hear everything clearly.

"Well if you won't tell me maybe Vicky will. Right, Vicky, you can come through." This was her cue. Vicky took a deep breath, went into the kitchen and walked straight over to Kev. She was glad to see that he was alone.

"We've got it all. Greg's been very useful," she said as she looked Greg directly in the eye. The sad fuck looked as if he were drugged. She always knew that as soon as Greg left that charity shop with the waistcoat he was a dead man walking. That hadn't particularly bothered her as she worked with him to deduce the number and where the security box was. Now after Greg's pathetic attempt to attack Kev had come and gone and as Kev led Greg through to the bedroom to do the business, she felt nothing in particular. She was glad that she had used Greg to work things out because he had found the number and now she would be safe. She wanted Kev to be quick and clean and leave no trace of them before they both got away as quickly as possible. If Greg had looked at her as he passed she would have stared him down, but he avoided eye contact and allowed himself to be directed out of the kitchen towards the bedroom. He was broken.

Vicky did feel something. Calm. She was coming near to the end of a very stressful day and as usual she was coming out on top. She put on her gloves and took the cleaning materials from her bag as it was time to wipe away all trace of her and Kev.

The sudden commotion came as quite a surprise.

CHAPTER EIGHTEEN

My eyes were stinging from my sobbing and I was shaking from the shock of the previous few minutes. It must have been some sort of police or SAS type raid, but I had no idea how or why they had made it here. Mr Cartwright was still sitting next to me. Vicky and Blondie – sorry, Kev – had been taken away and there were four men in black still in my flat. It sounded like there were others outside from the voices, radio noise and traffic movement that I could hear.

"This is now a scene of crime, son," Mr Cartwright said to me. I nodded. "Christ knows how you got involved in all of this, son, but I can tell you that your aunt is safe." Mr Cartwright had become my new best friend anyway, but this confirmed it. At this point I didn't think to question how he knew this news – the best news that I had ever heard. All I cared about was that she was safe away from that bastard in the mask. My body sagged in relief and my spirits soared.

Thank God, thank God, I said to myself. "Thanks so much," I said to him. "Where is she? Do Mum and Dad know? Is she okay?"

"Right, slow down, son; let's take this one step at a time. We need to get out of here. We can go downstairs to my house – me and Mrs C can look after you," he said.

"I'll take him downstairs to mine and bring him along to the station in a few hours once the dust's settled," he told one of the men who was presumably in charge.

"Go ahead. Keep in touch," was all the man said.

"C'mon on, son," Mr Cartwright said to me in a reassuring tone. I got up and followed him out of the kitchen. I didn't quite know what had happened or what was going to happen as I allowed myself to be directed by Mr Cartwright. He said goodbye to the man he had just spoken to and nodded at a couple of other black-clad men as we made our way out of the flat and down the steps. We went into Mr Cartwright's house through the back door which led directly into the kitchen and meant that we avoided the gaze of the numerous bystanders who had gathered at the front and were being held back by hazard tape and two uniformed policemen.

We went into the kitchen and Mr Cartwright shouted, "That's us back." His dog welcomed him eagerly and also wagged its tail at me. It was a black and white collie that looked quite old. Mr Cartwright tickled him behind the ear, saying, "Hi, son. Who's a good boy then?" A few seconds later Mrs Cartwright shuffled into the kitchen looking smaller and frailer than when I had last seen her. She was about five foot four at the most and her hair was grey with a few dark streaks in it; her face was very lined with a yellowy-grey complexion which looked as unappealing as it sounds. She had her slippers on and a pink fluffy nylon dressing gown and wore a strong-smelling lavender perfume or soap which partially covered the smell of stale urine.

"What a commotion!" she said in a quiet voice. "Is that it sorted then?" she asked her husband.

"Nearly," he replied. "We're going to look after young Greg for a while. He's been through a lot you know."

"I'm sure he has," she said. "Would you like a cuppa?" she

asked me. I noticed that she had very small brown friendly eyes. I was desperate for a cold beer and I think that Mr Cartwright sensed that. "Anything stronger, son – beer or whisky?"

"Can I have a beer please?" I asked him.

"Of course you can, my son," he replied.

"I'll be in the living room if you need me," Mrs Cartwright said and shuffled out of the kitchen. She seemed like a nice woman, I thought, and I wondered what condition she suffered from.

"Sit down," he instructed me so I sat down at the small dark wooden table in the kitchen. I imagined that this was where Mr and Mrs Cartwright would sit and face each other over breakfast. The kitchen, and I assume the entire property, could be described as tired and in need of some refurbishment. It looked like the sink and cooker were the originals from when Mr and Mrs Cartwright moved in – there were no modern appliances such as a dishwasher or tumble dryer and there was a fusty smell as well, but that may have come from the dog or even Mrs Cartwright, I thought rather uncharitably.

Mr Cartwright took a can of London Pride out of a cupboard, poured it into a pint glass and put it on the table. I noticed that the glass had a small speck of what appeared to be cereal that had hardened onto it. I was gasping for a drink and even though I much preferred cold beer, this would do. I went to pick the glass up but my hands were shaking so much I thought I would drop it, so I hurriedly set it back down again. I tried again with the same result. Mr Cartwright saw this, and to prevent me further embarrassment I think, said, "I'm going out back for a smoke. You have a couple of minutes' drink on your own then we can catch up on what's happened." He had such a kindly tone and seemed so sympathetic and empathetic.

Mr Cartwright went outside for his smoke and I tried having a drink again. I was still shaking as much as before, but not having an audience made it easier as I wasn't so self-conscious as I gripped the glass with shaking hands like an addict going cold turkey. I held the glass to my lips and gulped down several mouthfuls of beer. I set the glass down and then had another drink. It was doing the trick and I was gradually calming down. I had a third drink which just about cleared the glass, at which point Mr Cartwright returned. Without saying anything, he took another beer out of the cupboard and put it next to my glass. He sat down across from me at the small table. Mrs Cartwright had the television on very loudly in the living room.

"Apart from being your neighbour and living here, you might wonder what any of this has to do with me." I nodded. I could smell the tobacco from his breath and body. "Thought so. Well you've probably guessed that I'm retired." I nodded again. "Any idea what I did before retiring?" I shook my head. "Old Bill. Copper for forty years. Ended up as a detective with the Met. Been retired just over four years now, but I still keep in touch with my old mates. Once a cop, always a cop," he said with almost a glint in his eyes.

"You've got to keep in touch with your colleagues because the job drives you away from having normal friendships due to its demands, the hours, but mainly what we do. Most people have got a skeleton in the closet and don't want to be sharing it with a cop. I've seen it all my life at family gatherings or when you just want a few drinks down the pub; the mood changes and the way that people talk changes as soon as I get near. Anyway, that's the way it is and that's how it will stay. I don't go out much these days. As you can see, Mrs C doesn't keep great health, but when I do go out it's usually to the Police Club down Harrow way.

"Being a cop you develop certain characteristics. One of them is it makes you a nosey, suspicious bastard. Or is that two characteristics?"

I smiled weakly. I was intrigued – where were we going with this?

"Anyway last night, a few things happened that got me suspicious, then nosey. Another characteristic that you get is a sixth sense that something ain't quite right and that happened the minute I got up and came in here to make Mrs C a cuppa. I happened to notice through a gap in the curtains you and two others making your way towards the stairs. Nothing unusual in that apart from you hardly ever have guests round at that time – it don't happen often but when you do have people round it's usually after shutting time in the pub." I nodded. I was enjoying the moment in not having to speak or think and just listen. "I thought the body language of all three of you was strange. It didn't look like you had two friends with you. I can't see round corners so I couldn't see you go up the stairs but I listened and could hear chairs scraping, voices that didn't appear to be sociable and then I saw them leave which made me suspicious. Time to take Billy out, I thought." He looked over at Billy in the corner sleeping on his blanket. I had forgotten about him.

"I waited a couple of minutes and then went out the front with Billy and walked down Rathgar Avenue. I saw the blonde bloke further ahead on his own and out of the corner of my eye the girl, in the garden of number fifty-two, obviously watching your flat from behind a tree. She was a complete amateur – so obvious she stood out like the Blackpool illuminations. It was clear to me that something was wrong and that if your flat was being watched, even by an amateur, it was going to be serious. I did a circuit then went back to the house. I could hear you moving about upstairs. You learn in my game to think like the person you're watching and I thought that if they were watching you then they'd think that you may be trying to escape.

"I went outside with a bin liner and made a show of putting

rubbish in the bin and could still see the girl in the garden opposite. I went round the back to see if anyone was watching the house from the back. I made a show of getting a fag out and doing the 'old git not allowed to smoke in the house' routine. I didn't see anyone watching the back but then saw you opening the window and climbing down the drainpipe. I stubbed my fag out and stood in the shadows expecting you to see me, but you didn't and you went and hid something under my shed before climbing the fence and heading down Telford Road. Well this got me very interested and as I've said I don't get out much these days – I like to have something to keep me interested. I retrieved the object from under my shed, went back inside and saw that it was a wallet with your leisure membership card and a four-digit number on a scrap of paper. This got me very interested because I didn't have a clue what it was for and why you would hide it under my shed. I then watched your watcher from through the letterbox of my front door. I knew the girl was such an amateur that she wouldn't see the letterbox raised half an inch. She wouldn't even think to look at all around her and not just directly at your flat. Well after a while I could see her on her phone and then she left.

"I gave it five minutes, told Mrs C that I had some business to attend to – she knows not to ask – and went outside. I did a circuit of the block, again in sad-old-smoker-git mode, then went up to your place and went in."

"How did you get in?" I asked croakily.

"Old Bill, son. We know the tricks of the trade. I've got a little lock-picking set that will get me into seventy-five per cent of the houses round here in less than two minutes. Yours was no problem."

Time for a visit from the local crime prevention officer when this is all over, I thought, or maybe I should just ask Mr Cartwright.

"What surprised me was that you had left your phone on the kitchen table. I couldn't understand why you would leave your phone, or if you were being threatened why they would let you keep it. It took me longer to get into your text messages than it did to get into the flat even though you kindly didn't have the phone locked. It's four years since I regularly tampered with people's stuff – losing the knack. Anyway I looked at the text messages and froze when I saw that picture of the old lady and the person with the knife.

"I had a good look round and saw the ripped-up waistcoat in the bedroom, drawers and cupboards left open and then noticed the brown wrapping paper on the chest of drawers."

"What made you look at that?" I asked.

"A good cop looks for clues and as I said, son – instinct. Old lady in photo, old handwriting with an address on the wrapping paper, two and two together. It was time to call in some favours. I remember when I was in the force and climbing up the greasy pole that you have to be able to give and take favours and the trick is to know when you do either. I am careful that since I've retired I'm not seen as an interfering old bastard so it is usually them who contact me for some advice or if I remember such and such from way back. That way when I do contact them they know it's serious."

I think that he was enjoying this. He had a warm, deep, slightly croaky voice, caused by the smoking no doubt. You could tell that he had been a good cop who was caring and compassionate, but had the steel to change to hard bastard as soon as the job demanded it. Mr Cartwright told me that he then went back to his house with my phone and the leisure card and number, called an ex-colleague who is a detective in the force and arranged to meet him at their boozer. He told me the name and where it was but it meant nothing to me. I expect it was a hostelry with an environment where off-duty cops and ex-cops felt comfortable.

He didn't tell me the name of his ex-colleague but said that he was very interested when he was shown the picture on the phone of Aunt Isa and told of Mr Cartwright's hunch that she was Isa Braithwaite of Sycamore Avenue, Shirley, Solihull as shown on the wrapping paper. He told his friend about seeing me climb out of the back window of my flat, the blonde guy, his partner watching the flat, and of course the leisure card wallet hidden under his shed which contained the four-digit number on the scrap of paper.

His police contact left to get to the station and set up a team to start an initial investigation. He instructed Mr Cartwright to get back to his house, monitor events and report back on the hour with the promise that he would be kept in the loop, in an off-the-record way of course.

Mr Cartwright's ex-colleague had to get permission to set up monitoring of the calls and text messages, but given the nature of the suspected crime, he had that within the hour and then minutes after that, the cops had tracked the number of the phone that had sent Isa's picture to my phone and confirmed the location from which it was sent as exactly the one given by Mr Cartwright from the wrapping paper. The police soon traced the red van to an industrial estate on the edge of town and they quickly realised the connection between what I was doing with Vicky and Aunt Isa's fate.

They tracked the numbers that had received the text with the picture of Aunt Isa and got Blondie's number and from that number they got Vicky's as well as others. Then they tracked the text and phone conversations between him and Vicky throughout the evening and into the next day and could deduce that she was using someone, who they guessed to be me, to look for a numerical code. They could tell that after spending the night in Docklands we were in the Ealing area. They started picking up the messages from me on my new phone to Vicky. The number tracked to Solihull was obviously the person holding Isa, but they couldn't work out exactly what was going on and for what reason. They picked out addresses; mine, Vicky's, Eustace's and an industrial estate in East London as well as locations such as the leisure centre and Zach's garage, but they weren't bugging anything so they were reliant on trying to make out what the messages between the various devices meant.

Finally Mr Cartwright mentioned Eustace in that when I texted and phoned Vicky they picked up on my message regarding Eustace and Cassie. They understood that I had worked out that Eustace had hidden a security box in a car and with a code number that he had produced.

The police in West London and Solihull co-ordinated their surveillance and operations and Mr Cartwright was deployed as lookout at my flat. After waiting patiently all morning he saw me appear early afternoon, closely followed by Vicky and then ten minutes later by Blondie. The police were primed to pounce and Mr Cartwright contacted them as soon as I arrived and everyone was in place by the time Blondie turned up at my front door. At the signal for my front door to be breeched, West Midlands had covertly surrounded the dirty red van and stormed it at the same time. They arrested a thirty-one-year-old male and freed Aunt Isa.

I nodded at all of this and then said, "Do you know that Eustace is dead?"

"Dead. How do you know?" he asked. He was definitely taken aback and on reflection I think that he expected me to be gushing in my thanks for what he had helped achieve and full of admiration for how it had been done. If that was the case he was right, but I was still coming to terms with the whole sequence of events and their consequences. I gave him a brief summary of what had happened from picking up the waistcoat in the charity shop to finding the driving licence and number and returning the driving licence to its owner and finding him with a knife in his chest. I told him that was the first time I met Blondie and his partner, or Kev and Cassie as I now knew them. "What's the address?" he asked.

"You already mentioned it when you were listing the addresses identified from the phone monitoring," I said. "It's fourteen Clepington Road. I don't know if his body will still be there, but I was taken back to my flat by Blondie and Cassie and they left Eustace sat in his chair with a knife sticking out of him. That would have been about four or five o'clock last night."

"We need to get you along to the station, son, for a formal interview so that my ex-colleagues can start to fill in the gaps and work out what the hell has been going on."

I nodded. "I need to speak to Aunt Isa and my parents. How is she?"

"She's in hospital as far as I know. Had a traumatic ordeal." My heart sunk at this news.

"But is she alright?"

"She was knocked about a bit and has suffered mild hypothermia from being held in a van all night," he said softly.

"I need to speak to her." A force had appeared in me which I hadn't recognised before, one built of the injustice of Isa suffering this, but also from an inner strength that had developed over the past twenty-four hours in dealing with this shit, the very dangerous shit that I was up to my neck in. Mr Cartwright could sense my anger but also my determination in my need to speak to my aunt. I don't think that he knew or understood my guilt in that I felt responsible for setting this whole ridiculous dangerous chain of events in motion.

"It's probably best to phone your parents first to let them know that you're alright and then find out about Isa," he suggested. Rather guiltily I realised that I had hardly considered my parents from the moment the police crashed into the flat. Mr Cartwright got up and left the kitchen, returning a few moments later with the house phone. "Here, son, give them a call."

I dialled the number nervously and it was answered on the third ring by my father. "Dad, it's Greg."

"What the hell has been going on?" was his reply. He didn't sound very warm and didn't seem particularly concerned about me.

"It's a long story. How is Aunt Isa?" My tone was neutral.

"Not good. She's in hospital with hypothermia, cuts and bruises. The doctor told us he thinks that she may be traumatised. They have sedated her so that she can rest up tonight and they will assess her again in the morning."

"Oh my god. Can I see her?" The picture of her and that bastard with the knife flashed through my mind.

"What?" he almost shouted down the line. "After all that you've caused, you want to see her?"

"Dad I couldn't help any of this and I have been trying my hardest all night to get her free," I almost sobbed. I must admit I had expected some sort of sympathy, but no – it was all my fault. "Look, Dad, I have to go to the police to give a statement and I will probably stay in my neighbour's house tonight." I looked over at Mr Cartwright and he nodded in agreement. "But after I have spoken to the police, hopefully tomorrow I will come up to see you and Mum and Isa and tell you about everything that has happened."

"How have you managed to get tied up with these people?" Typical of my father, it was all my fault.

I didn't answer that and asked, "Can I speak to Mum please?"

"Just a minute."

"Oh, Greg – what have you been up to? Your father's in a terrible state. Poor Isa…" she tailed off.

"Look I'm sorry about all of this and none of it would have happened if I had had my way but I didn't. I have been held at knifepoint. I have seen a man who was stabbed to death in his own home, I have had a police raid on my flat…" I had raised my voice as I was telling her this and now I started to cry in dry, deep gasps. Mr Cartwright took the phone from my hand and spoke to my mother, telling her who he was and where we were just now and that we were going to the police station and thereafter we would come back to his and stay the night. He also told her that he would drive me up to Solihull the next day. This helped. I calmed down and we prepared to go the station. He phoned the police to tell them about Eustace and that we were on our way. He said a brief goodbye to his wife and we left the house.

Mr Cartwright had a two-year-old Passat which was parked in the drive. We drove pretty much in silence to the police station which was a few miles away and I have little or no recollection of the drive there. When we arrived at the police station, Mr Cartwright spoke into an intercom at the barrier which then lifted and we drove round the back to designated staff parking spaces. We got out and walked to a non- descript-looking door at the back of the building which had a keypad to the side of it. Mr Cartwright tapped in some numbers, there was a click and the door unlocked. We made our way into the building and had to go through a further two doors that required a similar procedure and we sailed through those.

Mr Cartwright nodded to a number of uniformed and civilian personnel as we made our way to the reception in what was a surprisingly clean and modern interior. He was greeted warmly by a uniformed sergeant at the front desk and they exchanged pleasantries and small talk for a few moments before we were told to make our way to Interview Room Three. I was totally unaware of police procedures but this seemed very relaxed and I expected a uniformed escort. I guess it was Mr Cartwright's clout.

We got to Interview Room Three and Mr Cartwright knocked lightly on the door. It was opened immediately by a uniformed officer who beckoned us in. Mr Cartwright shook hands warmly with a middle-aged man in civilian clothes and said, "Here's Greg, John, over to you. Let me know if you need anything more from me."

"Thanks," John said as Mr Cartwright left the room. I realised then that I still didn't know Mr Cartwright's first name. "Sit down," he said to me in a neutral tone.

The room was just like you see on television with a large table with metal legs fixed to the floor and a white Formica surface on top. There was no furniture apart from four chairs and there was one mirrored window where I expected we were being observed from outside and I guessed where Mr Cartwright might be. I sat down at the table as instructed. John and another detective sat next to him. The uniformed officer who had let us in sat behind me. "I am Detective John Stevenson and this is Detective Michael Brown. We are going to ask you about the events of the eighteenth and nineteenth of October 2014 in Ealing and other areas which involved the death of Eustace Barrington or Manley and the abduction of Isa Braithwaite. This will be taped and a transcript typed up. Do you agree to this?" I nodded. "Please confirm verbally," he asked.

"Sorry, yes I do agree," I said.

We started with formalities such as the date, time and location of the interview, my name, age, address and occupation before Detective Stevenson asked me to talk him through the events of the past day in sequence and stressed the need to include every detail however trivial it may seem to me. He asked if I understood. I told him that I did.

Both policemen were still very neutral to me. I obviously didn't expect the beer and support that I had got from Mr Cartwright but I felt that they displayed very little sympathy or empathy for me considering what I had been through. It sounded like Stevenson was from Yorkshire originally, but I couldn't tell where Brown was from because he hadn't uttered a word. He just sat and looked at me and occasionally jotted something down in his notebook. I noted that he had that white-paste effect at the corners of each side of his mouth. I bet he had halitosis.

I found it quite easy to retell my story considering that this was now the third time that I had done so. I began with my visit to the charity shop, being careful to name it and give its address and the time I went there. I kept to this level of detail as I recounted finding the driving licence, going to Eustace's, being taken to my flat, the photo of Aunt Isa at knifepoint on my phone, contacting Vicky and so on. Stevenson occasionally asked for clarity but was good at letting me speak and encouraging me onwards at the right times.

I had to explain about the code and the thought processes that had gone into working it out and of course the fact that I hadn't known that Vicky was working me like a puppet to look for a twelve-digit number in the first case. I was hoping that they were going to be impressed by me deducing that the number was made up from Eustace's running number, his time and his leisure centre membership number and my bravery in following Doug, sneaking into the garage and finding the location of the box. I suppose that I also expected a bit of sympathy from them at the nature of Vicky's betrayal but I didn't get that either.

I reached the end which was when the police virtually exploded into my flat and Mr Cartwright took me downstairs to his house. "Thank you for that," Stevenson said. "I have a few areas that I need clarity on please? When the blonde man and his accomplice that you now know as Cassie left your flat, you received a text to your phone with a picture of your aunt at knifepoint. You had previously left the house of someone that you recognised with him dead with a knife in his chest. Why didn't you phone the police?"

"Because I was scared."

"Scared?"

"Yes, scared." His tone was beginning to piss me off. Brown was scribbling a lot down now and surreptitiously showing certain notes to Stevenson. I started to explain my actions or was it to defend them? "I have never seen a dead person before, far less a murder victim. The people who had done this were holding my aunt so I didn't want them to harm her. I thought that if I could find the number then they would let her go. I also thought that they might be bugging my phone."

"You watch too many films, son," he said. I found that patronising remark offensive but tried to keep myself calm. I didn't mind Mr Cartwright calling me son, but not this prick. This was becoming difficult and I did think about reports of victims of rape, domestic violence and so on who ended up feeling as if they were responsible for the crime committed against them. "Let's move on," he said. "You lied about your car needing a MOT to the gym user called Doug who owns a garage called Zach's Motors then used Vicky to trick him out of the garage to allow you to break in to find out the location of the security box?"

"Yes." I was now expecting him to ask me for more details in my logic for working out the security box code and where it was located, but no.

"Did you know that you were committing a crime when carrying out these acts?"

"No."

"No?"

"Well, yes, but I wasn't committing a crime, I was trying to find the box and get my aunt free." Far from being impressed by my resourcefulness, they were suspicious of it.

"In your opinion, not the law's," Stevenson said as he stared directly at me. "Was Vicky working you or were you working Vicky?" was his next salvo. I didn't like the way that this was going. I had assumed that I was there to give a statement of the events of the previous twenty-four hours, which would back up the events that the police had monitored from the phone surveillance and backed up by the arrest of Blondie and Vicky. "You admit to coercing the Polish cleaner Piotr to elicit confidential information from his employer's membership records," he stated. I could only look at him and gently nod. I was then asked to go over huge chunks of my story again. Both Stevenson and Brown had increased their note-taking. "What is the number?" Stevenson asked.

"I can't remember it but Blondie has it – I wrote it down for Vicky but even if they don't have it now I can work it out for you." I repeated how the number was formed and how it would be easy to get the first two four-digit parts and they could get the third by contacting the leisure centre and getting Eustace's membership number. I noticed Brown pointing at one of his notes for Stevenson to read. Stevenson gave a brief almost imperceptible nod to his colleague.

"It all seems to have come to you a bit easy – how well did you know Eustace?" By now my heart was racing. I explained that I just recognised him because I had seen him in the leisure centre a few times.

"Is it a busy leisure centre?" he asked.

"Yes it is."

"But even though it is a busy facility in London, you recognise users of the fitness room?"

"Yes."

"How many?"

"Five or six."

"Name them."

I listed Doug, Brian and Eustace of course.

"That's only three."

"I don't know the names of the others, I just recognise them from seeing them in the fitness room."

"They are all men. Are you aware of any homosexual activity in this facility?" This was getting scary. Where was he going with this line of questioning? "Are you homosexual?"

"No," I almost blurted. It wasn't being asked about my sexuality that bothered me, it was the sudden confirmation that Mr Cartwright's ex-colleague doubted me and my story.

"Do you have a girlfriend?"

"No. Not just now. I broke up with my last girlfriend about six months ago. Vicky is – sorry, was – my best friend."

"How long have you known her?"

"Seventeen years."

I had lost track of time when Stevenson said, "Detain him so that he can continue to be questioned regarding breaking and entering, and accessory to kidnap, extortion and murder. Read him his rights and bang him up with the rest of them."

With that he left Interview Room Three.

CHAPTER NINETEEN

It felt like he had been hit in the chest by a cricket bat – no, what it really felt like was when he got hit in the chest by a cricket ball. He remembered that when he was only eight or nine and Brinsley Smith had thrown a bouncer at him – well it wasn't really a bouncer – Brinsley just threw the ball at him. It hit him square in the chest just above the ribcage and knocked him off his feet. He had fallen back onto the dusty ground and lain still for a few seconds before the pain hit and the tears started. He hadn't wanted to cry because he didn't want Brinsley to see that he had hurt him and give him that pleasure. He hated Brinsley, who at fifteen was two years older and several inches taller than Eustace's big brother David.

It was hard growing up in Wilton Gardens, Kingston, which they called Rema, and you had to be able to stand up for yourself, show no fear and walk the walk if you were to have any chance. Everything changed when he was eleven and his mother died and he moved from Jamaica to England with his father and David in 1967. They stayed at first with his uncle's family in Lambeth. It was a whole new cold, wet, scary world, but his father had got a job in a printers, they got their own flat in the area and the boys settled in and used their survival skills honed in Rema to get by. As the years passed Eustace now considered London as home. However after some local trouble involving a pregnant girlfriend and the subsequent stabbing of her two angry brothers, David returned to Jamaica in the late seventies. Eustace had not seen him again or spoken to him for over thirty years now. He had these thoughts as he was being held down by the young thug and Cassie.

He closed his eyes as he didn't want to see his attackers. He should have realised that a gorgeous young thing such as Cassie – so young, lovely and vibrant – would never have just chosen him, a middle-aged man, as her lover. She had come on so strong to him after her first spinning class that he had attended and had made a point of seeking him out to ask him about how he was getting on with it. She had offered him personal tuition and when she suggested that they could do a session at his house he couldn't believe his luck. He did enjoy that none of his mates could believe it either when they saw him with his new girlfriend. She was so good in bed and so much fun to be with that she had given him a new lease of life. The past two weeks had made him feel like he was thirty again. He was fit for his age and he did actually believe that she had fancied him.

The unexpected upturn in his fortune in the relationship department was welcome, but he had started to get wary when after only a week or so, her pillow talk would turn to the subject of what he did as part of his illegal activities and she would try to get information out of him that should have been meaningless to her. When he caught her going through his stuff after he had arrived home unexpectedly one lunchtime he definitely suspected that she was up to something. She had made an excuse that he knew was bullshit but as she was just wearing her tiny black see-through scants at the time, before he knew it, he let it go and instead of challenging her they ended up having a quick lunchtime shag. Thinking about it now, from the first time that they had made love she had become an almost permanent fixture in his house apart from when she was doing her classes. He had never visited her place and was unsure exactly where it was.

Although he suspected that Cassie was up to something, he had still got the surprise of his life when he left their lunch cooking away in the kitchen and answered the door only to be attacked by the two violent visitors who were helped by Cassie, grabbing him from behind and dragging him into the living room. At first he had thought that he could resist the young man and the two women by fighting back, but when that failed, his bullshit also backfired and taunting the young blonde thug had made it worse and now here he was on the way out.

He shouldn't have got greedy and should have just kept doing jobs in his manor; however he couldn't resist when he had met a friend of a friend who had promised easy money and lots of it. He had jumped in, got involved without proper planning and knowing who he was dealing with, gone way out of his depth and now was paying the ultimate price.

He was glad that he had split the security box code number into three and hid the three parts separately in the waistcoat, leisure card and his toolbox at Zach's garage. If the driving licence and number were found he thought they might find him. They might even wonder about the number he also thought, but by now Eustace was really past caring about that.

They continued to hold him down with his mouth covered and he kept trying to resist and grab the knife to pull it out but his strength was waning. His grip slackened and he finally let go of the knife handle. He didn't want to die.

Apart from thinking about the cricket ball incident, his life didn't flash before his eyes. The last thoughts Eustace had were: I wish that David was here and I wonder what became of Brinsley.

He had an odd taste in his mouth and then the lights went out.

CHAPTER TWENTY

When Stevenson had got up and gone and left Brown to do the formalities, I had gone beyond scared at the thought of spending my first night in a cell. After the events of the past day it was just yet more shit to deal with. I can barely remember what standard prose was read out for me to agree with and what paperwork I signed. I was led downstairs to the holding cells. My cell already had an occupant who appeared to be sleeping off large quantities of alcohol. I lay on the empty bed and stared at the ceiling.

I was awoken by the heavy cell door being opened, which surprised me because I didn't think that I would have fallen asleep in my grim surroundings. That, added to my sense of outrage at being incarcerated, had almost made me determined not to sleep and to lie and seethe all night at the injustice of it all. Given that I was sharing this small stuffy space with someone else that I had no idea what he was in for had made it all the more unlikely that I would have slept, but I suppose the adrenaline couldn't keep running for ever and the effect of the past twenty-four hours had taken their toll. The uniformed officer looked at me and said, "Stewart, you're wanted."

I got up from the concrete bed without looking at my roommate and walked out through the open door which was immediately closed loudly and locked behind me. I didn't know what time it was and momentarily had even forgotten what day it was. I was led through the labyrinth to the stairs and then upstairs to Interview Room Three again. Stevenson and Brown were there and it looked like they had both been home for the night because they were clean-shaven, wore different clothes and smelt lemon-fresh – bastards. They went through the same procedure as last night before the interview, only changing the day and the time in the standard text that they reeled off. I noted that it was 8.05 am.

"Following your interview yesterday, we've got a few areas that we need to explore further," Stevenson said. They were particularly interested in the twelve-digit number. "Tell me from beginning to end how you worked it out," Stevenson asked so I did. I started from the charity shop and the waistcoat all the way through to Piotr's handwritten note being put into my locker in the leisure centre and then confirming that it was indeed a twelve-digit number for a security box in the white Audi by sneaking in to Doug's garage. "But how did you know it should be twelve digits?" Stevenson asked, looking quizzical which disappointed me. When I looked back to my interview yesterday, on reflection I had thought that I was going to be treated sympathetically as the poor victim, that they would listen to my story and go all out to help me and get the bastards that did all this. I probably came over as a liberal wishy-washy wimp, so today I was not going to give an inch. I decided that I would attempt to meet their stares and would not be unsettled or side-tracked by their accusations, leading questions or aggressive suppositions put down as fact and I would tell my story, the truth by the way, clearly and unwaveringly.

"How many times do I need to tell you? I didn't know that I was looking for a twelve-digit number," I said evenly. "I found a four-digit number, Blondie was looking for a number and I thought that was it – the four-digit number I mean. It was only when I got Vicky involved that she started to subtly drop into my consciousness what the code may be for and how long it may be. I didn't realise this at the time and I thought that I was using logic and reasoning along with her to deduce that it was twelve digits, but she was manipulating me – she's very good at that. Yes, with the benefit of hindsight and twenty-twenty vision it looks strange that I started to look for a twelve-digit number and a security box so soon after finding a four-digit one, but I was being worked on and in my stressed, focused, single-track mind I was looking for the answer, not knowing that I was being steered by Vicky."

"For the record do you mean Kevin Osborne when you refer to Blondie?"

"Yes I do," I said in a tone that suggested that they knew perfectly well who Blondie was when I used that term.

"Tell me about your relationship with Vicky."

I started from the very first time that we met at Leicester University as Freshers in Autumn 1997 and described how we were soon in a group that socialised over the next four years and kept in touch quite well for many years after we had all left university. I did my best to go through the years from then up to now. I listed the names of all my friends in this group and gave details of when we had met up at weddings and other social gatherings. I gave as many details as I could recollect and told him about her husband John. I could give a very rough idea of how many times we met in a year but with no feeling of certainty. I tried my best to cover the past seven years, her London years, and detail how many times I thought that I had met her this year and where we had met up. I told him that we exchanged emails and texts from time to time and the nature of the messages that we sent each other. However this wasn't enough for Stevenson and he expected me to detail my every meeting with her which of course I couldn't do.

"Why do they call you the Professor?" Here we go, I thought, another sudden change of tack from Stevenson.

"I don't know who you mean by 'they'," I stated. "Blondie started calling me that in my flat when he was looking for the number. He asked me what I did for a living and when I told him that I was a college lecturer he called me that."

"You're hardly a lecturer, more like a teacher surely?" It was Brown – so he could speak after all. The first time he had spoken since he read me my rights last night. Cheeky bastard, but I wasn't going to rise to the bait.

"In your opinion," I said flatly. Brown stayed silent; he couldn't match my razor-sharp repartee.

Stevenson jumped back in and continued, "They both say that you were the brains behind this."

"What!" I exclaimed. This one did cause me to lose my cool.

"They are being held separately and have had no opportunity to converse since being arrested at your flat yesterday afternoon, but both of them have said that you killed Eustace after failing to get the number from him. Their stories are very similar," Stevenson told me.

I managed to hold back and not let loose with a self-pitying angry knee-jerk reaction, then took a deep breath and said, "If you have been monitoring their calls and text messages then you must know that they are working together so it is hardly surprising that their stories are similar. Also who else could they blame apart from me?"

"Cassie?" Stevenson said. Christ, I had forgotten about her.

"Yes they could have blamed her I suppose, but they don't know for sure if you even know about her, so why would they introduce someone else into the mix?" I countered. Stevenson just nodded as he wrote something down. He then moved on to other areas and he asked me about the white Audi's registration number. All I could tell him was that it was a customised plate.

"How many letters and numbers?" he asked.

"I'm sorry but I can't remember."

"Two, three, seven? Did it form a name? You must remember something." He wasn't giving up.

"I think that it may have been three letters and two numbers," was the best that I could do. The lengthy silence that followed suggested that they didn't believe me, but I genuinely couldn't remember. It hadn't been on the top of my list in the few minutes that I had given myself to find the security box after I had broken into Doug's garage.

The interview carried on for what felt like another hour or so with Stevenson asking me about my family, friends, job and relationships. In particular he probed my relationship with Aunt Isa. This is where I found it very difficult to remain calm and focused because I did feel guilty for what had happened to her and on top of that I felt an enveloping depression and sadness for drifting into the casual way that I had considered Aunt Isa over the past few years. He then held up a print of the picture of Aunt Isa and the bastard in the mask. "What did you feel when you saw that picture?" he asked. I looked at him, then Brown, and felt myself shaking. I shook my head at Stevenson and put my head on my arms on the cold white table. After a few minutes I looked up and asked for a drink of water. The uniformed officer reacted to a nod from Stevenson and placed a plastic cup of water on the table beside me. I gulped it down.

As I was finishing my drink, Stevenson stated that we were done for now and that I could go. He officially concluded the interview for the sake of the recording equipment and signalled for me to leave. The uniformed officer led me out of Interview Room Three and along the corridor to the front desk and told me to wait there. He pressed a bell which prompted a sergeant to come through to the desk and give me some paperwork to sign. He gave me my phone and wallet back, which were my only two possessions that I currently had access to, and then told me I could go. At this point Mr Cartwright appeared from the seating area in reception and said, "Come on, son, the car's outside," which was a pleasant surprise and I was so glad that he was here. This time we went out the front of the police station and had to walk on the narrow pavement around the side of the building to the staff car park. It was a bright, sharp morning which took my eyes a few moments to adjust to.

"I don't understand why they fucking arrested me," I shouted as soon as we were in the car. "I'm not a fucking criminal – look what I've been through for fuck sake. I've told them the truth all along. Look what I have suffered – assault, attempted murder, forced entry into my flat and he stole my laptop and my passport for fuck sake."

"They didn't arrest you, son," Mr Cartwright said softly as he stopped the car at the car park exit, rolled down the window and pressed the code to raise the barrier. "They detained you under Section 41 of the Police and Criminal Evidence Act 1984 for further questioning and now they have let you go. They can hold you for up to twenty-four hours before they must charge you or let you go. I tried to talk them out of it but to be honest I knew that I couldn't. I said that you would be with me but there is only so much that can be done unofficially and off the record. I shouldn't even being doing all this but anyway I digress. Think about it. Look at the level of the crimes that have been committed, look at all the missing bits – how can they bang Osborne and Monteith up and not keep you in overnight? A defence lawyer would have a field day if they did.

"I'll tell you the latest developments that I know on the road up to Solihull but let's get you back to my place first so that you can have a wash and some breakfast."

Yes, it had just dawned on me that my friends at the station hadn't even offered me breakfast. I'm sure that's against the rules – perhaps I should report it. With it now being Monday and having worn the same clothes since Saturday morning I was aware of my own smell. I was looking forward to a shower. "Thanks," I said warmly. We were making slow progress through the Monday-morning traffic, but were not far from home now which prompted me to ask Mr Cartwright, "When can I get back into my flat?"

"Don't know, maybe several days as it's still a scene of crime," he explained. My overworked mind then shifted elsewhere.

"Shit – what about work? I haven't told college." I had suddenly realised that I should be at work just about now.

"Don't worry, son, I've contacted them and explained the position to an extent and told them that you will be off for at least a week. Needless to say I was a bit economical with the truth." What would I do without him? He was wasted in retirement.

"I'll pack an overnight bag," Mr Cartwright announced. I didn't know what he was talking about.

"Sorry, what? Why?" I mumbled in response.

"So that I can bring you home in the morning – hopefully you'll be able to stay at your parents' tonight and you can spend time with them and have quality time with your Aunt Isa. I'll stay in a budget hotel nearby – there's plenty of them in Solihull."

His help at this time was invaluable. "You don't have to," was the best that I could come out with to express my thanks.

"I want to," he said with a mixture of steel and kindness.

"What about Mrs C?" I had dropped into Mr Cartwright's parlance.

"Her sister's coming round to stay – she can sleep in the room that you were going to stay in last night. Mrs C had made up a fresh bed for you, so that work ain't wasted," he said with a chuckle.

We were approaching Rathgar Avenue and I felt a sudden feeling of strangeness as we made our way up the familiar street. We got to our building and Mr Cartwright manoeuvred the car into position on the tiled area in front of the house. There was hazard tape around the stairs to my flat and a uniformed constable standing guard at the base of the stairs. Mr Cartwright nodded to the policeman who nodded back and we went into the house through the back door.

"Right, you get a shower, son. I don't want a two-hour drive sitting next to you smelling like that!" he said lightly. "Follow me, it's just along here." I dutifully followed, feeling slightly uneasy as he hadn't even acknowledged his wife on our return. I can't really explain why but I hoped that she wasn't in, or had recently visited the bathroom. Fortunately Mrs Cartwright wasn't in there and it actually smelled nicer than the kitchen. The shower was fixed above the bath and I noted with relief that it and the glass shower screen were relatively new.

The newness of the shower was offset by drab tiles around the bath and a weak yellowy light from an old-fashioned lightshade, not the type you would expect in a bathroom. There was a nondescript faded pinkish floral-patterned wallpaper throughout the room which again didn't really suit a bathroom. I undressed quickly and stepped into the bath, stood underneath the nozzle and put the shower on. Unlike at Vicky's I instantly got it working and surprisingly it had a strong jet of water which was such a welcome and therapeutic sensation. I didn't fancy using Mr Cartwright's soap on a rope which was a fawn colour with dark brown cracks in it, so I used a coal tar shampoo as my shower gel. The shower felt so good that I had to force myself to switch it off and get out. I stood on the damp bath mat and dried myself off with a towel that had been sitting on top of the toilet seat.

I now felt fresh but as I prepared to get dressed I was disgusted by the state of my pants. I put my jeans and hoody on a bit reluctantly as I felt that they were violating my new and sudden cleanness. The T-shirt, socks and pants were unwearable and I gathered them up and returned to the kitchen. Mr Cartwright had his back to me at the cooker and it looked like a fry-up was being prepared which got my juices going. I asked for a carrier bag to put my soiled items in, he handed me a bag and I put the smelly items into it and went outside and threw them into the wheelie bin. When I came back into the kitchen I half expected Mr Cartwright to tell me that I couldn't throw anything away as my pants could be crucial evidence. I asked him if we could stop off somewhere on the way to Solihull so that I could get some replacements, to which he agreed of course.

Breakfast was everything that I had hoped it would be – the works, which I greedily wolfed down. He had even given me a large glass of cold fresh orange juice which was nectar for washing down my food. He had a cup of tea with his and I had two coffees as well as my juice which again tasted surprisingly good. When we had finished he dumped our dishes and cups in the sink and left them unwashed.

"I'm touching cloth here," he announced. "Off to the bathroom then after that let's go."

"Okay."

When Mr Cartwright returned from his movement, he asked me if I wanted to clean my teeth. I could taste my breath and did desperately want to scrub my teeth and feel my mouth fresh again, but not with any implement in his house, so I politely declined. I said that I would nip for a quick pee and then I was ready to go.

I returned from the toilet, which hadn't smelt as fresh as

when I had showered, and Mr Cartwright was waiting for me carrying an extremely small seventies-style holdall which I assumed was his overnight bag. We left the house which we didn't lock, and again I felt uneasy that he didn't shout goodbye to Mrs Cartwright and, as far as I could make out, he hadn't even looked in on her in the time that we had been in the house. A stranger visiting Mr Cartwright at that house wouldn't have known that another person was living there.

We headed back down Rathgar Avenue and went to a local supermarket to get me some clothes which was becoming a regular occurrence. I chose basic items, however only the T-shirt came individually with both the socks and pants in packs of three. Mr Cartwright paid, by card I noticed, and I went to the toilets to put on my new clothing and came out feeling so much better.

Mr Cartwright asked for my parents' post code, set his sat-nav and picked his way out of the surprisingly busy car park. We made our way through the remains of the West London commuter traffic as we headed for the A40 and the motorway north. Radio Two was playing quietly in the background and it was still a very pleasant bright day.

As we drove I considered Mr Cartwright: he was old-school with a full head of black hair, which was gradually going grey, controlled by Brylcreem or some other substance that gave it a shiny, almost wet look. He wore horn-rimmed glasses that would have looked in place in the sixties, was about six foot one, quite heavy set, but not fat, always clean-shaven, never in jeans but flannels as my mother or Isa would call them. It struck me as I observed him that he was always quite well dressed and always slightly better dressed on a Sunday. Today he wore a tie, which was normal for him. I never wear ties unless a formal occasion requires one, but I think the current fashion is for short, wide, colourful ties. Mr Cartwright wore a long, thin, plain maroon tie over his lightly checked shirt and it was tucked into his trousers. He had a grey V-neck sweater on and his black anorak was lying on the back seat.

We were now on the motorway. I have always hated motorway driving. I passed my test when I was eighteen so have had my licence for nearly twenty years but am an inexperienced driver, having had little need to drive regularly over the years. Mr Cartwright was a very smooth driver and had a calm authority as he dealt expertly with the constant need to move lanes and react to situations on the busy carriageways. He was the type of person that I would expect to wear driving gloves but his hands were bare. As he drove, he told me the key developments: "Kevin Ian Osborne, Victoria Elizabeth Monteith and Darren Roderick Jackson have been charged and are still being detained and questioned. Douglas Zacherelli was brought in and held overnight for questioning but wasn't charged. They have found Eustace's body at fourteen Clepington Road and despite the assailants having worn gloves at times they have found prints all over the property – amateurs. The Audi suspected of containing the security box is missing." I noted the introduction of cop speak. "What do you know about Cassandra Lewis?" he asked.

"Cassie?" I explained that apart from seeing her at Eustace's and her then accompanying Blondie to my place, nothing apart from seeing her face on the poster on the wall of the leisure club, the chat in the fitness room between Doug and his mates and putting two and two together to link her with Eustace.

He nodded and said, "No sign of her by the way. Osborne and Monteith have made no mention of her so far. The cops are visiting the leisure centre today as a lot of things seem to revolve around it." Then he went on to, "How did you work out the number and put two and two together with the garage? I know how the number was made up because you told me, but apart from the running number which you found by chance, what made you think of the other two parts? How did you link it to the garage?"

So I went over my thought processes explaining that I now knew that Vicky had manipulated me into looking for a twelve-digit number, but I had just started thinking laterally using what little information on Eustace that I had, and that of course I would have got nowhere if I hadn't seen his picture from the race in the local paper by chance. I told him that I thought if the code was indeed made up by Eustace then the numbers would be in the sequence that I had found them because in a way they were chronological – race number, race time and then bag swap in the leisure centre. "You're wasted as a lecturer – should have joined the Met!" he said with a laugh.

"Not what Brown would say!" I replied.

"I know. Cheeky bastard."

I asked him about the police raid on my house. "It was standard procedure in a potentially life-threatening or hostage situation," he explained with more cop speak.

"Do you know anything about the person who took my aunt? I forget his name," I asked.

"Darren Jackson? He's a bad one, a right bad one." I flinched at these remarks. "He's been inside more than out since he was about fifteen. Started off with the usual things – gang fights, petty theft, vandalism, affray – but he soon moved into car theft, housebreaking, drugs – you name it. Did a five-year stretch at Bedford for firearms offences, got out after three and a bit. Osborne was in there on a two-year stretch and they probably met then." Before he could elaborate his phone rang. I was surprised that he was on Bluetooth, despite his house having fairly basic appliances – what with satnav and Bluetooth, his grasp of new technology was better than mine. He let Stevenson know that he was on speaker phone and that I was in the car and then continued to have a conversation regarding the case. Stevenson made no acknowledgement of my presence.

I noted that Stevenson didn't refer to Mr Cartwright by any name and reckoned that he must have been Stevenson's superior when he was in the force so he didn't want to call him boss, but Mr Cartwright was too formal and his Christian name (whatever that was) was too informal. Mr Cartwright told him that we were on our way to Solihull for me to see my parents and Isa and that we would almost certainly stay overnight. Stevenson acknowledged this and asked Mr Cartwright to ensure that I did not divulge details of the case to anyone, to which Mr Cartwright agreed. How could he agree to that? I wondered. I needed to try and explain to my parents and Isa why this terrible thing had happened.

"We still haven't found the car or Cassandra Lewis. Greg, if anything springs to mind let Mr Cartwright know straight away." I was surprised that he called me Greg, not Stewart or even suspect three, and also surprised that he was asking me for something rather than demanding it. I told him that I would. He then asked Mr Cartwright to keep in touch and let him know when he was back in London. Mr Cartwright said he would and the call ended.

"Don't worry, son, Stevenson is just going through procedure. He knows that you will have to tell them something of what happened. Let's face it, with your aunt being kidnapped, they know a fair bit of what's happened already. By the way and strictly off the record, Stevenson believes you and doesn't think of you as a suspect." I trusted Mr Cartwright and that came as a relief.

"Did you know of Eustace?" I asked.

There was a slight hesitation before he said, "Yes. Yes, I was aware of him as a petty small-time local crook. Nothing too serious – clocking, vehicle ringing, cut and shuts."

"I know what clocking is but what are vehicle ringing and cut and shuts?" I asked.

"A ringer is a stolen vehicle with its identification numbers replaced by a set from another written-off model and with bogus documents. A cut and shut is where the remains of two or more vehicles have been welded together to create a new model."

"Ah," I grunted.

"Do you know what Vicky does for a living?" he asked.

"I know that she works in the City."

"Yes, but as what?"

"Something in finance," was all that I could add.

"She works as a PA to a fund manager for a company called Whighams Asset Management. Heard of them? It's a good job, but ten a penny and not one that would get you a fully paid-up two-bedroom apartment in Canada Water." Knowing what I did now, I wasn't surprised at this news.

As we turned off the M40 and headed towards Solihull, I felt a knot in my stomach. I really, really wanted to see Isa, but was scared at what I may see. I was also extremely nervous at meeting my parents, which sounds ridiculous, but the tone of my father and the nature of my call to them last night had surprised me. I had truly expected, if not sympathy, at least some support, but I had received neither. In between talking to Mr Cartwright, I had been thinking a lot about my parents on the way up to Solihull and my relationship with them. I had always thought that we got on well, but when I think about it what was the relationship? As I had gone from gawky student leaving home for the first time to college lecturer in London, what had our relationship become? A standard call every Sunday evening, two to three visits a year, one of which was Christmas, and that was it. I always felt some warmth emanating from my mother, but on reflection little or none from my father and I don't recall him once ever telling me he loved me.

I think that they were both disappointed that I hadn't settled down yet. Why? Why was this so important? Yes, you can get happy unions that span decades with a relationship that defines them like Isa and Bill had, but for every one of them there are probably lots of Mr and Mrs Cartwrights, or to a lesser extent my parents. Were they happy with each other? Their life was one of boring routine conducted pleasantly enough on the whole, but there appeared to be no spark and I do think that a lot of their reason for being was now channelled through their offspring.

I think my career path has disappointed them, my father in particular. He didn't think of it as a real job and I may be wrong but I sensed a slight racial overtone to the way he considered me teaching foreigners when I could be doing something more worthwhile. Whereas Frances got her History degree, taught for a few years, married a good stolid professional and had now got the standard two kids. Job done.

I overruled Mr Cartwright's satnav system and directed him along the final few streets to Blenheim Road, Shirley. I had phoned ahead when we turned off the M40 so they knew that we would arrive soon. We were now driving along very familiar streets and I always had mixed feelings when I returned as an adult: on the one hand they stirred happy memories and a sense of belonging because this was where I cycled and ran along as a child, but on the other I was glad that I didn't stay there anymore. The speed bumps were quite new – I would have enjoyed flying over them on my BMX, I thought.

It was eleven forty-five; I took a deep breath and got out of the car and Mr Cartwright followed a respectful distance behind. I walked up the familiar path and went to open the door and go in, but it was locked. After all that had happened, a sensible step

I suppose. I rang the bell. It took a while for it to be answered by my father. "Hi, Dad."

"Hello," he said formally.

"This is Mr Cartwright," I said as I stood aside.

"Hello, Mr Cartwright, and many thanks for everything you have done to help. Don't know what we would have done without you." He glanced at me as he said it. We were still on the front step.

"Come in," my mum said from the hall. I dutifully took my shoes off as I always did and Mr Cartwright followed suit. It's funny, I thought, but no one ever does this when they come into my flat. We went into the lounge. It looked odd seeing Mr Cartwright in his socks and flannels. "Would you like a cup of tea?" my mum asked.

"Yes please," Mr Cartwright replied.

My mother went into the kitchen. "So what happened, what's caused all this? Isa's in a hell of a state," my dad said accusingly. As I was about to speak, Mr Cartwright stepped in.

"Greg can tell you some things but remember this is an active investigation with a lot of missing parts at the moment. It covers murder, extortion and of course kidnapping." He said this evenly but I got the sense that he wanted my father to know what I had been through as well as Isa.

"I understand," my father said somewhat meekly. He was definitely intimidated by Mr Cartwright. My mother returned from the kitchen and we drank our tea whilst Mr Cartwright gave a brief overview of what had happened, emphasising that I had become involved in this quite by chance. On hearing the story retold by someone else emphasised to me the sheer horror but also randomness of it all.

"Can we go and see Isa now?" I asked. I was desperate to see Isa and I also wanted out of the house.

"Let's have some lunch first," my mother insisted. "Are you going back to London Mr Cartwright?" she continued.

"No, I was hoping that Greg could spend a night with you and I'll take him back down tomorrow."

"Where are you staying?"

"I'll find a hotel somewhere in the neighbourhood," he replied. Even if I stayed the night there was still another room available here, but I noted that this option wasn't offered to Mr Cartwright.

"Would you like to stay for lunch, Mr Cartwright?"

"I would love to," he answered and sounded genuine as well. We had lunch in the dining room and it was a grim affair conducted mainly in silence and I was so glad for Mr Cartwright's presence. My mum is a good cook but this situation was affecting us all as lunch consisted of a watery vegetable soup and sandwiches.

It was finally over and time to go to the hospital. Mr Cartwright thanked my parents profusely for their hospitality and made a point of giving me a hug as he said goodbye. He handed me a note of his phone number which I had forgotten to ask for in the car. "Keep in touch, son," he told me.

"I will," I promised.

We left the house and I went with my parents whilst Mr Cartwright got in his car to find a hotel. We drove in silence and gathering tension towards the hospital. When we arrived it took ten minutes to get a parking space which didn't help my dad's mood. We made our way through to the main reception of the standard large NHS hospital where doctors, nurses and ancillary staff battled away to deliver a valued service. The customary hospital smell is always off-putting but I couldn't hold that against them. My parents knew the way and didn't need to ask directions. We took the lift to get us onto the third floor. "It's just along here," my father said and I dutifully followed.

We came to a small four-bed ward. It must be the next one, I thought, because all the beds were taken and Isa wasn't there. My father walked up to the bed of a very frail old woman with pale skin and I thought that he must know her; maybe she was one of Isa's friends from the Women's Institute. It was only when he said, "Hello, Issy, my love," that I realised that it was Isa. Issy was his pet name for her. He had called her that since he was a 'wee boy' as his father would have described him. She was propped up but with just her head and a part of her neck not hidden by the bedcovers. A drip ran from a tall metallic wheeled stand next to the bed and presumably into her left arm.

Holy Christ it's Isa, I thought. Holy mother of God. I realised that I must have been staring at Isa with my mouth open and made an effort to pull myself together so as not to upset her. I moved up to the foot of the bed. Her face was sagging and there were several very black lines merging under her eyes. She smiled at me which in some ways made her look even more pitiful. Her pallor was an even more upsetting version of Mrs Cartwright's. "Greg," she said in a husky whisper. I had to almost push my way past my father who seemed reluctant to give up his space.

"Aunt Isa," was all that I could manage at first. I was desperately trying to think of what to say. There was no point asking how she was. We hugged, we have always hugged. By hugged I mean that I sat on the bed and put my arms around her. Isa raised her arms and rested them against me. She has always been so proud of me and Frances; throughout my life I have hugged Isa way more times than either of my parents. I wanted to hold her tight but was scared to hurt her. While I was doing this, I knew, and I think that she knew, that things had changed and would never be the same again. I had caused this – unwittingly, but I had caused this. I knew that Isa would never blame me but perhaps there would be something at the back of her mind. She would be upset that I had given her gift away; I had lied to her, a small lie but a lie just the same. She had been through something that no one should have to experience and I had caused it. What the hell could I say? "Isa, I am so sorry that all this has happened. It was a cruel set of circumstances." My nerves and sense of upset caused me to choose such clumsy words.

"Were you up to no good, Greg?" she whispered.

"No. No. Of course not. Nothing like that. A freak set of circumstances led to all of this. I witnessed a murder and then the people thought that I had something of theirs which I didn't and that was when they took you. I don't really think we should talk about it now though, Aunt Isa. Let's wait until you are out of here and better," I said softly and Isa nodded her head.

"You're a good boy, Greg. I knew you couldn't have been involved with that, that beast..." Her quiet voice had risen and she broke off and then started sobbing. My mother rushed to the bed and cuddled Isa's head against her breast. Isa was quietly mumbling into the fabric of my mother's cardigan and her body shook slowly and gently. I stood silently at the side of the bed. "Best you two go for a cuppa and give me and Aunt Isa twenty minutes together," Mum said.

Dad and I mutely agreed; we both nodded and turned to make our way out of the ward. I got in step with him and followed him to the café area which was one floor down. We sat at the sparse table with very hot cups of coffee from the vending machine.

For a minute or two neither of us spoke. Then it all came out: "She's more of a mother to me than a sister. She's looked out for me all of my life and now look at her. Christ knows what she's been through. Look at her, look at her..." His voice had got very loud and other people in the café were looking at him, or trying not to look at him. "You did this, you did this to her, you…" He suddenly got up and walked out. Perhaps just as well because I was speechless and would have struggled to answer him. I absolutely understood his pain and his anger at the way that Isa had been treated, but he seemed unable to grasp that my role in this was unwitting – I had not gone out to cause any of it. Through his pain he needed a scapegoat and I was it. I, his only son, was solely to blame – did he care what I had been through, had he even bothered to ask how I was?

I nursed my coffee with shaking hands for another five minutes, but it was still too hot to swallow; however at least the café occupants had stopped looking at me and got on with their own business again. I left the coffee and went back to the ward. Isa was talking with mum and she had a cup of tea. My father was standing near to the bed. Isa looked marginally better than when we had left but she had lost all of her spark; the vibrancy, the feistiness had gone. Her dull eyes told me that.

A consultant arrived with a nurse who pulled the curtain around the bed. When this was done he told us that they were going to do a few checks on Isa and it would be best to leave her for that and then allow her to get some rest. He told us that her full assessments would start tomorrow. We put our heads through the gap in the curtain one at a time and said our goodbyes to Isa and told her that we would be back at seven. My voice trembled as I spoke and I struggled to look directly at her. She whispered, "Bye, son."

We had an uneventful and silent drive home and spent the late afternoon watching television, again mainly in silence. I assumed that they watched these programmes every day as part of their routine now that they were both retired. Occasionally one or other parent would make a functional remark such as "I'll put the kettle on" but there was no chat as such. We had an early tea, the details of which escape me, suffice to say that by now it was obvious that my presence in the house was uncomfortable and that the effect of the past two days had blown our relationship apart. After tea, we drove back to the hospital, me in the front feeling depressed and angry.

Isa looked marginally better. As ever my father spoke to her first and had the prime spot sitting on the edge of her bed. My mother had a chair which she brought up close to Isa and I stood behind it. The conversation was stilted and a bit forced, although that is often the case with hospital visits I suppose. After twenty minutes or so, my sister turned up. She hugged and kissed both Mum and Dad and said, "Hi, Greg," to me on her way to position A1 at Isa's bed. Frances and I have always been quite close even though our lives have drifted into different areas. I feel that I can chat freely and openly with her and have always valued that. Her brief acknowledgement of me was clear evidence of her views on the cause of Isa's misfortune.

For the next twenty minutes it was mainly Fran and Mum talking and to be fair they did a good job in finding happy, useful things to talk about. When it was time to go and we said goodbye I felt a little bit more optimistic. That was soon dispelled in the car on the way back; the interminable silence started and in a way had its own noise. I couldn't stand it any longer. "Stop the car," I said firmly.

"What?" my father asked.

"Stop the car please." We were near the town centre.

"Why?"

"I've had enough – from the moment that I spoke to you on the phone you've basically accused me of causing all of this. I want you to understand that I didn't mean this to happen. I didn't knowingly cause anything. All you have done is blame me – don't you understand what happened? I found a driving licence and returned it to its owner. He was sitting in a chair with a knife in his chest and the people that did it were still in the same fucking room." My voice was getting louder. My mother gasped and I don't know if it was at my story or my swearing. My father was still driving but had slowed down and was looking for a parking place. "They stripped me bollock naked, then ransacked my fucking flat. They held a knife at my throat and told me that they were going to kill me. They sent me a picture of Isa with a knife at her throat and gave me twenty-four hours to find a code number or she would be dead. I didn't know what the fuck I was looking for and they gave me twenty-four hours to find it. Oh and by the way they took my laptop, passport and driving licence.

"Look what I have been through. I'm your fucking son for Christ sake and all you can do is blame me for everything. Christ knows I feel bad for Isa, I can't believe what's happened, but stop blaming me," I shouted. I was finished – there was an eerie silence.

"Oh, Greg," my mother said in almost a sob from the back. We had now come to a stop. My father said nothing. He stared ahead. I waited for him to say something but he didn't.

"I'm going for a drink – if you go to bed before me leave a key under the plant pot," I said. I unbuckled my seat belt, opened my door and got out. I closed the door with a slam and walked off. The car didn't move. I didn't look back and made my way to a bar that I hadn't frequented since I was about twenty. It had changed names several times since I was last in and was now called the Liquorice Bar and like many town-centre establishments was the type of place I could just sit and not feel the need to engage in banter with the locals.

I went into the noisy environment and the physical layout seemed similar to what I remembered of it. There were several large-screen televisions warming up for Monday-night football competing with a juke box and the noise of several fruit and other gaming machines. I ordered a pint of lager and sat at the bar. I gulped it down and it felt good. After ten minutes I ordered another and it was at this point after the initial pleasure of the first pint had worn off that I realised that I was not a good solo drinker. I didn't mind having a couple of drinks while I waited for companions to turn up, but the thought of spending all night in a bar drinking on my own depressed me. I stared blankly at the televisions, played with my phone and noticed disappointingly that it was only eight thirty. Despite the bar being barely occupied it took what felt like ten minutes to get served while the barmaid busied herself at the other end of the bar and chatted to a customer who appeared to be the off-duty chef. I ordered a third pint and drank it slower than the first two. I finished my drink, left the bar and went home via an off licence where I bought a cheap bottle of red wine.

I ambled home because I was in no rush to get there. When I did get there I was disappointed to see that the lights were on. I tried the door, it opened and I could hear the television from the living room as I passed but didn't go in. I went to the kitchen to get a glass then went upstairs to my room. It had been redecorated several times since I had left home and retained no trace of me. Unfortunately the refurbishment had not included fitting a telly.

I sat on the chair next to the chest of drawers, put the bottle down and opened it then poured a large glass and stared out of the window which looked out onto the front. As it was dark there wasn't much to see but my reflection. I closed the curtains, picked up my phone and speakers and found a decent radio station. I filled my glass a second time, lay on the bed with my back against the headrest and my drink on the bedside table and listened to the music and drank hungrily. By the time that I got to the third glass I had consumed much of the bottle. I noticed the hall light which had been coming in from under the door was now off.

I poured my fourth and final drink. I needed to pee but wasn't going to go for a while because I didn't want to bump into either parent. I put the glass down on the bedside unit. I still had another couple of large gulps to go.

I lay back on the bed and for the first time in my life I genuinely wished that I was dead.

CHAPTER TWENTY-ONE

After a fitful night's sleep I got up and went to the bathroom. I had fallen asleep in my clothes so there was no need to get dressed and I approached breakfast with a great deal of trepidation. My outburst in the car hadn't been cathartic for me and in fact it had probably stirred up my sense of injustice and anger even more. I wondered how it had affected my parents as I came downstairs and went into the kitchen. "Morning," I said flatly as I entered the kitchen. They both replied, which was something I suppose, but then we drifted into the familiar silence again. I couldn't stand this; I needed some form of normality.

When they were speaking with the consultant yesterday, both my parents had mentioned that when Isa was well enough to get out of hospital she would be staying with them. I felt that this was a good move because she would be in safe company although it also made me sad that she felt she couldn't stay in her own home anymore, her home of at least fifty years. I didn't know which room she would stay in but assumed that it would have to be the dining room as it was the largest and of course on ground level. I wondered what would happen to all her possessions. "Do you want a hand to help get Isa moved in here?" I asked. There was no response. I could tell that my mother wanted to answer but that she was leaving it up to Dad to do so. He said nothing as he angrily ate his cereal. I was about to ask again when he let loose.

"Lying in her own shit. Eighty-three and lying in her own shit. Beaten up by a masked lunatic thug. Lying in a freezing cold van all fucking night. He slit Misty's throat and left her lying in the garden. Misty was her life. You didn't even tell us. You didn't even call the police. You went on a wild goose chase for some fucking number." I had never heard him so loud and again with him being old-school I had never heard him use the F word. My mother started crying silently, still sitting at the kitchen table.

Yes he was angry. Yes he was upset. But so was I. "I fucking told you what had happened. Put yourself in my position – what the fuck would you have done? I have seen someone they have just murdered – somehow they sent me a picture of Isa with a knife at her neck. I was fucking terrified with what I was up against. I thought that they would be able to tell if I had contacted the police and then she would be fucking dead. I tried my best, Dad, I really fucking did. I am so sorry that you think it's all down to me and that I can't change your mind." I thrust my phone at him. "Phone him, phone Mr Cartwright, he's ex police, he'll tell you again what happened and that it wasn't my fault."

My mother's crying was now very loud and heaving. I thought, or hoped, that she could see my point of view, but by showing that level of understanding it would be somehow disloyal to my father. "I've got to go," I said. I left the kitchen and went into the hall, put my trainers on and left the house. I phoned Mr Cartwright and asked him to pick me up at the end of the street.

"Something up?"

"Yes, they blame me for fucking everything."

"I'll be there in fifteen minutes," he said. I started walking down the path and out of Blenheim Road towards the main road.

This would have been the ideal time if I was a smoker to light up and inhale whilst I brooded at the injustice of it all. I hadn't shaved since Friday morning and I was nervously playing with my developing beard. I had become lost in my thoughts and was unaware of time passing and didn't notice the car arrive until Mr Cartwright sounded the horn which gave me a bit of a fright. I quickly got in and we headed off.

"Morning, son." It was good to hear Mr Cartwright's reassuring deep tones. "You seemed a bit upset last night," he stated, which quite surprised me.

"What do you mean?"

"In your texts."

Fuck. What had I written? I must have been more pissed than I thought. Time to come clean – after all I had nothing to hide from Mr Cartwright. "Sorry, I can't remember sending them. On the way back from the hospital, I had a huge bust-up with my dad who blames me for everything. I got out of the car in the town centre and had few pints then got a bottle of wine and finished that in my bedroom."

"Don't worry, son, thought as much," he said reassuringly. I surreptitiously looked at my sent messages which were a bit aggressive and self-pitying but nothing to get too embarrassed about. What worried me was that I was so pissed that I had no recollection of sending them. The amount I had drunk was a lot I suppose, but something that I would have handled much easier until recently.

The visit had been totally draining for me. I had been massively relieved when I heard that Isa was safe, had so looked forward to seeing her again and couldn't wait to get up the road to see her. However, it had been far worse than I had feared. Seeing Isa as she was in the hospital was shocking because I had naively thought that when she was rescued she would maybe need a couple of days in hospital and then be physically well enough to get home and recuperate there. I had not expected to see her in that state and I truly worried how long she would have left, because that wasn't Isa.

On top of that, the feeling of resentment from my father was obvious but I definitely sensed it from my sister as well and my mother's lack of support for me was another worrying factor. On reflection Isa was the friendliest, and, dare I say it, most forgiving towards me. However, things had changed and they would never be the same again.

This whole unending episode had got me questioning relationships. I thought that I had known someone well and that after what seemed like an eternity we may become a partnership, but then after her ultimate betrayal I realised that I had not known Vicky at all. She was prepared to have me killed for Christ sake. Was it like that with most people? Not to the extreme of Vicky of course, but thinking you know someone but not knowing them at all.

The behaviour of my dad had come as a major surprise to me. Of course he was upset and shocked by what happened to Isa, but he wasn't listening to me. He didn't want it confirmed by anyone else that it may not be my fault. Why not? I was his only son. I'd not been any real bother to my parents apart from a mild adolescent rebellion. I had got my degree; I had a stable job that I liked. I did my bit and kept in touch and remembered birthdays and always came home for Christmas, but he was not giving me any support or empathy. Although we had not had a particularly close relationship when I was younger, he was still a good dad to me. He took me swimming, taught me to ride a bike; we went fishing and watched Birmingham FC every fortnight. As I grew from gawky adolescent to cocky teenager, some of my mates' dads seemed quite young and a bit of a laugh whereas mine always appeared old-fashioned; however he was always civil with my friends when they came round but hardly welcoming. It was a content upbringing though and from student to adulthood we hadn't really ever fallen out, but now? It got me questioning family life and the meaning of it.

Now I had never felt so lonely. No Vicky, no family it would appear. Just my mates. I had liked my simple life for the past few years: beers, mates, bit of training, football, curry, good undemanding job, but now I started questioning it all. Madness "One Step Beyond" was playing quietly on the car radio and it got me thinking. They seemed to be all about having your mates, meeting up and spending all week looking forward to meeting up. Now I was suddenly aware that I was losing that as I got older. Would I remain the token right-on old git at the college as I stayed single and a continuous stream of new mates from college came and went as the years passed?

What is happiness? Up until Saturday afternoon I had considered myself happy, or content at the very least, but now I was questioning this. In two or three days I had gone from this simple unquestioned contentment to wondering if I wanted a future at all. I even considered if I had a drink problem, or was I developing one? When reflecting on things it seemed that all of my best times over the years had revolved around drink and it was also my crutch in difficult times. Over the past few horrendous days, whenever it had been possible, my way of dealing with a crisis was to reach for a beer. Little things got me thinking, like my dad and Vicky swearing – I had never heard either of them say *fuck* before.

So many things were whirling around in my head and I had felt the need to offload and before I could help it I was away… I told all of this to Mr Cartwright in a straightforward, hopefully non-self-pitying manner. He had listened and let me speak.

I thanked him for listening to me and not judging or criticising, but just listening. I needed that. "That's the least I can do, son. My son is about your age and being with you reminds me of him. There's not much in my life these days and trying to help you has helped me. It's hard to explain, but nowadays it's an emptiness, a yearning for something that you might have had or think that you might have had but it ain't around anymore. Me and Mrs C, we go through the motions. I like her very much, she's the mother of my son, but do I love her now? No. I pity her and try to help her but like you would do for a favourite pet.

"With Robert, my son, we just drifted apart. He went travelling, I suppose over fifteen years ago now. He's a mechanic and very handy at other trades so he could work his ticket wherever he went. Don't know where he got that from – I'm useless. Worked too many nights and weekends to have the time or inclination to do DIY. Of course I didn't properly see him grow up – too busy in my career. I wasn't really there for him if you know what I mean. Yes I might have been physically there but my mind was usually elsewhere thinking about the job. I didn't have the interest that I should have had and kids can sense that. His mother was always there mind – she was healthy back then. Broke her heart when he emigrated…" he said as he drifted off right on cue and the words hung in the air for a few moments.

"When he met an Aussie bird we knew that was it. She's been over here once. We couldn't make the wedding because by then Mrs C couldn't handle the travel. We keep in touch by Skype and email, but I've never actually met my grandsons. Two of them and they say 'Hi, Papa' in an Aussie accent. That breaks my heart – it shouldn't but it does. Lovely little boys, eight and six, typical Aussie blonde and tanned outdoor types and I've never even met them."

"Whereabouts in Australia are they?" I asked.

"What? Oh, Perth, so it's about as far away as you can get," he said with a resigned sigh. "I just wish that he was here…wish that I could pop round the corner and meet up and take the boys fishing or to the football. But no, none of that. I've worked for forty years, work that has destroyed my paternal bond and what have I got now? Nothing, nada, nothing to look forward to.

"It's funny how it gets you but you start to resent things, little things – his wife calls him Robbie – it's not, it's Robert. She speaks to us but you can tell she's just going through the motions to keep him happy and the kids are thinking 'let's get out of here'."

"What's wrong with Mrs C?" I asked. I felt the need to change the subject, although I didn't suppose that this would cheer him up.

"She's diabetic, got emphysema and arthritis. Three for the price of one," he said with a bitter laugh. "It's all about keeping her stable, warm and comfortable. Can't remember when we last went out and did anything. We get a few visitors from time to time but that's it. Don't know when Robert will be back again, if ever – probably for his mother's funeral." I could see that Mr Cartwright's eyes were moistening behind his glasses and his steering had wavered slightly. He quickly straightened up and we carried on in silence for a few miles. "I'm sorry," he said, "you shouldn't have to listen to a tired sad old bastard and his tales of woe."

"Don't be sorry," I said. "You've listened to mine and let me slobber all over you. You've listened to me again today and I'll never forget the support that you have given me over the past few days. If it wasn't for you, Isa and me would be dead. You prevented that and I am forever grateful." It was my turn to get emotional.

"Thanks, son, I appreciate that," Mr Cartwright said in a quiet voice. "Look, I need a break after all this emotional stuff.

There's a lovely tea room down the A40 just ahead if you fancy a stop to stretch our legs and get a cuppa and a scone. I told you I don't get out much!" he said with a slight chuckle.

"Sounds like a plan," I said. I felt sorry for Mr Cartwright.

"Years ago, me and Mrs C sometimes stopped off here on our day trips," he said as we turned off the motorway and followed signs for Oxford. After five or six miles we left the main road and went along a narrower B road and followed the brown tourist board signs.

"There's the sign ahead," I said. I could see a sign for the Cottage Tea Room and we took a right into the car park which was behind a hedge. The café was a picturesque whitewashed building sitting on its own and, reflecting its name, it was a converted old cottage with an extension that had been added as the sitting area.

"Don't look like much sign of life," he said with a sigh. We got out of the car and walked up to the front door. We didn't need to try the door as a sign indicated that from 1 October to 1 March the tea room was only open at weekends. Shit, I thought. I had wanted Mr Cartwright to get his cup of tea and a scone.

"Sorry about that, son. Don't know about you but I need a leak; think I'll go around the back."

"Me too," I said.

We went round the back which had a yard that overlooked a field. There were trees down one side that led to the field and we each chose a tree to pee against. Mr Cartwright finished first and I was just finishing when I thought I heard him say, "Where's the car?" Which I didn't understand because ours was the only one in the car park. I finished peeing, had a shake and turned round. I realised that I wasn't mistaken and had heard him correctly because Mr Cartwright then said, "Where's the fucking car?" It was the first time that I had heard Mr Cartwright swear; he looked very angry and was pointing a gun directly at me.

CHAPTER TWENTY-TWO

"I watched both the interviews. You made out that you are all wide-eyed and innocent, but you've got a brain, some steel in you and a sense of determination. I meant what I said yesterday – you're smart. There are plenty of detectives with thirty plus years' experience who couldn't have worked out what you did and I'm one of them."

Was this the third major shock or the fourth? Eustace, Vicky's betrayal, the police raid on my flat – yes the fourth. Despite my newfound friend and confidant standing pointing a gun at me I didn't stare at him open-mouthed. I was definitely shocked – yes, but I genuinely wanted to know what was driving him. When had he decided to do this and why? What was his reasoning?

The events of the previous day culminating in meeting up with my parents and then seeing Isa had thoroughly depressed me and the thoughts and feelings that I had just imparted to Mr Cartwright in the car were genuine. Having so recently had a knife held against my throat thinking that I was going to die meant that I wasn't so scared anymore and now I was less clear on the point of surviving anyway. Perhaps being held at gunpoint was my fault as well – in this moment did I even care?

He continued, "I told you that a good cop has instincts that ninety-nine percent of the time are correct. My instinct is that you know where the Audi is and I want you to tell me. I know that you're lying and I'm past the point of no return. I've got fuck all to lose now. Tell me where the car is, or at least using that good brain of yours, where you think the car is." As he was talking I had become aware of some form of movement behind Mr Cartwright. I was focused directly on him and didn't want to shift my gaze. He asked me again where the car was.

"You should know me by now, I'm not a good liar," I said. "You know more about me than my parents. I'm not lying – I don't know where the fucking car is. The last time that I saw it was when I left Doug's garage yesterday, I mean Sunday. Why don't you hold a gun to him?" I looked directly at him as I spoke. There was definitely movement behind Mr Cartwright as a shadowy dark figure was silently and slowly making its way towards him.

"Son. You know me better than most as well. I've got nothing to live for and nothing to lose. Getting the car and whatever is in the security box might just make my last few years a bit more enjoyable."

Time to play for time. "Why are you doing this? You don't even know what's in the car," I stated.

"Yeah you're right, I don't know what's in it but it must be fucking important to have caused this carnage. If I get my hands on it I've still enough contacts on the other side of the law that can do me a favour for a small fee."

"What about Mrs C?"

"What about her? I've gone through the motions but let's face it, what have I got to look forward to apart from caring for that ungrateful old bitch? Our marriage is in name only – it ended before Robert went to Oz. I've looked after her long enough. She's better off dead, does damn all but watch TV and piss her pants."

Next my masterstroke: "What about Billy? You can't go on the run with him." That got him.

"Ah well, er, yeah, he'll keep Mrs C company. I would miss him but you've got to make sacrifices."

The black-clad figure was approaching and was just two or three feet behind Mr Cartwright. "You haven't thought this through, Mr Cartwright. You're a clever and I thought honourable man, but something bad has clicked in you. You've got greedy and even if you get whatever is in the car you don't know what you would do with it and where the fuck you would go. Unless you know a lot of bent cops that you could pay off they would catch you in five minutes." This got him; I could sense a slight wavering in his gun hand. "Put the gun away. Let's get back in the car and go home," I urged him. "Let the cops find the car and pretend that this never happened. Let's both get on with our lives." I was remaining calm and he could see that I wasn't scared.

Mr Cartwright looked steely and determined but I think that I had sown a seed of doubt. Before I could know for sure, the black-clad figure stole up from behind him and in a flowing set of movements knocked the gun from Mr Cartwright's hand, yanked his neck back and held a knife against it. The figure then wrenched his arm behind his back and kicked the gun away from the two of them and towards me. I moved forward slowly and carefully, picked the gun up and held it gingerly. I had seen this type of situation in films and at this point someone usually flicks the safety catch, but of course I had no idea about these things so I held the gun lightly, pointing it straight to the ground with my hand down my right side. Mr Cartwright's expression was one of anger, surprise and I think resignation as well.

"You bastard, you little fucking bastard," he spat at me. This confused me. What had I done? "You devious little bastard. You've had us followed all of this way." I couldn't believe it. He thought the person holding him was part of my team.

I looked straight at him. "I'm not that fucking clever or that fucking desperate," I said. All the while the figure held Mr Cartwright. He was dressed in black motorbike leathers and had a crash helmet on. It looked like Mr Cartwright was being held by a giant Power Ranger.

"What the fuck are you going to do now, Professor?" he frothed. Good question. I didn't have a clue what to do next but luckily the figure spoke for the first time.

"Shut up." As he said this he pressed the sharp knife onto Mr Cartwright's skin. "Point the gun at him," he instructed me. I did as I was told. The voice was muffled through the full-face helmet and I couldn't be sure but the black figure's accent sounded Eastern European.

CHAPTER TWENTY-THREE

The figure – it was hard to think of it as a person – took out what looked like the plastic that is used to hold a four- or six-pack of beer together and secured Mr Cartwright's wrists; I realised that these were some form of handcuffs. He roughly searched Mr Cartwright, patting him down with one hand whilst still keeping the knife against him with the other. He took out Mr Cartwright's wallet, phone and car keys one by one and threw them onto the ground. The figure found nothing else and I was going to tell him that Mr Cartwright's anorak was in the back of the car but thought better of it. The figure then picked up Mr Cartwright's belongings and told me to move towards him. I did so. "Give me the gun," he instructed and I was happy to comply. He handed me the wallet, phone and car keys and told me to take them to the car. I nodded.

"Stay in the car," was his final order and I nodded again and the butterflies kicked off big time. I walked slowly back from the yard and round the side of the building to the car park and over to Mr Cartwright's car. It was locked and it took me several attempts to press the correct part of the key fob to open it. I got in, sat in the passenger seat and closed the door. I put the wallet, phone and car keys on the driver's seat.

This latest surprise was at least to some extent welcome in

that it saved me from facing a gun from a desperate man, but who and what was this black-clad figure? It sounds ridiculous but despite it all, I didn't hate Mr Cartwright or even resent him. I pitied him. I saw him as someone who had grafted all his life and as a result of that graft had basically lost his family and now the much longed-for retirement was in fact a vast empty black hole. Whilst I was thinking this, I saw activity in the passenger-seat wing mirror. The figure was moving a motorbike which was parked underneath a tree against the car park wall. I hadn't even seen it when I had made my way back to the car. He rolled the bike along the path back to the yard and was again out of sight.

I wondered what he was up to and a sudden thought struck me: I am sitting in a car with the keys whilst the figure and Mr Cartwright are round the back. Time for a quick getaway.

I picked up the wallet and phone and put them in the glove compartment and then picked up the keys. I clambered awkwardly over the gear stick and under the steering wheel to the driver's seat. I familiarised myself with the dashboard layout and played about with the indicator, windscreen wipers and gears then put the keys in the ignition. Was this a good idea? Would this be another crime that Stevenson would add to my list of felonies? Also, and more pressingly, the black-clad figure was menacing, was carrying a gun and what was he doing to Mr Cartwright right now? He had a motorbike so would be able to catch up and follow me and I had a feeling that my evasive driving skills would be no match for his angry pursuit. However, my newfound resolve, bravery and what-have-I-got-to-lose mentality kicked in and I started the car. It came to life silently and smoothly. There was a tap on the window at my side. It was the figure. He tapped again on the window with the handle of the knife and was looking in.

"Turn off the car," he said and made a gesture to indicate

that as well. Decision time. Fight or flight? Neither. Compliance. I switched off the engine.

"Get out," he instructed. I did so with shaking hands and rubber legs. The adrenaline from my aborted attempt at escape was now draining away and my strength and resolve were following it. This figure was a far more frightening prospect than Mr Cartwright. What did he expect from me and what was he going to do with me? Mr Cartwright obviously believed that I knew more than I had let on and that I could find the missing Audi and its cargo which was the cause of this whole mess. I hoped the figure wouldn't think the same.

"Walk round the front. Get in the passenger seat," he told me. His voice sounded calm and was definitely Eastern European. This got me worried because I immediately started thinking of Russian mafia and the hits that had taken place all over the world to right the wrongs of slighted oligarchs. I had read some of this type of information when I was trawling the net searching for the number and investigating illegal money transfers and other activities at Vicky's on Saturday night.

I got in the car and while I was doing that he put a number plate that he was holding onto the back seat. I guessed that it was from the motorbike as it didn't look like he would be using it again. He leant into the car and picked up Mr Cartwright's anorak and then still standing outside the car went through the pockets. There was a linen hankie and a small notebook which he flicked through. Then he surprisingly leant in through the driver's side and handed the notebook to me. He chucked the anorak and hankie onto the back seat and asked me for Mr Cartwright's phone. I took it out of the glove compartment and handed it to him. He opened the back of it, took out the SIM, dropped the phone to the ground and stamped on it before picking it up and hurling it into the trees beyond the car park.

He took a lighter from his pocket and melted the SIM, letting the globules of metallic plastic drop to the ground. The figure took off his helmet and put that on top of Mr Cartwright's anorak on the back seat and closed the door. He got into the car, disabled the Bluetooth and put Mr Cartwright's gun under the seat. The figure was Piotr.

CHAPTER TWENTY-FOUR

As these bizarre events continued to occur this had shot into my surprise top ten at joint number two. Vicky's betrayal still held on to the top spot, but Piotr's appearance had joined Mr Cartwright in second place. By dint of the relative time lapsed (three days) in this fast-moving nightmare, Eustace with the knife in his chest had dropped to number three.

"Hello, Mr Stewart," he said with his small boyish smile as he started the car.

"Call me Greg please, Piotr."

"Of course, Greg." He smiled again as he moved the car out of the car park and onto the road. I expected that we were heading to London, but how could I know? I turned sideways and smiled back. I was waiting for him to tell me what was happening. Instead he said, "Are you well?" What an odd question, but it seemed genuine and I felt that he was perhaps deferring to my seniority in terms of being his lecturer. Maybe he wanted me to get things going.

"I have never been so confused and frightened in my life, Piotr," I started with. "Since Saturday, one thing after another has happened to me or to others that have been very frightening and surprising. Do you understand?"

"Yes," he nodded.

"I keep thinking that I can trust someone then they let me down." This didn't do justice to how I felt but I was trying to keep my English at a basic level. He nodded and briefly looked from the road to me with sympathetic eyes. "I have had big arguments with my family and I think the police may still think I am to blame for all of this, but I don't know anymore. I am so glad that you have saved me, but I don't know anything anymore," I sighed.

Piotr didn't say anything but concentrated on the road with a sad expression, so I started to tell my story in order that I could explain about the number that he had helped me to find, the reason for it and the consequences that had followed. I started from handing back the driving licence and seeing Eustace with the knife in his chest and had got to the part where I returned to Doug's garage and was just about to talk through how I broke in when he said, "I know."

"What?"

"I know," he repeated.

"How do you know?" I asked. We were approaching the M40 slip and it was beginning to rain. He then started to tell me his story.

Despite his baby features and his quiet, demure, reverential nature, Piotr told me that he had been a member of the Legia Warsaw ultras, one of Poland's most feared gangs, and had risen to be one of their lieutenants. He explained that being in the ultras was a lifetime commitment and more than just soccer violence, it was for honour and a sense of regional, and when required, national pride. He ended up in prison for a stabbing and on his release was still involved in trouble which mainly involved sudden random acts of extreme violence in defending his ultra honour. He was unemployed and had become a marked man amongst rivals in the ultra fraternity. He used his driving skills to steal cars and motorbikes to make a living and by now his wife was expecting their first child, so for the good of the family and at her insistence they moved to England. They travelled on false passports so that Piotr would elude his ultra brothers who would not forgive his betrayal by leaving them and his rivals who obviously wanted to slit his throat. Also he wanted to evade the Polish Army which was calling up many reservists who had moved abroad.

Piotr didn't like London much and he found it hard to get work because his English wasn't as good as many of his countrymen and he didn't have a trade. He signed up to an agency with his false credentials and through it got the job in the leisure centre. He ended up at my college to improve his English and his daughter Ania was born here. His wife didn't work and I couldn't see how his work at the leisure centre would be enough to live in London to support himself, far less a wife and child, but he explained that two nights a week when his wife thought that he was working at a restaurant he was in fact stealing motorbikes and Eustace was adapting them and selling them. This did not surprise me; not because I had always secretly suspected it, but because from now on nothing, however unlikely or ridiculous, would surprise me again.

Piotr explained that from his work at the leisure centre he had got on nodding acquaintance with Eustace because he was a daily visitor, and after a while they would chat briefly which led them to become friendly. He thought that this was because they were both outsiders to an extent and Eustace respected Piotr. Doug and the rest of his group were not like that unfortunately. Piotr got to know that Eustace was a mechanic and from overheard conversations, mainly from Doug and Brian, realised that his work was sometimes outside the law. Mr Cartwright had mentioned that this was one of Eustace's lines of work, as of course had Vicky.

Doug and his friends probably thought that the foreign cleaner wouldn't understand them, but as he said, "I understand English better than I speak it, but you are changing that, Mr Stewart!"

"Greg," I reminded him.

His arrangement with Eustace worked well and he was making a good living. He hated working in the leisure centre and also lying to his wife about the restaurant work but had to do so to keep up his front. When he was contacted by me on Saturday night he wasn't at home, but was making his way back there after stealing a BMW 650i and hiding it in his lockup in East London where he did most of his exchanges with Eustace. Despite thinking that nothing would surprise me again, my mouth was beginning to drop open. I was concerned at the amount of implicating evidence against himself that Piotr was giving to me which if I passed on would leave him in serious shit. I sensed that he may want to use me Vicky-style to help find the final missing pieces of a jigsaw. The worrying thought based on recent evidence was that if Piotr wanted rid of me he wouldn't fuck it up. However by now I just wanted to see all of this to some form of conclusion no matter what might happen.

Piotr continued with his story and told me that when he met me and Vicky on Sunday he couldn't believe that Eustace was dead. "I not look surprise when you told me?" he asked. I remembered that we used Google Translate to tell him but didn't recall a shocked reaction.

"Surprised?" I emphasised the ending of the word in true teacher fashion. "No," was all that I could add.

When he left the Bridge Café he was determined to help us because it might help him. He couldn't believe that his friend and business partner was dead. He had no worries about getting Eustace's membership number because the receptionist was stupid and lazy.

Hearing that Eustace was dead had reminded him about some recent strange behaviour. He would often pass the time of day with Eustace, but not indulge in any long chats or anything to indicate that they had a connection outside the leisure centre. That worked well, but a few weeks ago Eustace was with someone, a middle-aged man who spoke with an Eastern European accent which Piotr thought was Russian. The pair of them were acting suspiciously and stopped speaking when Piotr walked past. Eustace had barely acknowledged Piotr as he came up to them from behind pushing his buffing machine, which was unusual. A few days later when Piotr was dropping off a bike he asked about it but Eustace dismissed it then changed the subject. However, Eustace then asked him to steal a good sports car and promised him a special payday. Piotr stole a nice Audi A7 Sportback, but hadn't been paid yet.

"Is it white?"

"Yes."

A couple of weeks later he saw the man in the leisure centre again, this time with his running gear on and a number on his vest. He was in the locker corridor and seemed to be waiting for no one to be around before he used the locker which was difficult because the leisure centre was so busy that day. Piotr blended into the background and watched as the man finally unlocked his locker, but far from taking his stuff out and going for a shower he took a large bag out and then unlocked and opened another locker and put the bag in it before locking it and leaving, still wearing his running gear. Piotr hovered around that area and after about thirty minutes Eustace appeared and he too had a running vest on with a number and he went straight to his locker, took out the bag that had been left earlier and also left without having a shower and changing.

"This must have been the day of the Ealing Half Marathon,"

I interjected. Piotr nodded and continued with his story.

On the Sunday after he got the membership number for me and when his shift was over, he checked Eustace's address from the leisure centre database as he had never met him at his house. Then he went to 14 Clepington Road to have a look. He also took my address because he couldn't understand how I or the pretty redhead was involved. He could see no signs of life and was about to break in through the back window when he saw Doug approach in his Mini, have a quick look and then speed away again. Piotr stepped out from his hiding place and made his way to Doug's garage because he knew that's where he would have come from. When he got to the garage he saw the door wide open and Doug's car parked there. Suddenly Doug slammed the door shut, jumped in his car and screamed away.

Piotr then looked for a motorbike and found one in what sounded like the lane that I had hidden from Doug in. He stole it and made his way to my flat and watched and waited. He saw Mr Cartwright and the subsequent police raid on my house with Vicky and a blonde man being led away. By this time a crowd had gathered and he mingled in with it. When the crowd dispersed he found a good observation spot and eventually saw us leave and he followed us to the police station. He followed Mr Cartwright home and followed him back to the station the next day and on the return trip to the Cartwright's house with me. He tailed us to my parent's house in Solihull and followed Mr Cartwright to his hotel. He must be good, I thought, because Mr Cartwright obviously was completely unaware of being followed.

"You must have been away for two nights. Was your wife not worried?"

"Maybe. She knows not to ask," he said calmly.

He knew about, and was suspicious of Mr Cartwright because Eustace had warned him about him, saying that he was bent and couldn't be trusted. He didn't know who had killed Eustace, but thought that Mr Cartwright might have a good idea. Christ, I had forgotten all about him.

"What has happened to Mr Cartwright?" I asked Piotr.

"I don't think that he will be coming home," was his enigmatic and worrying reply.

"What did you do to him?"

"Nothing."

"Nothing?"

"Yes. Nothing. I tell him that I have recorded him talking to you. I cut the plastic handcuffs off. I left him."

By now we had approached the outskirts of London, but we were not following the familiar route to Ealing and instead we appeared to be heading for the East End.

"Where are we going, Piotr?" I asked softly.

"We go to my lockup," he replied. After all that had happened, part of me expected him to be getting ready to finish me off after he had told me everything. Perhaps he still was.

CHAPTER TWENTY-FIVE

"Piotr, I know that you have disabled the Bluetooth and disposed of Mr Cartwright's phone and I'm sure that you know much more about this than me, but aren't there cameras everywhere on roads now that check for licence plates? Surely the police will be able to track this car and will have filmed evidence of where it's been?" I said this as we continued to make our way through London.

"Don't worry," he said as he picked his way towards our destination. We were following signposts for the North Circular and Wembley and after a while passed Neasden Junction then Staples Corner, familiar names but despite my many years in London not places that I had visited or passed all that often.

"But they will be able to track us," I bleated.

"Yes, but we are not worried. We are the good guys." He sounded so relaxed as we continued on through streets unfamiliar to me.

"The police will want to interview you – Mr Cartwright said that they were at the leisure centre today."

"I know."

"When will you go back?"

He gave a very small shrug and said, "Don't know."

I saw a sign for the Blackwall Tunnel and Stratford and not long after I saw Leytonstone and Leyton signposted. We soon turned right onto Leytonstone High Road, made a few more turns and arrived at the lockup. It was behind a house and accessed via a narrow private road. Piotr got out of the car and unlocked and opened the door, which was a standard up-and-over metal one. The garage was about the size of two average-sized cars, had lighting and power points inside and there was also a long bench with plenty of storage spaces underneath.

Piotr got back into the car and drove us inside, we got out and he pulled the roller shutter door fully down before retrieving Mr Cartwright's gun from the car. He pulled a three-door metallic filing cabinet to one side and then knelt down at a floor safe and typed in a combination which opened the door. He put the gun into the safe and because he was leaning over as he did this his back prevented me from seeing what, if anything else, was in the safe. He closed it, put the filing cabinet back in place and asked, "Tea?" as he made his way to the bench which had a kettle on top of it.

"Yes please." I think my voice quavered a bit as I replied.

"No milk, sorry," Piotr said with his back to me.

"No worries," I tried to say calmly. I was steeling myself for Piotr to turn round with some form of weapon demanding details on the Audi; however he turned round with a cup of tea and handed it to me.

"What do we do now?" he asked. This took me back. Piotr had literally been in the driving seat for the past couple of hours and now he was asking me what to do. On Sunday he had taken the right option every time: Eustace's, Doug's garage, my house, back to Mr Cartwright's and then Solihull. I had just expected that he would know what to do next. I took a long sip of my tea, which was refreshing, and gave his question some thought.

"We need to find out who the Russian is," I said finally, "I think from what you say that he must have been constantly watched and needed a way to transfer his goods to Eustace. The race that day meant that he would blend in with all the other runners and make the transfer." Piotr nodded at this but said nothing. "I am guessing of course but it sounds like the Russian has ripped off a Mr Big. If it was a simple theft, he wouldn't need to go to such measures. The cops would probably not even know to track him and wouldn't have the resources to do so. Also look at the shit that this has caused – whatever is in the Audi must be serious stuff and someone is extremely pissed off that they don't have it."

I looked at Piotr for his reaction and all he said was, "Easy."

"Easy?"

"Yes. Easy."

"How? What do you mean?"

"Camera." He made the universal sign of a camera with one outstretched arm and the other doing a circular motion. "CCTV. We find Russian. He a film star." He explained that the CCTV at the leisure centre was an old-fashioned system using recordable DVDs which were downloaded periodically and then recorded over. The locker area in the leisure centre was well covered by cameras and he explained that we just needed to go onto the system and copy the correct recordings.

"Brilliant," I exclaimed. "If we see him with his running vest on then we can use his number to check his name from the race entry database."

"Yes, of course."

"Can you get into the system?"

"Of course," he said. He then explained that if they had a more up-to-date system we wouldn't have needed to go to the leisure centre at all because it could all have been done remotely and he could have got the access details.

I nodded whilst contemplating that DVDs were now considered old-fashioned and then asked, "How will we get into the leisure centre though?" Again came the stock answer.

"Easy," he replied with a smile. He held up a set of keys which I presumed were for the leisure centre so I suppose that he had a point. I was going to ask how he got them but even I was not that naïve and realised that a motorbike thief who has access to all the keys in the building would have no problem in getting a set copied.

"We wait 'til centre closed, then we go in," Piotr explained.

"When is that – is it ten?" I asked. He nodded. I looked at the time on my phone and it was only approaching three, so we had plenty of time to kill. I realised that apart from some cereal that I had picked on in my parents' house I hadn't eaten a thing all day. Piotr must have been a mind reader.

"Stay here. I go and get food."

"Okay."

He pulled a cover off a bike and rolled up the garage door then pushed it outside. He came back in and got his helmet from the back of Mr Cartwright's car then told me, "Pull door down. Let no one in. I text when on way back. Okay?"

"Okay," I answered. As I pulled the shutter down I could hear the roar as he kicked the bike into life. There were a couple of chairs in the garage so I brushed the dust off one and sat down. There was no reading material, radio or any other music-playing device that I could see in the building. When Piotr was here it was obviously for intense undistracted work. I was going to listen to some music on my phone but then thought better of it as I may not hear anyone approaching.

As I sat and waited, I tried to go over and piece together what had happened up to now and why. From this I hoped something would jump out at me for future use. With Blondie and Vicky inside and I assumed saying nothing, the cops would be no further forward. They would have spoken to staff at the leisure centre but not got anywhere. Mind you they hadn't spoken to everyone yet and Piotr would be near the top of the list, having been on duty on Sunday and his role in getting part of the number having been detailed by me. Mr Cartwright was of no relevance to the investigation but of relevance to the cops because of his relationship with me, so how long before they reacted to his non-appearance?

To me the key players at the moment were Doug, Cassie and the Russian. What did Doug know about the Audi? Where was Cassie and did she know anything? After all, she was in theory Eustace's girlfriend but had almost certainly been planted into that role at the behest of Blondie. Hopefully we could get the Russian's race number so we could get his name and from there possibly a lead.

I checked my phone and it was now nearly six. Whilst I had been lost in my thoughts, Piotr had been away for almost three hours. I was getting ever hungrier but now beginning to panic as well. I had remembered to save his number into my phone but thought that under the circumstances I shouldn't call and I would give it another hour. Then I realised that from what the cops had told me previously they could track me from my phone and I supposed that was a very real possibility when they didn't hear from Mr Cartwright. They knew that he was probably going to stay overnight so they would probably expect to hear from him on his return to London, which I expect that they would work out as around now...

My phone went. It was a text from Piotr: Back in 5. At six thirty Piotr finally returned. I heard the bike approaching and opened the door a couple of feet and kneeled down to look under the door to see if I recognised who it was. It was dark by now and there didn't appear to be much lighting in the parking area outside or in the lane for that matter. The bike drew up and Piotr got off swiftly and was over and pulling the door up in seconds. He rolled the bike into the lockup and pulled the shutter back down. I didn't ask him where he had been and he didn't volunteer any information. He opened one of the storage compartments on the bike and took out a bag which he handed to me. The bag contained two large baguettes, crisps and juice. I took a tuna baguette, ripped off the cellophane cover and started to devour it then opened a bottle of orange juice to wash it down.

"We still have some time," he said as he looked at his watch. "I will tell you what we are going to do." I nodded to show my agreement and understanding. He told me how we were going to operate on our way to the leisure centre, when we were inside and on our way back. His briefing took over forty minutes as he detailed the layout of the reception area, the operations room for the CCTV which was also where the disks were stored and copied, the PC that they were copied to, the alarm system and so on. He was slow and deliberate and I of course helped in my teaching capacity in getting him the correct word or sequence as and when required.

After he had finished I asked if he had a laptop for us to watch the films on and also to go onto the race website. "Yes," he said and went over to a cupboard below the worktop and took out a laptop. He picked up two memory sticks and put them in his pocket. I suddenly thought of Eustace's leisure membership number and asked Piotr if he would get that again from the computer. "No need. Still got it." Phew, one less thing to worry about.

My stomach was sore from the combination of suddenly eating quite a large amount on an empty stomach and nerves. He made us another cup of tea which helped a bit; however, I needed the toilet, unfortunately not a pee. There was no way I could get through the next few hours without going. "Piotr I need to go to the toilet – where can I go?" I asked rather desperately.

"Hold it in."

"I can't. I haven't even had a pee since lunch time."

"Okay," he said as he opened a cupboard door underneath the bench. He took out a plastic container, emptied some screws from it onto the work surface and then handed it to me. "Use that." It was originally a container for ice cream. I looked at him. He was serious. "I no look," he said as he handed me the lid. "You need this as well." He handed me a large kitchen roll. I went round the other side of Mr Cartwright's car, pulled down my trousers and pants and squatted. I was worried that I would miss the small target, so I made sure that I had got my bearings before pushing. The turtle head slid effortlessly onto its target followed by what seemed like an endless gushing of pee. Finally I was finished and my log floated in its yellow sea which was almost up to the top of the box. I tore off a strip of the blue paper from the roll and gave myself a wipe and delicately sat the soiled paper on top of the contents of the box, gingerly put the top on and hoped that it clicked shut.

"What do I do now?"

Piotr gave me a thick industrial bin liner. "Put it in there, we get rid of later." So I did and carefully set the bag down on the floor.

He took out leathers and a helmet for me from a metal wardrobe situated in the corner of the garage and told me to put them on. I had never worn leathers before. "On top of my trousers?" I asked seriously. Piotr laughed loudly as he thought that I was joking. I realised that I should take my jeans off and pulled the leathers on. They had a funny smell and were slightly too big for me. I put the jacket on over my hoody.

"Let's go," he said and gestured with his arm. I went outside, remembering to take my bin liner of effluent with me which I disposed of in a wheelie bin. Piotr killed the lights in the garage, came out, pulled the door shut and locked it. I didn't want to tell Piotr that I had never been on a bike before. I pulled the full-face helmet over my head and immediately felt claustrophobic. I hoped that I would get used to the feeling and went to get on the large bike. It was a BMW 650i which was probably the one that he had stolen on Saturday night. Piotr stopped me and climbed on first, then signalled for me to get on, which I did awkwardly. I sat astride the large machine and he turned round and signalled for me to grab him by the waist. I did so and he kicked the bike into life and we growled slowly away from the lockup and down the lane to the main road. When we were on the main road we accelerated smoothly and I held on, occasionally looking to my side at the whizzing grey of the road. I was scared but excited at the same time. We then went round a corner and I continued to sit straight and hold on as the bike twitched a bit and almost skidded. Piotr slowed down and we pulled up at the side of the road. He raised his helmet and from underneath he said, "You lean, I lean. Understand?" He made the motions as well. I nodded and he pulled his helmet back down and we started up again. I began to get the hang of it; holding, leaning and praying as we went round corners.

We zipped through the quiet streets, but it still took around forty minutes before we were in familiar territory and approaching the leisure centre. He parked the bike round the back of the facility and we cautiously circumnavigated it and noted that there were no lights on apart from the security lights. From Piotr's briefing I knew how we were going to operate and to follow him and react to his hand and arm signals. When he was happy that we were safe, we made our way to the front door and were quickly underneath the awning which helped shelter us from view. Piotr unlocked the door in seconds and we entered the building. There was something strange, however: the alarm wasn't going off. He had said in his briefing that it beeps for forty-five seconds with the beeps getting quicker and louder until the alarm gets switched off – but nothing.

He indicated for me to follow him to the reception area. We went behind the desk and went straight to the alarm. It was switched off. He put his fingers up to the front of his mask in a *shush* gesture and then indicated for me to follow him. I did and we made our way out of the reception office area and across the large foyer.

I couldn't hear anything, but like a hunter tracking his prey, Piotr seemed to know that there was a presence in the building and where it was. He was certainly wasted as a cleaner. We stood outside the First Aid room. Piotr took out his large knife and then slowly tried the handle, which turned easily as the door was unlocked. In a split second he burst into the room brandishing the knife.

We were greeted by a pair of thrusting bare buttocks on the first aid bed which suddenly stopped their movements. There was a scream from the body below the buttocks and the man on top rolled over, revealing a naked female. I recognised the female: it was the receptionist who had dealt with me on Sunday and who Vicky had performed her fainting act in front of. The man appeared familiar too and I realised that he was one of the leisure attendants that I had seen sitting bored on poolside or wandering around the building. Being charitable she would be at least forty-five, but was more likely pushing fifty, and he was probably mid-twenties at the most. They stared at us and Piotr's knife in particular in open-mouthed mute terror.

Piotr handed me the knife and indicated to me to make sure that they didn't leave. I don't know who was the most nervous, my naked prisoners or me trying to look menacing and control my shaking. Piotr definitely made a better Power Ranger. I presumed that he had gone to the operations room to boot up the computer and access and copy the recordings that we needed. Fortunately he returned within ten minutes – he was good at this – but it was a long ten minutes for me.

During that time my hostages continued to stare at me, but barely moved. I was so grateful for my black full-face helmet in hiding the fear in my eyes. The leisure attendant stood at the side of the bed and the receptionist crouched on it with her legs crossed and arms over her chest to try and protect her modesty. She had large folds of flesh that helped to do that as well. Some of her frizzy brown-grey hair was matted and stuck to her forehead. On his return, Piotr gestured violently towards them to get up and to get out of the room. They meekly complied and in their terror had given up their futile attempts to hide their nakedness. He indicated that they should walk towards the cleaning cup-board situated next to First Aid. The door to this small room was already open and inside were the usual cleaning tools of the trade along with the smell of disinfectant and damp mops. He stood to the side and pointed sharply for them to go in. The leisure attendant momentarily hesitated before Piotr raised the knife and made as if to move forward towards him. He realised the futility of his hesitation and went into the room followed by the shuffling receptionist. I noticed that she had what appeared to be a flower tattoo on the left buttock and what was definitely a dolphin tattoo on the right one of her dimpled and sagging bottom.

Piotr took a roll of bin liners out of a box, pulled one bag off the roll and went back to the First Aid room. He returned with their clothes stuffed in the black bag. He then suddenly smashed the room light with the handle of his knife in a single violent thrust and closed the door of the pitch-black room without a second glance. He locked it and I could hear no noise whatsoever coming from inside. He went back to reception, set the alarm and we calmly walked out of the building and locked up. He threw the black bag into a wheelie bin and we went back to the bike.

On our ride back to the lockup I tried to imagine the horror that we had left behind for our prisoners. No one was dead of course or even injured, but we had left our couple from their illicit tryst naked and imprisoned. What would it feel like when they were discovered by their colleagues the next day? I thought that the leisure centre opened at seven during the week and as it was only eleven o'clock now, they would have probably seven hours locked up together before any staff arrived – what if they needed the toilet? I suppose they had buckets in there, not like me, and at least they could wear bin liners. They'd better watch their bare feet on the broken light bulb though.

I suddenly remembered that the receptionist was called Irene as I had a mental picture of her with her clothes on and her name badge on display. I imagined that she was married and wondered what the reaction from her husband would be when he inevitably got to know about it. I didn't know what the leisure attendant was called but expected that it might give him some bragging rights when his mates heard about it.

We were expertly whizzing through the now quieter streets and like the outward journey I didn't take in any landmarks as I held on to Piotr and pressed my head into his back. I quickly forgot about Irene and her toy boy because I was looking forward to watching the disks and identifying our Russian friend.

CHAPTER TWENTY-SIX

Piotr plugged in the laptop and booted it up. He took out the disks and confirmed that he had also taken tonight's recordings and disabled the camera which was a relief. As he stared intently at the images on the laptop I pulled up a chair alongside him and noticed a few whiskers had appeared on his chin. The films were in colour but were granular, low pixelated images with colours merging and faces blurred. They did, however, display the date and time and so we quickly got to the point where there were runners arriving back at the leisure centre and Piotr appearing in shot from time to time. He would speed up, then pause, then return to real time and after a short while he paused the recording and said, "That's him."

Piotr pointed at the screen, then rewound slightly so that we could see the man come in and look around slightly furtively as he fumbled with his bag whilst he walked slowly up the corridor. Then he disappeared from shot before he reappeared briefly before going out of shot at the other end. Two people had opened and emptied their lockers and gone away whilst others were just arriving. He came back into shot as another two runners went past his locker and he quickly opened his locker, took a bag out and moved quickly to an adjoining one, opened it and put the bag in. He then turned and left. We watched all of this and let it run for a few seconds then rewound and froze the picture. There was his number in the picture – number 1837. Piotr's IT skills were better than mine and he froze the film and saved the still shot before emailing it to me so that we would both have an image of him. Piotr then moved the film on and we saw Eustace come in wearing his running gear, go straight to his locker, take the bag out and then leave.

"Go to marathon site," Piotr instructed me. I leant over and typed in the address, then clicked on the results link and typed in the number. The database showed that runner number 1837 completed the race in 92 minutes 56 seconds, so he was just ahead of Eustace, and was called Oleg Artamanov. He was in the Veteran Men's category which ranged from forty to forty-nine years. Like Eustace he wasn't in a running club so we couldn't get any further detail from that.

I started the familiar routine of Internet searching. There were plenty of people with the full name and hundreds more with the surname, however nothing obvious jumped out. Whilst I was doing this, Piotr was making numerous phone calls mostly in Polish and all I could make out was the occasional mention of Oleg Artamanov. I presumed that he was calling his contacts in the black economy.

Piotr made us a cup of tea which was welcome as it was now after midnight and I was definitely flagging. Considering what appeared to be Mr Artamanov's line of business I wasn't expecting to find many overt references to him or it and that was proving to be the case. By now my mind was wandering and I was staring blankly at the screen when I was roused from my inertia by Piotr's phone ringing. He answered it quickly and spoke in short guttural bursts which I noticed he did in his own language. When he spoke in English his voice was much quieter and gentler. He hung up and said, "Artamanov is an in-out business." He was moving his arms across each other to help try and mime what he was meaning.

I was puzzled. "In and out business?"

"Yes."

"Ah! I get you. Import and export business?"

"Yes," Piotr smiled.

"Where?" I asked.

"Neasden. We go now."

"Okay," I agreed but I don't think that I had much choice in the matter. Before we left, we wrote down the security box code by visiting the race website to get Eustace's time which I had forgotten in all the excitement of the previous few days. I could remember his race number – 2339 – and Piotr knew and had noted his leisure centre membership number. That done we donned our leather jackets again, put the helmets on, left the garage and locked it up before getting on the bike and heading for Mr Artamanov's business. As before, I hung on to Piotr and remembered to lean into the corners and we arrived there in around thirty minutes. Despite being relatively close to my own patch the area was unfamiliar which for me is true of most areas of London. We had stopped at a small industrial estate similar to the one that Doug's garage was in but smaller. This one contained six units and was surrounded by a fence supported by two-metre-high spiked grey metal posts and was flanked by what I think was the North Circular Road to the rear. We drove slowly into the estate.

"There," Piotr said as he pointed. It was the first unit and the sign indicated that the business was called OA Imports UK. We went past slowly and I noted that like Doug's garage this had an office area alongside a workspace, or in this case I imagine a storage space. The office area was accessed through a normal door and the larger area could be accessed from a roller shutter. It was bigger than Doug's because it also had first-floor offices. Piotr continued to drive and we arced round the cul-de -sac and then slowly passed the unit again. There was a landline and a mobile number on the company's sign and Piotr took a photo of it as we passed. Unsurprisingly there was no sign of life at this time of night and so without stopping we made our way out of the estate.

Back on the main road Piotr picked up speed and I held on with no idea where we were off to now. After a while when I plucked up the courage to have a look I started to recognise some landmarks and realised that we were heading back to home territory. We were in fact heading to Piotr's flat which was a second-floor maisonette in West Ealing. The flat was very small and consisted of a kitchen, one bedroom, a living room and a bathroom. It smelt of cooking, wet laundry and nappies and was very untidy with toys, magazines, clothes and cups in every room. Piotr didn't make any allowances for the fact that it was now after one a.m. and went into the only bedroom and wakened his wife who came through in her pyjamas. She was small and pretty but appeared downtrodden and tired. He didn't introduce us so I did, telling her that I was Greg and she said hello and told me she was Brygida. She didn't appear to speak any English apart from the very basics. He spoke to her sharply and she left the room and returned with a blanket for me, then said something to him and returned to the bedroom. He told me to lie on the couch and get some sleep. That sounded like a good idea so I lay down but had to change direction because my right shoulder was on a damp patch of the settee. After that I dropped off straight away.

I was woken just after six by the baby crying and then Brygida moving about in the kitchen. I thought that there was no point in trying to sleep and also I felt sorry for her so I pulled the blanket off and got up and said hello. She gave me a tired sad smile and said good morning back. She made a feed for the baby and sat down in the living room to administer it, after asking me if it was okay to do so which made me feel bad. I tried talking to her but we couldn't understand each other so most of the time we sat in a slightly awkward silence and exchanged the odd bashful smile. When the baby had been fed she fell asleep in her cot easily and Brygida asked me if I wanted breakfast to which I eagerly replied yes. Breakfast consisted of some thick spicy sausages cooked in a frying pan together with a couple of eggs. As it was cooking it smelt delicious which must have roused Piotr who then appeared.

We ate our breakfast that included second helpings and he told me to have a shower which was another good idea. The bathroom was like the rest of the flat in that it was tired, but unlike the Cartwright's, the shower was simply a rubber hose attached to the two bath taps by nozzles and the jet of water was barely a trickle. I did my best to at least clean myself but was certainly not refreshed and invigorated when I returned to the living room.

"Are you ready?" he asked. I said that I was and wondered what he had told his wife. We left the flat and I was pleased to see him give her a peck on the cheek and that he lifted his sleeping baby to give her a kiss and a cuddle. We then set off to return to Mr Artamanov's business to see if anyone had turned up; they hadn't so we found a café and had a cup of tea and after half an hour drove past the business again, but there were still no signs of life. We went to another café and Piotr found the photo of the business on his phone and noted the phone numbers. He withheld his number and phoned both the landline and mobile numbers that were on the sign but didn't get an answer or even an answerphone message on either. It looked like we were hitting a dead end. "We go back to my house to think," he said and I nodded. We got back onto the bike and I adopted my usual back-seat position.

I was not paying attention to where we were going when the bike came to a sudden stop. It appeared that Piotr was taking a phone call, then he started the bike up and we continued on our way. After about ten minutes we slowed down; I couldn't remember the way back to Piotr's and didn't recognise where we were. We had stopped outside another garage. Between lockups and garages this would be my fourth in a couple of days, I realised. Piotr cut the engine and got off. I followed. "Where are we?" I asked.

"Hounslow," he replied.

He had only been in this country a short while, but if he wanted to work legally he would make a great taxi driver because he already had The Knowledge. This time we were not in an industrial estate but what was grandly called The Vines Business Village. It looked just like an industrial estate to me and the building was again similar to Doug's garage and about the same size. It too had a roller shutter door which was down and padlocked. We walked around the building and there seemed to be no signs of life. What appeared to be a kitchen window looked out onto the small yard at the back which was basically empty apart from some litter. A standard domestic-type door with a mortice lock opened out onto this area.

Piotr glanced round then took out a chain with different keys on it from his jacket pocket and tried a couple on the lock – within seconds we were in. We walked along the short corridor into the garage area. There was only one car in the workshop, a large black Audi. I recognised it, but the last time that I had seen the car it had been white and in Doug's garage. "That's it," I said to Piotr, "that's fucking it! How did you know it was here?" I asked.

Piotr nodded then made a shushing motion with his finger against his lips. The last time he did this was in the leisure centre.

Surely not again, I thought. He slowly made his way to a large grey bashed metal wardrobe which appeared to be the only hiding place in the garage area. When he got there he pulled both doors wide open and lunged inside. The figure cowering inside didn't have a chance and he was on top of them in an instant. He violently yanked the figure from the wardrobe onto the dirty cold concrete floor and knelt on top of it. The figure offered no resistance and he turned the person around. The last time I had seen her she was on the leisure club flyer. It was Cassie.

CHAPTER TWENTY-SEVEN

"Get off me, you bastard," she screamed. He did. This was the first time that I had heard her speak since she had let me into Eustace's. She looked drawn and tired but still incredibly pretty. She brushed herself down and then stood up. It looked like her heart was still beating rapidly.

"Piotr, what the fuck are you doing here?"

"Hello, Cassie," he said. She looked confused and a bit frightened then looked over at me and recoiled when she obviously remembered who I was.

"What the fuck are you doing with *him*?" She was obviously baffled why the quiet Polish cleaner from work was with me and how we had tracked her down. Come to mention it, I was keen to find out how we had tracked her down as well.

"Where were you going with the car?" he asked.

"Just getting away. Kev's after me. He'll kill me. How did you find me?"

"I work with Eustace. I know who he knows. I ask about the nice Audi and I find it."

She didn't know what to say, so I said, "Kev and Vicky are both inside."

"How the fuck would you know?" she spat out.

"Because they were lifted at my flat just before he could slit my fucking throat," I growled back. She was surprised at my response and so was I. "Remember my flat? You should do coz you fucking ransacked it." A lot of pent-up anger was coming out.

"Didn't have a choice. Kev made me do it."

"Quiet, both," Piotr said loudly. Cassie had quickly realised who was the boss. "Stay still. Stay quiet," he told her. She gave a small nod. "Greg. Open it." He gestured towards the Audi. I walked over to the car and they followed me. I opened the rear passenger door, leant over and picked up the rubber mat.

Pardon the pun but were we approaching the end of the road? I retrieved the piece of paper from my wallet and knelt down and started to punch the numbers into the security box keypad. I had put the first four in with barely a glance at the paper as they were now etched into my memory. Then the next four – 9326, ninety-three minutes and twenty-six seconds – which bizarrely made me think not a bad time for thirteen miles, especially at his age. Then the last four: 7126. Were they in the right order and were they even in blocks of four? We would soon find out. I pressed enter; nothing happened immediately then there was an almost imperceptible whirring followed by a small click and the door opened by a few millimetres. I opened it wide and we looked inside. Piotr pulled me out of the way and went to retrieve the goods.

He took a metal box out of the car and set it down slowly on the floor. This was what had caused so much grief. It was about ten inches in length and six inches wide and had numbers and Russian Cyrillic script on it. It also appeared to be soldered closed. He took the box and went over to the workbench at the side of the garage and using a vice to secure it and what appeared to be a form of chisel he worked methodically to break the seal. He opened the box and stared at the contents. We had moved over to watch.

"Fuck!" he said with wide eyes. "Fuck, fuck," he repeated.

Cassie and I looked at each other blankly and Piotr swore again.

CHAPTER TWENTY-EIGHT

"What is it?" I asked just before Cassie. We were now standing beside Piotr.

"Polonium."

"What?"

"Polonium. Kills people."

We were looking at the box which Piotr had carefully opened. There were four small metallic-looking bottles that were larger than phials but smaller than an average aftershave bottle, and similar to aftershave bottles they were set into a hard foam base in the box. I had vaguely heard of polonium, but I didn't know why. I made a mental note to look it up when I had a moment.

"Poison. No good. No good. They catch us, they kill us." He made the sign of death by drawing his finger against his throat. This was the first time that I had seen Piotr genuinely scared. It seemed like we had stumbled upon something of possibly international consequence. In terms of serious badness we were suddenly on a way bigger scale from hotwiring bikes.

"How do you know?" I asked.

"I do. Polonium found first in my country. I read about it."

"Has this come from Poland?"

"No. Russia."

Piotr told us to stay put and he went into the kitchen area

from where he was making a number of calls. Whilst he was doing this I got talking with Cassie, or to be more accurate she just started talking without any invitation from me. She began with, "'Consider it done', that's what he said. He was speaking to Vicky on the phone on Sunday afternoon and was pissed off that she had called him. He wanted everything done by text so that I couldn't listen in I suppose. He told me to make him a cup of tea when his phone rang. I went out of the room but I listened in. 'Consider it done' – I just knew what it meant. It was obvious that you and her were getting close to getting the number and that you must have worked out who I was. I decided it was time to run."

"Where were you?" I asked.

"We were shacked up in the usual place, a small lockup in Bow just off the Northern Approach." I wanted to ask her how she escaped from Kev but before I could she was off again. "It's so sad, coz I've known Kev for years, we've got family connections. We both come from Southend. He's a few years older than me and has always been flash as far as I can remember. Always in trouble with the law, but seemed to come out smelling of roses most times. A couple of years ago my big sister got in serious trouble, developed a bad habit and ran up massive debts to dealers. She whored, stole and shoplifted, anything to get money. She took a few beatings and she still owed thousands so she went to Kev to help her out and he paid off the debt and got the heat off her. I'll always be grateful for that and Kev knew it." She was on a roll and speaking quickly and animatedly: "Kev's been inside for attempted murder – got out after two years on appeal." Mr Cartwright had told me that as well. "He's a good guy underneath." Mr Cartwright hadn't told me that though.

Her story unfurled. Kev and Vicky met through cocaine, as you do. He was dealing it and she was taking it, but most of what she got from him she sold on to her contacts at vastly inflated prices. Vicky's role in her financial services company meant that she built up contacts which occasionally led to her sleeping with a few of them. She soon realised that most of them took cocaine and wanted a clean, comfortable way of getting it. Therefore, it was only a matter of time before she formed a partnership with Kev. It flourished and they leapt headfirst into their lifestyle.

They would have parties for a selected few clients who could test the product in convivial surroundings with call girls on hand. Cassie was brought in as additional fluff to keep them happy and occupied which she did once or twice a month. "I never went all the way with any of them mind," she reassured me. "I was part of the setup and did little jobs for Kev – pick-ups, drop-offs as well. He looked after me."

At one of these parties in August, after a few lines a Russian she hadn't seen before suggested an interesting proposition to Kev. He had a valuable package that he would like to move on and Kev agreed to meet to discuss it. He didn't tell Cassie what it was about, but for a while he seemed a bit strange, but almost happily strange. Several weeks later Kev was incandescent with rage and so was Vicky. In between the rage was an unmistakable fear. They cancelled several coke parties and both became increasingly agitated. "That dirty fucking cheating Russian bastard," she heard Kev shout on more than one occasion.

Vicky was no use. "That stuck-up cow was okay when things were going well but couldn't handle it when she wasn't in control. Kev was calling the shots or trying to and there was nothing that she could do coz she didn't know where to start. She had no contacts."

Cassie realised that they must have been ripped off big style in some way by the Russian. She asked Kev but was told that the less she knew the better. She could sense his stress and did feel some sympathy for him after what he had done for her sister so she comforted him and after a stress-busting shag he confided in her. Kev had brokered a deal with the Russian that for two kilos of high-grade cocaine he would get the package. Kev had approached a Russian crime syndicate through a contact from one of his parties and told them that he had a very valuable package that they may be interested in and told them what it would cost. After several meetings, they agreed to pay half upfront and half on delivery and he promised them that he would deliver in three weeks. I asked her what sort of money we were talking about here. "He never said what the product was that the Russian had, nor how much it was worth, but two kilos of pure coke could be worth up to two million," she told me.

Kev arranged the cocaine transfer for 1 October as he needed the time to get that quantity and quality. It was made on time and carried out as arranged. He then went to the agreed meeting point for the Russian's package and there was no one and no goods. Kev was panicking because he had set a date of 20 October to hand over the goods. He used all his contacts and called in a lot of favours, and she thought that he spent most of the upfront payment on buying information, before he eventually tracked the Russian down.

"I don't know who he went with or what he did but he came back with a name – Eustace, a description and a name of a garage in Ealing. It took a day and a half of watching but eventually we found him. We followed him to his house and the leisure centre and Kev told me to join the place and make contact with Eustace. I had two weeks absolute max to get the info.

"I made up some posters, false qualifications and watched a few DVDs – went along and asked if I could take some classes. They said they had enough instructors and would put me on a reserve list, so I asked if I could hire the hall three times a week

– they didn't need to pay me and what I took was my own. That's how I started – I went into the fitness room and got talking to the guys that go there all the time and persuaded them to come to my classes. After the first class I got talking to Eustace and the rest is history." So is Eustace, I thought.

"I tried to get snippets out of him, but didn't get much. I would go through his stuff when he was out. He was out a lot; on jobs, at the leisure centre or running. I didn't get much though apart from a list of contacts that I saved into my phone."

"Do you know how the Russian and Eustace got together?"

"I've been thinking a lot about that. You wouldn't believe how busy Eustace was. Mainly with hot motors that needed changing. In his line of business you don't advertise – word on the street gets you work if you're good. The Russian would have contacted Eustace that way I think. His business isn't that far away; out in Neasden or Willesden I think I heard Kev say."

I nodded. "Yeah, Neasden. They were both runners and have been in some of the same races, so they maybe met at one of them."

"Yeah, maybe; like I say he didn't talk about his work much but he was always taking calls. In the couple of weeks that I was with him, his phone never stopped. He didn't tell me about any codes or any of the stuff that Kev wanted, but he mentioned that he was working on a lovely Audi at Doug's. He just said that it was a cracker, that most of the cars he did were much lower down the scale."

"When I went to Eustace's, why did you take me through to where his body was?" I asked.

"Coz Vicky said that she had seen you buying the waistcoat with the number in it at a charity shop and, when you turned up at the door, Kev thought that you would have the number and was going to take it off you."

"Was he not bothered that I saw Eustace?"

"No."

"So he would have killed me if he had got the number?"

She didn't reply, but the silence told me everything.

I moved on.

"Did you know that Piotr was working with Eustace?"

"Hadn't got a clue 'til he said it just now," she said with a wistful laugh.

"How did you get away from Kev and get the Audi?"

"I had a bunch of car keys that I had taken from Eustace's when me and Kev left on the Saturday night. Kev didn't know that I had them. When I heard him say 'consider it done', I knew it was time to go. I took him his cup of tea and told him that I was going to the toilet. He was so intense and distracted that he barely acknowledged me. He sometimes mentioned a Plan B, but I don't think he had one. He was seriously worried. The toilet is next to the kitchenette – I put the light on and closed the door then went into the kitchenette, pulled up the window and climbed out. It's only just over five minutes' run to Pudding Mill Lane Station so I ran there without looking back. I was panicking about him chasing me and that it being Sunday the service would be poor but I got to the station and a train was pulling in. I jumped on and it was a Lewisham service so I got off at Canary Wharf, changed and made my way for Ealing."

"Did you head straight to the garage?"

"Yeah. I still had the keys so I thought that I would get one of the cars that Eustace was working on. I wanted the Audi – not for any cargo that everyone else is bothered about, but to sell it. It's an A7 so I reckon it's worth forty-five grand new, so if I sold it at least that would give me a start."

"How did you get the Audi?"

"That was the easiest bit surprisingly. I had the garage keys, but I didn't need to unlock the door coz it was broken. Doug's car wasn't there and there was no one inside." She must have arrived as Doug was looking for me I guessed. "The hardest bit was opening one of the big doors so that I could drive out. All the while I was panicking, but not coz of Doug – I could easily talk my way out of it with him – but Kev in case he was after me. Anyway, I jumped in the car and was off."

"How were you in here alone?"

"I got in touch with one of Eustace's contacts and promised him £10k if he would spray and sell the car and let me stay here. I've slept in the car for three nights, two of them here. About an hour ago he looked a bit strange but said that he had urgent business and might not make it back today. I said that he had promised to get the car sold tonight, but he told me not to worry and that he would get it off my hands tomorrow. I believed him, and let's face it there was nothing else that I could do. So I thought that I would be here another night and before I know it you two turn up."

"You must realise that you are an accessory to murder," I reminded her.

"I know. I didn't want any of this to happen of course. I just thought that I was helping Kev out. I quite liked Eustace – he was a bit of a laugh and very fit. Good in bed too. I felt bad for leading him on but I couldn't get the info that Kev needed. I thought that Kev would just scare him a bit and get whatever info he needed and piss off and I would do the same. But Kev was different I think coz he was so scared and he just snapped at Eustace's and stabbed him in a wild fury. It was horrible. Eustace was writhing about in his chair with his hands on the knife handle and his legs flapping and Kev was pushing him down and shouting for me to help. It must have been ten minutes before he died. Horrible, fucking horrible. Of course I feel bad but I didn't stab him and

Kev shouldn't have done it." She was trembling and her eyes were wet. I almost felt sorry for her.

"What are you going to do? The cops have been interviewing all the staff at the leisure centre so they will be looking for you and Piotr." As I said this Piotr joined us.

Cassie ignored my question and asked him, "How did you know that I was here?"

"I work with Eustace. I know his friends. I ask his friends. One of them tell me about white Audi re-spray. I tell him to go for a break."

"What next?" I asked him.

"May be a long day. Get us some food and drink." It was only early afternoon when he said this and I didn't expect that reply. I was hoping for a plan for what we were going to do next with a container of lethal chemicals, a stolen car and an accessory to murder. However in some ways, I considered, it would be good to get out for a short while and take everything in on my own whilst I went shopping.

"Piotr I don't have any money." I looked at him plaintively. He peeled off £40 from what looked like a large wad and handed it to me. That seemed like a lot but I took it and went on my way. It had started to rain and I pulled up my hood as I left the business village. I had no idea where to go and trusted to instinct. I could see a school nearby so headed for that because there are usually a few outlets around schools catering for the hungry kids. I was aware of the constant aircraft noise from Heathrow, which I hadn't noticed when we arrived on the bike but it was now annoying me. There was nothing near the school so I kept going and trudged further down the depressing nearly empty street and eventually I found a mini market. The shop didn't have pre-packed sandwiches but did have rolls so I bought six rolls along with packs of ham, cheese and chicken as well as packets of crisps, chocolate, juice and a four-pack of beer.

I carried the bulging carrier bags back to the garage and went round the back, set them down so that I could open the door and then picked them up and went in. It was very quiet as I walked into the garage area and the deadly package was still sitting on the bench where Piotr had put it. However the Audi that was now black was nowhere to be seen. Where were they? I went out of the building and round to where we had parked the bike which was gone as well. Fuck. I was now beginning to panic. What were they doing? It dawned on me that the package was dangerous as an entity but also being associated with it would probably lead to a permanent position in the foundations of the next city office development. Had Piotr decided it was too dangerous and the pair of them had fled? My mind was whirring. Had he done this because he trusted me to do the right thing and deal with this, or did he not give a fuck and just wanted away? What should I do?

I decided that I would have to take the polonium, but where to? I picked up the metal box and looked for something to put it in but couldn't find anything so tipped the contents of one of the carrier bags onto the floor and put the metal box in that. I took the other carrier bag with me. I left from the back of the building and just started walking head down and purposefully in the direction that I had gone in previously. I had no real idea of what I was doing so I decided to walk and think. I tried to appear normal and I didn't get the feeling that anyone was watching me.

The carrier bag that I had taken with food in it had the four-pack of beer so I sat on a park bench and had a can quickly followed by another. Not having eaten for some time I got a bit of a buzz which actually helped me think and what I decided was that I would go to Artamanov's business, break in and leave the package there. That would restore the link between him and Eustace and Blondie and Vicky. The only problem was finding my way back there again. I racked my brain for the street name and couldn't remember it but then suddenly thought that if I searched the company name I would get it. I got out my phone and did so – Kestrel Park, Neasden. I hadn't noticed when we were last there that it was very close to Neasden Underground station which was a bonus.

Next: how would I get there? I was getting into this new technology and used an app to find the nearest Underground station, Hounslow West, which was only a few minutes' walk from the park that I was sitting in. I hadn't eaten anything and put the crisps and fruit on top of my deadly cargo in an attempt to hide it.

I arrived at the Underground and got my ticket. The journey required a change at Green Park which I think from now on for me will always be associated with deep shit. I sat on the busy train, holding my carrier bag on my lap, avoiding eye contact and staring vacantly at nothing. I kept thinking about Piotr and Cassie and also kept hoping that there wouldn't be an incident on the journey which caused my cargo to be found.

When I got off and left the station I found the estate easily and OA Imports UK was still unoccupied, but there was life in the other units. Now what should I do? Having broken into Doug's before, this wasn't new territory for me; however that was on a Sunday morning in a deserted industrial estate – this was Wednesday afternoon and may be too risky here. I went up to the office door and tried it: no response. Same with the big garage door. I went down the side and round the back and the door there was locked as well. Perhaps it was the influence of Piotr, but as I had approached the front of the building and gone up the side of it to the back, I surreptitiously looked for signs of CCTV but saw nothing. This didn't really surprise me because I reckoned in Artamanov's line of business he wouldn't want a record of what was going on there.

There was a large grey waste container in the back yard which was chained to a railing near to the back door. Presumably this would be unlocked and wheeled to the front for emptying once a week. This would have to do. I looked around to see that the coast was clear and then raised the lid enough to lean over and carefully put the metal box into it, before covering it with some cardboard.

I then made my way out of the estate walking briskly back towards the station feeling somewhat lighter. I wanted to get out of the area quickly. I needed to check some things online and after that it was time to visit Detective Stevenson.

CHAPTER TWENTY-NINE

It was time to face the music. I was sitting in Interview Room Three again. I had called the police less than an hour after I had returned from Artamanov's and asked to speak to Stevenson and here I was back in the station. I sat facing Brown and Stevenson; Brown still had that paste at the edge of his mouth. "Well, Greg – we've been wondering where you've been and we haven't heard from Mr Cartwright either. So have you got something to tell us then?" Stevenson started with.

"Yes."

"Okay, whenever you're ready." He went through the recording formalities again and asked me if I was ready to start. I said that I was.

"I know why Eustace was killed and for what. I also know where the goods are and suggest that you go and get them as a priority." There was a brief silence. I think that I had surprised them. Stevenson took a small breath and then asked me to elaborate. I then continued, "Eustace had made a hidden storage area in the white Audi as you know. It had a code as you know. The security box contained polonium from Russia that a Mr Artamanov got his hands on. The polonium is now at Artamanov's import/export business in Neasden which is called OA Imports UK. I am sure that Artamanov is dead." Again a pause. I think that even Brown was impressed because he asked a question.

"What is polonium?"

"It is a very strong form of poison that I think is radioactive."

"How do you know all this, Greg?" Stevenson's voice sounded softer.

"I looked it up on the Internet."

"No, how do you know about this stolen polonium and where it has been hidden and how is it connected to Eustace Manley, Kevin Osborne and Victoria Monteith?"

"From what I have seen and heard," I said.

"You will need to be a lot more specific than that," he countered. I had carefully worked out my story and it was time to recite it. There would be no mention of Piotr or Cassie. I told them how after I had left questioning the last time, I did as instructed by Stevenson, and had racked my brains to try to remember if I could think of anything unusual that I had seen or heard. I kept trying to remember any time that I had seen Eustace in the leisure centre. I then adapted Piotr's tale of the suspicious activity regarding Eustace and the Russian on the day of the half-marathon with me taking the role of Piotr watching them in the corridor. Then I pulled out my trump card.

"I have got a photo of Artamanov," I said.

"Let me see it," Stevenson replied. I took out my phone and showed them a picture from just after the start of the Ealing Half Marathon. After dumping the polonium at Artamanov's I was wondering how I could get a photo of him and Eustace together when it dawned on me that with them having similar times in the race that they may have been together near the start. I did a trawl of the photo gallery and amongst the many bobbing head shots I eventually struck gold. I said that I recognised Artamanov from that and used his number to work out who he was. I then tracked down his company and when it became obvious that there was nobody there I did a search and found the polonium abandoned in the wheelie bin. They both looked quizzical to say the least. "How did you know it was polonium and why didn't you bring it to us?" Stevenson asked.

"I didn't know it was polonium at the time, but I took photos of it and then did an Internet search."

"What did you use to take the photos?"

"My phone."

"Have you saved the photos?"

"No. I deleted them." As I said this I realised that they could easily establish if this bit of the story was true by taking my phone away and analysing it. However they moved on and I was asked to repeat the story from beginning to end and give clarifications at certain points. They cross-referenced my story with notes from the previous interviews. Stevenson asked me a lot about the Audi, about Doug and about what happened in Solihull. I could answer truthfully about most of that and did so. However, when I told him that I had overpowered Mr Cartwright after he had threatened me and tried to get information out of me and that I had left him in the back yard of the Cottage Tea Room and taken his car, it sounded weak as piss.

"Where is the car now?" Stevenson asked.

"Probably stolen. I left it with the keys in the ignition in East London." Brown made a few notes. We had been at it for over three hours now and they were seeing through me. They tried the tactic of silence again. I had no more to say so I let the silence hang. Time for Stevenson to come in from left field.

"Blondie, as you call him – Kevin Osborne – is dead." I stared and said nothing because I didn't know what to say. "On remand in Belmarsh. Fight in prison. No witnesses." He let that hang. I still didn't know what to say or think for that matter. I hated that bastard for what he had put me and Isa through.

In fact on reflection I didn't care that he was dead. "Thoughts?" Stevenson asked.

"Nothing. None really," I said a bit half-heartedly. "How was he killed?"

"Stabbed."

"Oh."

We weren't really getting anywhere with this conversation and Brown as ever was contributing nothing. Stevenson moved on. "Cartwright's dead. Found hanging from a tree in the grounds of the Cottage Tea Room, Oxfordshire, near the A40." I didn't say anything but my mouth fell open.

"Used his tie." So the long thin one did the job. Just as well he wasn't wearing a modern one, I thought. Poor bastard.

I was ready for the next step.

"Read him his rights and give him a bed for the night."

CHAPTER THIRTY

Four Days Later

My phone rang – the number was withheld. I hadn't had many calls because most people didn't know my new number. As I couldn't access my old phone, which along with my laptop had been kept as evidence, it meant that I couldn't get into my contacts to tell them of the change.

It was approaching one o'clock on Monday afternoon and I was reclining on Phil's sofa watching television. Phil didn't have satellite or cable so I was forced to watch Freeview and over the past few days had enjoyed watching the unchallenging regular daytime fare of antique sales, home improvement and buying property abroad programmes in the empty flat. I had been staying in Phil's box room since I left the police station last Thursday morning after my second overnight stay. I could now move back into my own place and all I needed to do was collect the new keys from the police station. They had kindly replaced my broken front door; however I had no inclination to move back just yet. I wanted Mr Cartwright's funeral over and done with first as I couldn't face having to see Mrs C or their son and I didn't want to be the subject of endless prying eyes and hearing snatches of conversation about me as I entered or left my property.

I answered the phone. "Hello, Greg, it's Detective Stevenson."

"Oh hello." My heart was beginning to flutter, as I was naturally set into a default position of always expecting the worst when I spoke to him.

"I would like us to meet up for a chat, just to go over things." His voice sounded a bit mellower than the other day.

"Okay," I said with a sigh, "when do you want me over?" There was no point resisting his request. I had the feeling that they had found Piotr and Cassie, or worse they were causing carnage like a latter-day Bonnie and Clyde and he wanted to question me on them.

"You don't need to come to the station. Let's go for a drink and have a chat." I didn't expect this.

"Yeah, okay. Where about?" He gave me the name and location of a pub in the city centre, explaining that it was best to meet out of his manor. This took me aback as well. "What time?"

"What about six o'clock tonight?"

"Yeah. Okay," I mumbled.

"See you then." With that he hung up. I watched the television, but without it really registering as I kept thinking about Stevenson's call and our impending meeting. Round four.

My phone rang again and I took a call from Ealing Council regarding Brygida, Piotr's wife. Two days ago I ventured out to visit Brygida. She is totally in bits having been left with a baby, no income, doesn't speak the language and is here on a false passport. Piotr's disappearance had come out of the blue and she had no plan or even any idea of how to cope. I had told her to come clean about the passport and I would contact the Social Work department to seek assistance for her. They offered an appointment for the following week and asked if I could attend along with her and I agreed.

Eventually I got up, had a shower and dressed in jeans and long shirt. I put my fleece on, which needed a wash, and wrote a note to Phil before taking one of his jackets and leaving the flat. It goes against the grain for me to be heading into central London at rush hour but the Tube journey which involved one change was tolerable. The chosen pub, The Grapes, was in a narrow lane just off Regent Street and looked quite small from the outside. As I was approaching the front door I heard, "Greg." I looked round and there was Stevenson behind me. He wasn't smiling but he looked approachable.

"Hi," I said.

"Thanks for coming," he replied. He wasn't in a suit but was wearing jeans, an open-neck casual shirt and a leather jacket.

"That's okay."

He held the door for me and beckoned me inside. We went into the busy pub which was larger than I expected and had a Victorian-style interior with a varnished horseshoe-shaped bar. He told me to find a seat whilst he went to order us a drink. I asked him for a pint of lager and found a table and seats not in the corner as I had hoped for but in between two other sets of furniture. I sat down and whilst I waited noted that our neighbours on both sides appeared to be foreign tourists with A–Zs and pamphlets laid out on their tables which relaxed me a bit. Stevenson arrived quite quickly; he sat down and we raised our glasses, then he came out of the traps: "I know that you are lying and other people are involved. I must say that you have surprised me in what you have worked out and how you have got it. You would make a good cop."

"Hah! That's what Mr Cartwright said." I was trying to remain cool.

"You worked out a lot on your own, but I don't believe that you overpowered Cartwright yourself and got away. We know that Cartwright had a gun and he would have taken that with him to Solihull and aimed it at you at the tea room. We always knew he was bent and would shift from side to side. We worked on the basis of better the devil you know, keep your enemy close." I was waiting for him to ask me how I did it. "The post-mortem showed marks on his wrists which perhaps came from some type of handcuff. We found an abandoned motorbike hidden in the wood next to the tea room and we haven't looked yet, but I'm sure that we can get footage of Cartwright's Passat heading back towards London with two figures in it. Also we have had a few whispers, nothing official yet, about some strange goings on at the Nelson Leisure Centre involving two leather-clad figures breaking in on Tuesday night which we may have to look further into. We still have a couple of staff members to interview, Cassandra Lewis of course, who has disappeared, and Piotr the Polish cleaner who got you Eustace's membership number."

Fuck. My heart sank just as everything appeared to be falling into place and smoothing over. I felt that I was slowly drifting towards an abyss before sinking into it. But why had he brought me here to tell me this and presumably arrest me? I couldn't think of anything to say so said nothing. After a pause of perhaps thirty seconds he appeared to go off on a tangent: "London has always been a major city obviously, but now it has soared to be international with a capital I," he said. "There is and will be massive investment – Russia, Middle East, the Far East. When you get that amount of money coming in and being spent it attracts dirty money and illegal activity as well. At the level that we work at we will never get to the Mr Bigs who are number one or two in their organisations. They are too well insulated and never actually go near to whatever product they are involved with. We have to go further down the food chain and pick off the number fours, fives and sixes and occasionally if we get lucky maybe a number three. I would put Osborne and Monteith as a four or a five in the scheme of things. Darren Jackson aka Daz at number six, just hired muscle. So they all have been or will be dealt with. Result." He took a sip of his beer and continued, "We have found out a lot about Osborne and Monteith over the past few days and if they had stayed in their comfort zone of dealing to acquaintances and holding coke parties then they may have been okay, but I doubt it. They were doing well, but it all came too easy and they thought that it would stay that way. They were too inexperienced, didn't have enough contacts and were far too cocky; they thought that they could do anything. They moved to a whole new level and were so out of their depth that when things went wrong they couldn't cope and they panicked. Look at the way the behaved at Eustace's – they were caught on CCTV from around the area before, during and after their time in his house. They left prints and DNA everywhere and they brought in a shit-for-brains psychotic thug to kidnap your aunt. It was a piece of cake to track him down and take him out.

"We will probably never get near to finding out who the cargo was for. Mr Big will be seriously pissed off at not getting the product but content in the knowledge that Artamanov is almost certainly dead and Osborne is definitively dead and all key players will know that. By the way no one has been seen or heard of at Artamanov's business premises, so they are either dead or in hiding. Mr Big will be satisfied that we have got the polonium and not a rival. That means that when another batch becomes available and he gets his hands on it, it will be even more valuable.

"For what it's worth my instinct is that Osborne and Artamanov arranged a deal – coke for polonium. Artamanov got greedy when he realised that Osborne wasn't a big player and he thought that he could probably get away with double-crossing him and get the coke and keep the polonium. This is where he brought in Eustace to customise the car so that he could make his getaway, however he underestimated the rage and fear that Osborne had. It's a guess, but from whispers that I've heard, there was someone trying desperately to track Artamanov down who was paying big sweeteners for information and I would guess that person was Osborne. He would have been given an upfront payment for the polonium and probably spent most of this in finding Artamanov. My instinct is that Osborne killed Artamanov because how else would he find out about Eustace? At that stage the Mr Big in the background wouldn't have known that the polonium hadn't been delivered. Osborne only got so much info from Artamanov and by the time that he tracked down Eustace he was panicking, which would explain his violent rage there."

Well, like Mr Cartwright, that was pretty good instinct. I tried to look at Stevenson neutrally and interestedly as if all of this was news. I hoped that my eyes weren't flickering too much and I was making an effort to minimise my swallowing. Having a pint glass to look at, play with and drink from helped.

"Another gut feeling is that someone left the polonium at Artamanov's business to make the connection between him and Osborne. It is highly unlikely that an international gang would use a wheelie bin to hide a very valuable and dangerous product, but I suppose stranger things have happened. Pickles the dog found the World Cup hidden in someone's garden in 1966."

I choked on my drink and could feel beer coming down my nose. Stevenson was not adding anything else so it was time to edge away from this, "What sort of damage could this batch of polonium cause?" I asked.

"A few drops in a drink would guarantee to kill you. It's away being analysed so we don't yet know the strength, but seeing as there were four bottles of the stuff – major damage. Polonium is serious shit – remember that Russian double agent that was killed in London? That was polonium. They reckon ten million dollars' worth of the stuff was used on him which was way too much but shows you its value. Also it's easy to smuggle because it doesn't set off radiation detectors."

I did recall the case he was talking about. And to think that I had this stuff on a couple of trains...

He changed tack again, which suited me. "From our perspective we have got a result. We worked well in partnership with West Midlands Police and arrested three key players in murder, kidnapping and extortion. One of them is dead and the other two will serve serious stretches. On top of that we have got Monteith on various Class A drug violations and would have had Osborne on them as well.

"Not forgetting of course that we have found the polonium and will hand that part of the investigation over to Special Branch to review. One downside coming out from this is that there might be a mole in our organisation given the short time it took from Osborne being banged up on remand to being killed. Not many people out there could have known that, but still that has helped to expose our potential problem so that we can now go out to trap the bastard who may well be a protégé of Cartwright. So even having said that...yes, all in all a satisfactory result."

"Will Special Branch be interested in me?" I asked.

"They will be aware of you obviously, but know that you have no direct link to any of the top-level stuff. You were just a pawn some way down the food chain." This had to be his favourite analogy. Phew, that was a relief. He then continued, "They should be able to trace the source of the polonium when it has been fully tested and will then decide if and how they find out how Artamanov got his hands on it. That decision will be overseen and approved at government level because of potential political sensitivities if it is indeed from Russia. They will be keen to find the Audi to see if there are any other hidden compartments and it could of course contain the coke if that was indeed the payment used for the polonium." I hadn't thought of that, which could be a nice little earner for Piotr and Cassie; however I felt their chances of staying at large were slim now that Special Branch, and no doubt Interpol, were involved.

Time to change tack. "What about me? What are you going to do?" I asked.

"Son we are meeting here unofficially and hopefully no one is listening in. Use your brains, Professor – we know some off-the-record stuff that will stay off the record and just now you will be considered only as a witness. At the moment we are not interested in looking to see that you had accessories because it serves us little or no purpose and Cartwright being dead suits everyone including him. You will have to give evidence in court of course." Thinking about the court case made me shiver and started an unwelcome tingle in the pit of my stomach. "It looks like the case will go to court in March or April, but it shouldn't be drawn out. The evidence against both of them is compelling – fingerprints, DNA, text messages, tracked movements. Osborne's death in prison can't be used directly as proof of their involvement in all of this, but rest assured that our prosecutor will drop its implications into the jury's consciousness."

"How long will Vicky and that bastard Jackson get?"

"If they both plead guilty and they have good lawyers, she will probably get six to eight as accessory to murder and Jackson will get around the same for kidnap. Monteith will be looking over her shoulder for the rest of her life when she gets out. If she makes it out of prison alive."

I nodded and asked, "What will happen with Doug?"

"Doug has told us that he acted almost as a fence for Eustace and he let him use the garage for a monthly retainer. Eustace had a set of keys and most of his work was done directly between himself and his clients. Sometimes Doug swapped keys or money with regular trusted clients. He got a number of phone calls on Saturday afternoon and Sunday morning from some anxious regulars who Eustace had told he would see on Saturday afternoon. You were probably there when he received a couple but they were about regular jobs, not the Audi. Doug said that he was unsettled by the Audi because this type of car wasn't what Eustace normally dealt with and he felt that there was something different happening and he wanted it out pronto.

"We basically believe his story. Like you, he had no direct involvement in the big picture. He knows that we know that he was aware of Eustace's illegal activity in his garage which may be of use to us in the future – if we need some ear on the ground for stuff then we can squeeze him a little.

"At the risk of repeating myself," he said as he leaned back, "it's what I call a result."

"So what now?" I asked Stevenson.

"Let's have another drink," he said warmly.

Sounds like a plan. I had finished my drink and was in desperate need of another. I got up and pushed my way through the crowds to the bar to buy a drink for my new friend.

CHAPTER THIRTY-ONE

I have developed a nervous tic in my right eye and haven't been sleeping well over the past few weeks, awakening in sweaty terror from my nightmares. They are recurrent and usually involve seeing Eustace with a knife in his chest whilst talking to me quite naturally, or Isa speaking in a strange high-pitched voice to no one in particular and laughing manically before having her throat slit. I wake as the bleeding starts.

It has been two months now since my return to the flat and it was a struggle to go back having become comfortable sleeping in Phil's box room with my routine of daytime television and undemanding tasks, along with his company at night. My flat still has the broken kitchen door which I should have replaced as the police gave me the details of a joiner to carry out the work for which they would pay, but I can't be bothered. It has barely been tidied since my return and I have had a number of run-ins with the landlord which have become quite heated.

I have been back to Solihull twice since my ill-fated visit to see Isa in hospital. One of the visits was for Christmas and I stayed for four days. It was tolerable in terms of my relationship with my parents as my dad and I considered each other's point of view and trod warily around each other. I accepted the shock that he must have felt together with his old-fashioned values of male pride being dented in not being able to do anything for his sister. From his side I think that Mr Cartwright's betrayal and the forthcoming court case demonstrated that I had been an unwitting and unfortunate pawn in a very dangerous game.

Isa was still very frail and hollow-eyed with the stuffing knocked out of her. She is staying in what was the dining room of my parents' house and they have done a good job in getting her main possessions and items of furniture in there to make it as homely as possible. She tried to be sociable, but would spend hours on end in her room alone and any time that I went in to see her, always mindful to knock first, she would be sitting holding and staring at pictures of Bill and Richard. So desperately sad, as she had always been a battler and I hoped that she still had some fight in her, but being honest I feared that this had now been lost forever.

Over the past three months my thoughts have been dominated by Aunt Isa and the events of that week in mid-October. I have been off work since then and am on full pay which will reduce to half in another three months. At the moment I feel unable to return and my doctor has set the wheels in motion for me to undergo counselling because she feels that I may be suffering from some form of post-traumatic stress disorder. I don't know if I want to continue in my job, which I had really enjoyed, but now with my loss of confidence I am unsure if I can face a class again and speak confidently and not worry about how they are judging me. It is hard to explain, but I now feel that everyone is looking to use me in some way, which might sound ridiculous, but after Vicky, Mr Cartwright and Piotr, perhaps not. I have lost confidence in my ability to judge people – Christ I opened up more to Mr Cartwright than to any other person as an adult. I have been let down so many times recently and under such circumstances that it makes me question how well we really know people. Such is my paranoia that I'm worried that I will wake up from a session of hypnosis only to discover that my therapist has teased my bank details out of me and cleared out my account.

Stevenson keeps in touch periodically, but he hasn't shared much apart from that psychiatric profiling of Vicky indicates that she may have an underlying psychopathy or narcissism which drives her needs and subsequent actions, meaning that she carries out actions with no empathy. Perhaps, but as far as I'm concerned something triggered this. Maybe something such as her divorce or the new job in vastly different circumstances did it. Who knows? One for the professionals to try to get to the bottom of after she's sentenced and they have a few years to work with her. I regularly think of Vicky and her family. What is she thinking right now? What about her parents – are they primarily concerned with her wellbeing or dealing with the sense of shame brought upon the family?

The court case is getting closer and I am dreading it. Stevenson assures me that the defence counsel will recommend that they both plead guilty given the mountain of evidence against them as it will be their only hope of getting a lenient sentence. I hope so because if not I will need some serious coaching, particularly when I am being questioned on Mr Artamanov and the polonium.

I keep thinking of Piotr and Cassie. I now realise that from the moment that he had gone to the leisure centre on Sunday morning Piotr had decided he was going to disappear, hence the lack of concern regarding traffic cameras when driving Mr Cartwright's car on our return to London. It seems that Piotr and Cassie have run off directionless with, as far as I can see, no sense of purpose. I believe that they will have formed a hasty partnership on discovery of the polonium and that when I was sent for food, Cassie would have taken the Audi and Piotr the bike. Piotr had Mr Cartwright's car in his lockup as well and I expect that the vehicles were sold quickly at knocked down but still substantial sums to give them some ready cash. I had forgotten to ask Stevenson if Mr Cartwright's car had ever been found.

Stevenson told me that a brother came over from Jamaica for Eustace's funeral, which made me realise that I had hardly thought of him as a person or the effects of his murder on his family.

Trying to look at this horrendous episode positively – I have been resourceful, determined and brave. I have dealt with massive shocks and truly dangerous situations and kept going and prevailed. Unfortunately that doesn't outweigh the negatives. I am changed and feel broken. I don't have the will or the energy to channel these newly found positive traits in a useful, meaningful way at the moment.

I have visited Mrs Cartwright, which was painful. Her tiny eyes misted over as she told me with her quiet dignity pretty much the same sorry story of her marriage that I had already heard from Mr Cartwright. He had missed out telling me about the affairs, drinking and wife-beating though. Robert came over for the funeral; ironically his father's not his mum's. His family stayed in Australia and he came alone. Mrs Cartwright told me that she was moving out into a retirement complex and was looking forward to it. She has since moved and their flat is empty and up for sale. The Cartwrights were not noisy neighbours, but with them gone I have noticed the complete silence from below.

It's made me think a lot about growing old – what do my parents look forward to? Do they both think the same or does Dad have different views on aging to Mum? What do they expect from and look forward to from their children? Grandchildren?

Well Frances has come up with the goods there, what about me? Are they happy if I am happy or do they expect more from me? I'm thirty-six and unmarried and so am I still in their eyes directionless? What do they see as the direction that I should follow?

What is happening to my life? My content, happy status quo has been kicked into touch and I am veering from up to down and back to up violently and suddenly many times in a day. I constantly question myself on my future, my family and what is doing the right thing. Conversely, despite my lack of confidence I have become much more argumentative and confrontational. I have had my hair cut back to the wood and feel in some way empowered by this. I will look for issues and complain about the slightest thing to a shopkeeper or ticket collector. I don't give way on a pavement or if I hold a door open for someone who doesn't acknowledge it I will confront them with a sarcastic "You're welcome."

I have had a couple of one-night-stands as I needed the physical comfort and sense of release but didn't want any commitment. I am ashamed to say that one of them was with Brygida, who I had kept in regular contact with. I had gone round one evening to help with some form filling and Brygida told me that Piotr often moved the wardrobe about in the bedroom and didn't let her in when he did so. It was worth a look so I moved it, rolled back the carpet to find a couple of loose boards which I lifted and underneath found a bag containing various denominations of cash which came to approximately £4,000. This unexpected boost made Brygida the happiest I had seen her. She gave me a hug and a great big kiss and one thing led to another. I crept out of bed in the early hours and made my way home in a welter of self-loathing and disbelief at my behaviour.

I haven't been back to the leisure centre, but I have been

back in the Bridge Café a few times, valuing the genuine warmth that can still be found. London Isa is called Gladys and I look forward to my visits. Obviously it is close to Doug's garage so I always wear a hoody or hat and make my way quickly into the café. I have never seen Doug since the day I broke into his garage. Another flip side to visiting the café is that Gladys reminds me so much of how Isa was and how I wish she would return to that state. So whilst I look forward to the visits and enjoy them at the time, they leave me pining for what used to be. That's the way it is these days.

I now truly value friendship and think that I have that with Phil and Dave, but after what I have been through who knows? Both of them have been a great support to me with the normal things that I enjoy so much such as the pub, football, curry or just some banter. They sometimes give quizzical looks when they see me in a period of morbid self-reflection but they now know not to probe. Their black humour helps and I may be asked if I have taken a hate-the-world tablet that morning. Dave did offer a suggestion once of getting a tattoo with a Chinese symbol to reflect my inner strength. Er, thanks, Dave, but no…

I have lots of decisions to make, but that is for another day. Yes it's time to move on. I like the area and have always felt comfortable here, but this is also where all the shit has happened and I don't want a daily reminder of it. I have secured a new flat with a six-month lease on the other side of the park from Eustace's house. I don't at this stage want to commit for any longer because I truly do not know what I want to do. I need the court case to be over first. One day at a time.

CHAPTER THIRTY-TWO

We had put my possessions into boxes, suitcases and holdalls and had moved the last of them downstairs and into the van. Dave was already sitting in it and Phil had closed the van's back door and gone to sit in the driver's seat ready to make our third and final journey to my new flat.

I returned upstairs and went round each room in turn to convince myself that I hadn't left anything. I went into my bedroom last to get my hand luggage which consisted of my laptop in its bag and a holdall containing my college books, a few favourite novels and a couple of new as-yet unread ones along with some folders of general paperwork. I took a final look around the room and noticed that the birthday card from Aunt Isa was still on the chest of drawers. I was definitely taking that to my new home.

I picked up the card and felt something flutter behind it, so turned it around and there, stuck to the back with a tiny piece of tape, was a small envelope. *Greg* was written on the front in spidery handwriting. I opened the envelope; it contained a gift receipt from Aunt Isa just in case I had wanted to exchange the slippers.

I put the receipt back in the envelope, turned the card round and looked at it for several seconds then carefully put it on top of the pile of books, folders and paperwork in my bulging holdall and zipped it closed.

I picked up the holdall, put the laptop bag over my shoulder and walked slowly out of my empty flat then closed the door behind me and locked it for the last time.

ACKNOWLEDGEMENTS

Thanks to Mags, my first proofreader, and Jenny, my second; to Dad for his wise counsel; David for naming convention and all my family for being around; ATJ for getting me into writing and alongside Steve for designing the book cover; Euan and Gordon for getting me into running and Kelvin, Sandra and the team at the Ealing Half Marathon. Thanks also to Rowena and Emily at SilverWood for their knowledge, guidance and support.

Finally to my late mother, who after reading an early draft in her hospital bed advised me to get rid of the swearing. I tried, Mum, I tried...

Lightning Source UK Ltd.
Milton Keynes UK
UKHW01f0051090518
322318UK00001B/20/P